CHRISTOPHER
PIKE

FINAL FRIENDS 3

THE GRADUATION

*Hodder
Children's
Books*

a division of Hodder Headline plc

First published in the USA in 1989 by Archway Paperbacks,
a division of Simon & Schuster

First published in Great Britain in 1991 by
Hodder and Stoughton, a division of Hodder Headline plc.

ISBN 0 340 53139 8

Printed and bound in Great Britain by
Cox & Wyman Ltd, Reading, Berkshire

Hodder Children's Books
a division of Hodder Headline plc
338 Euston Road
London NW1 3BH

INTRODUCTION

In FINAL FRIENDS Book 1, *The Party*, senior Jessica Hart returns to school a week late from summer vacation. Her old alma mater has been closed, and Jessica is now attending Tabb High. Jessica no longer has a locker of her own; she has to share one with a young man named Michael Olson. Although Jessica is charmed by Michael, she sees him more as a friend than a possible boyfriend. Michael, however, develops an immediate crush on Jessica. Michael has attended Tabb since his freshman year and is the smartest person in the school. Jessica is one of the most attractive.

Jessica's three closest friends have also been transferred to Tabb: Sara Cantrell, Polly McCoy, and Polly's younger sister, Alice. Sara is the most interesting of the three – witty and overconfident. Polly, on the other hand, is rather neurotic and suffers from poor self-esteem. But it is Alice who is Jessica's favourite: a sweet frail girl with a gift for painting. Alice has a mysterious boyfriend – Clark. Neither Jessica nor Sara knows much about Clark, only that he used to go out with Polly.

As a joke, during a morning snack break, Jessica and Polly add Sara's name to a list of students who are running for school office. There is to be an assembly in the afternoon during which all the candidates have to speak.

Michael teams up with his friend Bubba during fourth

1

period. The two boys are 'Mentally Gifted Minors' and work on projects of their own choosing at this time. Bubba is a short, round version of James Bond. Everything goes his way, in every department – including romance. Yet Bubba is not above a little subterfuge and theft. Stealing computer codes from Tabb's administrative offices, he shows Michael how he is able to alter certain school records. To Bubba's displeasure, though, Alice walks in while Michael is using the codes Bubba has stolen. Bubba wants Alice to swear to keep the codes secret, but Alice just laughs at his paranoia.

Although Michael and Alice are close friends, Michael does not know of Alice's relationship with Jessica. Nor does Jessica know of Michael's friendship with Alice. Michael and Jessica are the two most important people in Alice's life. Alice has purposely kept them apart so that she can introduce them at 'the right time'. Alice has decided the time has come. She makes Michael promise to meet her at the football game that night, telling him she knows a girl he is going to fall in love with. Michael does not realise the girl Alice is talking about is Jessica.

During the afternoon assembly, Sara's name is called out, and Jessica and Polly force her to talk. Sara quickly denies that she is running for school office and also ridicules all the candidates who are running. She is elected school president by a landslide.

Another newcomer to Tabb High is Nick Grutler, an ex-gang member from a violent section of Los Angeles. Nick is tall, black, and powerful. He is also very shy. During P.E., Nick gets dragged into a heated dispute and fight with a bigoted young man named The Rock. Nick makes short work of The Rock, but only the intervention of Russ Desmond, a gifted long-distance runner, saves Nick from being expelled.

Leaving school that same afternoon, Nick meets Maria Gonzales, a quiet Hispanic girl. Maria lends him a quarter for a Coke, and they have a pleasant conversation, which leaves Nick feeling confused. Few people have ever treated Nick with anything but contempt.

Leaving school about the same time, Sara accidentally steps across Russ Desmond's path while he's in the middle of a cross-country race. The resulting collision sends Sara into the bushes. Russ stops to help her up, and Sara is immediately taken by Russ's great body and indifferent manner.

Later, Jessica and Sara convince Polly to pursue Alice's idea of having a party, where all Tabb's new and old kids can get to know one another. Polly is unsure at first because it will have to be at her house. Jessica is anxious to have the party so she can invite Tabb's handsome quarterback, Bill Skater.

Unlike the girls, who are all rich, Michael has to work full-time at a local 7-Eleven to help his divorced mother pay the bills. He is at the store when Nick stumbles in after an exhausting afternoon searching for a job. After giving him a trial task, Michael offers Nick a job. Soon, though, they are held up, but it is only a joke hold-up. It is only 'Kats'.

Michael knows Kats mainly through Bubba. A couple of years older than Michael, Kats attended Tabb the previous year but never graduated. He works at a local petrol station, aspires to be a Marine, and is pretty much a loser. During the mock hold-up, Kats uses a real gun, infuriating Michael. Kats collects guns. He has a secret passion for Alice McCoy.

Michael and Nick arrive at the football game that night at half-time and are met at the gate by Alice and her boyfriend, Clark. Alice persuades Clark to wait while she dashes off in search of the girl she has told Michael about. Michael speaks to Clark for a few minutes and thinks he's very strange – almost frightening.

Alice does not find Jessica, but Michael does run into Jessica on his own, and soon realises the girl Alice has been speaking of is Jessica. Because he also notes Jessica's interest in Bill Skater, he does not reveal this fact to Jessica.

The most beautiful girl at Tabb is a cheerleader named Clair Hilrey. Bubba has decided she is to be his. Calling upon his considerable powers of persuasion, he talks Clair into going out with him the following Saturday. Bubba has also taken an interest in Sara, whom he sees as a kindred soul.

Also during half-time, Polly bumps into a drunk Russ trying to chop down the school's varsity tree. Because he stopped to talk to Sara that afternoon, Russ lost his race and has been kicked off the cross-country team. Thinking that Polly is Sara, Russ allows Polly to take him home. Polly keeps his axe. She also falls in love with Russ, for much the same reason she fell in love with Clark before – because he shows her a tiny bit of attention.

The following Monday at school, Michael and Nick attempt to ask Jessica and Maria out. But before Michael can ask Jessica, she asks him. Jessica has been having trouble with chemistry and is hoping Michael can tutor her. Jessica's timing is unfortunate; she never learns of Michael's intentions towards her. She continues to see him as just a friend. Nick's invitation goes more smoothly, however, and he sets a date with Maria for the following Saturday.

The evening of the big date comes. Jessica has been playing the matchmaker. She has talked Russ into taking Sara out, even though she has assured Sara that the date

4

was Russ's idea. Predictably, Jessica has to call Russ when she is out with Michael to remind him that Sara is waiting for him. It seems Russ has forgotten about the whole thing.

Michael and Jessica, Nick and Maria, Bubba and Clair, and Russ and Sara run into one another at the movies. Everybody's been having a great time except Sara, who blows up when Russ asks her to pay for the movie. When she realises that it was Jessica who talked Russ into asking her out, she runs off in shame. The big night ends with Michael taking Jessica and Sara back to Jessica's house. Michael does not kiss Jessica goodnight, much to her disappointment. Jessica is still keen to get to know Bill Skater, but she has already begun to fall for Michael. Only Michael does not know.

The night of the party arrives. Half the school shows up. Polly feels she will go nuts trying to keep up with everybody. She gets into an argument with Alice. She feels Alice has lied to her and has invited Clark to the party. But Alice swears she hasn't even spoken to Clark. And it is true that Polly has not actually seen Clark in the house. The whole issue gets rather confused, but then, Polly has a reason to be confused. She accidentally sticks her wet fingers in a light socket and gets an electric shock.

The evening abounds with interesting events: Jessica flirts with Bill, and Michael gets depressed and wants to leave; Bubba flirts with Clair, and Clair tries to get Bill into bed: Kats tries to hit on Alice, and Polly tries to hit on Russ; The Rock tries to humiliate Nick in the pool, and Nick almost drowns him; The Rock tries to get revenge on Nick, and Polly stops The Rock by throwing chlorine in his eyes.

Eventually the party comes to a close, and soon only the principal characters are left in the house. Michael,

Jessica, Sara, Maria, and Nick are in the living room. Polly is outside by the swimming pool. The others are 'around'. Nick suddenly stands. He has to go to the bathroom. Jessica advises him to use one upstairs.

Nick walks towards the stairs and sees Bill bent over the kitchen sink, upset. Upstairs, Nick notices Kats outside on the second-storey porch. Nick passes several closed doors in his search for a bathroom. In one of them he hears water running. In still another he thinks he hears someone in pain. But he enters none of the rooms until he comes to the last room at the end of the hall. The door is wide open, the light is broken. He stumbles inside, uses the bathroom, and then heads down the hall towards the stairs.

He is at the top of the stairs when the sound of a gunshot explodes through the house. Instinctively, Nick runs down the stairs, accidentally banging into Maria, who is running up the stairs.

Michael, Sara, Jessica, and Polly join Maria and Nick upstairs. Together they enter the dark bedroom at the end of the hall. They turn on a corner lamp. Kats, Bill, Bubba, Clair, and The Rock – in that order – come up behind them.

On the floor, in a pool of blood with a gun in her mouth and a hole in the back of her head, is Alice.

They bury Alice a few days later. Everyone assumes it was a suicide. But Michael knows his dear friend would never have killed herself. When Jessica does not share his point of view, he yells at her, breaking her heart and his own.

FINAL FRIENDS Book 1, *The Party*, ends with Michael vowing to find the person who murdered Alice.

FINAL FRIENDS Book 2, *The Dance*, begins two and half months after the death of Alice McCoy. Jessica Hart has driven to Michael Olson's house, hoping to patch up their differences, but she is unable to bring herself to knock on his front door. It is only by chance that Michael notices her car parked on his street. Thinking that Jessica is visiting another girl who lives on the block, he hurries over to apologise for yelling at her after Alice's funeral. Jessica just wants to put the whole incident behind them, so she suggests they go out to a movie together the next day. Michael agrees.

Michael continues to be haunted by Alice's death. He is now convinced that she was murdered, and he fears her murderer may strike again. Michael wants to study Alice's autopsy report, which he hopes will give him a clue to what really happened the night of the party. Unfortunately, the detective in charge of the case will not let him see it until he first obtains a signed permission form from Alice's guardian, an elderly aunt. After picking up the form, Michael drives to the McCoy house, where Alice's older sister, Polly, still lives with her aunt.

Polly has had a difficult time since her sister died. Her aunt has had a heart attack, and Polly has been staying up most nights, caring for her. But she is happy to see Michael. She takes his permission form and promises to have her aunt read it.

Polly stays up late after Michael leaves. The night is stormy, filled with thunder and lightning. Suddenly Polly hears a banging at the side of the house. It is Clark – Alice's mysterious boyfriend. He denies having killed Alice, but does admit to having gone to the party. In fact, he acts surprised when Polly does not remember his being there. He takes Michael's permission form and puts it in his back pocket, telling Polly he will take care of it.

Russ Desmond also visits Polly the same night. He needs a place to stay. Earlier in the day Sara Cantrell had visited Russ at the supermarket where he worked. They got into a fight, and Sara ended up locking him in the store's freezer. He had to chop his way out with an axe and was subsequently fired. His dad has kicked him out of his house. But Polly welcomes him with open arms to hers.

Sara has more problems than her fight with Russ. She accidentally left Tabb High School's homecoming dance money in the store's freezer. When Sara realises it is gone, she turns to Bubba for help.

He offers her his assistance on two conditions: she must turn over to him whatever money she has left, and she has to have sex with him. Desperate, Sara agrees to his terms.

Jessica and Maria Gonzales are nominated to the homecoming court the next day, along with Clair Hilrey. Jessica notices that Clair is troubled, and wonders why. Jessica doesn't have any troubles. Right after the court is announced, Bill Skater asks her out for that night. Forgetting about her previous commitment to Michael, Jessica accepts.

Michael and Nick Grutler play basketball after school that afternoon. Michael, a guard on the varsity squad, tries to talk Nick into going out for the team. He agrees, but only after he has had an unpleasant conversation with Maria. Since the night of the party, Maria has refused to speak to Nick. He feels he has to prove himself to her and hopes he can do it on the court. Unknown to Nick, however, Maria has been avoiding him only because her parents have forbidden her to go out with him. She still cares for him.

Michael pays a visit to 'Kats' on his way home from school. Kats is at the top of Michael's list of suspects. But after confronting Kats about the night Alice died, Michael feels confused. Kats seems to be telling him the truth when he says he didn't kill Alice.

8

When Michael gets home, Jessica calls to say their date is off. She doesn't explain why. The turn of events depresses Michael, though not nearly so much as it does Jessica. Once she realised she had made two dates for the same time, she assumed she would be able to reschedule Michael, not knowing how busy he was. Her guilt chases her all night. Yet it is not enough to prevent her from trying to seduce Bill. She doesn't get very far. He doesn't even kiss her goodnight.

Needing time to be alone, Michael goes to the desert that night to hunt a comet with his telescope. He remembers a remark Clark made to him the one time they met. Michael feels the remark may help him locate Clark.

Nick joins the basketball team later and plays brilliantly. But Michael gets kicked off the squad when he questions the coach about his qualifications for the job. To further ruin Michael's day, Bubba tells Michael that Jessica was out with Bill the night she was supposed to be out with him.

Learning from Polly that Clair was at the family clinic and looking ill, Jessica starts the rumour that Clair had an abortion. Jessica does this hoping Clair's reputation will be ruined and she'll be out of the running for homecoming queen. Yet her conscience plagues her to no end.

Jessica and Michael take the SAT on Saturday morning. Having got no sleep the night before, Jessica swallows several Valium, thinking they're caffeine pills. She begins to pass out right in the middle of the test, and Michael tries to help her by slipping her his answers, not realising they have different tests. She does terribly on the test, but something good comes out of the experience. Jessica realises that it is Michael, and not Bill, whom she loves. But she doesn't tell Michael, and he continues to long for her without hope of ever having her.

Nick finally settles his differences with The Rock, who had mistaken Nick for a pusher who sold drugs to kids in East L.A.

Sara makes amends with Russ, also. She goes to cheer him on to victory in an important race. But being Sara, she inadvertently gets him disqualified. Russ doesn't mind.

Homecoming finally arrives. In the basketball game before the dance, Nick leads the team to a heartstopping victory. It is a happy moment. Maria's parents and Nick's father meet and Nick and Maria finally get back together. As the dance begins, most of the school is in an upbeat mood.

But Michael doesn't join in the celebration. With Bubba's help, he has tapped into the files of the coroner who performed the autopsy on Alice. He is amazed to discover that in addition to having severe brain damage caused by the gunshot, Alice also suffered a broken nose. He wonders who could have struck her in the face, and why.

At the close of the dance, the homecoming queen is announced. To Jessica's immense shock, it is not her, but Maria. Regrettably, Maria is not given long to enjoy her victory. While helping Sara clean up after the dance, she ascends the homecoming court float one final time. As she is standing on top of the queen's tower, the float suddenly collapses beneath her. She lands at an awkward angle and damages her spine.

It is a night of hard falls. Someone chops down the school's varsity tree. It crashes into the school, demolishing the snack bar.

Polly returns home from the dance and just misses catching Clark leaving on his motorcycle. The door to her house has been left open. Inside, she finds her aunt dead.

Michael, Nick and Jessica spend the night at the hospital, waiting for Maria to come out of surgery. Sara spends the night trying to get Russ out of jail. His fingerprints have been found on the handle of the axe that was used to chop down the varsity tree. He is in big trouble.

Maria is finally moved from the operating room to intensive care. Jessica goes in to see her. Maria is paralysed from the waist down, and she blames Jessica for ruining her life. Stricken with guilt, Jessica runs crying from the hospital, telling Michael to stay away from her, that she is no good. Only a few minutes later, while studying another school's yearbook in the hospital parking lot, Michael finds a picture of Clark. It is Michael's first lead to the strange guy's true identity.

FINAL FRIENDS Book 2, *The Dance*, ends with Michael promising to find Clark.

CHAPTER ONE

The last day of school began early for Sara Cantrell. As
ASB president, she had inherited the job of passing out
the yearbooks. No one else had wanted to do it. The task
called for a crack-of-dawn rising. The books had only
arrived the night before and had to be unpacked and
sorted into alphabetical order. The yearbook club had
been late sending the book to the printers. There had
been some concern – so the rumour went – about the
quality of the athletic photographs.

The price of vanity. Did I not say it months ago?

Sara smiled with glee as she squatted on the floor of
the recently reconstructed snack bar and tore open one
of the boxes and pulled out a copy of the annual. The
cover was dark blue, featureless except for a silver name
tag on the top and a tiny gold rope emblem in the lower
right corner, which Sara had to assume bore some
relationship to Tabb High's bronco-bull mascot. Quickly
she turned to the sports section. A moment later she was
laughing her head off.

'Where are your glasses, Jessie?' 'Bug off, Sara.'

In the basketball section in particular, and to a lesser
extent throughout the football and wrestling pages, every
other picture looked as if it had been shot underwater.
There was a blurred photograph of Nick Grutler going
to the basket with what could have been a swollen
pumpkin in his hand.

13

'I love it,' Sara said aloud, noting something else unusual about the basketball section. Michael Olson, who had been dropped from the team at the start of the season, was in more pictures than anyone else. And a couple of those were remarkably sharp. Jessica must have slipped on her glasses for a second here and there during the game against Holden High, Sara decided. No doubt there was going to be talk when the rest of the basketball players saw how he had been favoured.

They'll talk all day, and talk all night. Then nobody will see anybody again.

The graduation ceremony was to be held at three in the afternoon in the football stadium. The time had been moved up to accommodate nearby Sanders High's ceremony. Sanders's stadium was undergoing major renovations. Sara thought it was a bum rap that Sanders's ceremony wasn't first. She would have the sun directly in her eyes when she addressed the stands. She still hadn't figured out exactly what she was going to say in her speech, although she had stayed up half the night worrying about it. She simply had too much on her mind. There was the all-night party aboard the cruise ship she still had to pay for, and then there was Russ Desmond. Last Christmas he had been sent to a juvenile hall in northern California for chopping down the varsity tree, which fell on the snack bar. He was being released – temporarily – to attend graduation and receive his diploma. She was supposed to pick him up in downtown L.A. at the bus station at one o'clock. She hadn't seen him in over five months.

He's probably forgotten what I look like.

Sara set aside the yearbook and, with a razor blade, began to cut open the boxes. Although the books had not been packed alphabetically, she was pleased to see they had been grouped according to class, simplifying

14

her job somewhat. But there was still a lot to do. Tabb High had a student body of over two thousand, and more than half had ordered annuals. She wished she had Jessica to help her, the new clear-sighted Jessie who now wore her glasses wherever she went. But her best friend, bless her lazy hide, was getting her full measure of beauty sleep this morning.

The first knock at the window came two hours later, an hour earlier than Sara had anticipated – she had less than half the annuals unpacked. Two junior girls wanted their books *now*. Sara had no sooner found them than two more students arrived. It must have been because it was the last day – no one came to school this early usually. From that time on she was running. She quickly gave up checking receipts and IDs. If anyone felt he needed to steal a yearbook to be happy, she wasn't going to stand in the way.

Fortunately, before the big rush started around eight-thirty, three sophomores on the student council came to her rescue. Now she was able to take people's names and call them out to her helpers, who would hand her the right book a moment later.

Michael Olson and Clair Hilrey appeared at eight forty-five.

Sara had seen neither of them since January. Both had chosen to leave school at the semester. Apparently both had had enough units; and that was all that mattered, although Michael's GPA must have been about twice Clair's. The word going around was that Clair was making big bucks modelling and Michael was working for the government on some top-secret space laser. But, Sara knew, you couldn't believe everything you heard, although Clair had been on the cover of the May issue of *Seventeen*. Looked pretty damn good, too, and hadn't Jessica scowled when she had seen *that* magazine.

Clair had on baggy white shorts and a thin red blouse, perfect for the weather – the temperature was already close to eighty. She'd always had a tan, even in December, but now she was chestnut brown. It went without saying she was gorgeous.

Michael looked different. It was possible he hadn't cut his hair once since he'd left school. Black as night, and now curly, it hung way past his collar, practically on to his shoulders. He had lost weight, especially in his face. He appeared more handsome than she remembered, less a boy, more serious.

'Hi, Mike,' Sara said. 'Hi, Clair. Been a long time. How are you both doing?'

'We're just as happy as can be.' Clair giggled, squeezing Michael's arm. Michael smiled faintly and nodded.

'It's good to see you, Sara,' he said. 'Busy?'

She glanced past them at the line. 'Yeah, but I can take a minute off.' She called behind her 'Michael Olson and Clair Hilrey. They're both seniors. And, Lori, take the window for a second.' She had their books a few seconds later and carried them with her as she slipped out the side door of the snack bar. The carpenters were still working on the building's south wall; it was covered with plastic instead of stucco. The varsity tree had been awfully heavy.

Clair immediately opened her yearbook to the homecoming court pictures. Michael peered at the page over her shoulder. Clair made a face.

'That photographer – what an amateur,' she complained.

'You look fine to me,' Michael said.

'I'm supposed to look sexy, not fine,' Clair said. She studied the page a little more, then added reluctantly, 'But that is a nice picture of Jessica.'

16

'Very nice,' Michael agreed.

'Have you seen Jessie, Mike?' Sara asked. Clair quickly glanced over her shoulder at Michael.

'I've got to go,' she said, suddenly closing the book. 'I've got to find Bubba. Nice to see you Sara.'

'Catch you at graduation,' Sara said.

'I'll be along in a minute,' Michael told Clair. When she was gone, he said, 'No, I just got here. How's she been?'

'Great,' Sara said, which was something of an exaggeration. After Maria Gonzales's crippling accident the night of the homecoming dance, Jessica had gone into as deep a depression as she had when Alice died. She hadn't even returned to school after Christmas vacation to finish the semester. If Sara hadn't brought her work to her, Jessica might have flunked out. Her spirits had improved somewhat when she finally returned at the start of the new semester. Yet Sara continued to worry about her. Jessica wasn't interested in going to the movies, going shopping – hardly anything any more. Sara had had to use every bit of her considerable persuasive skills to talk her into going to the senior prom in May with Bill Skater. Afterwards Jessica told her she'd had a wonderful time, but Sara didn't quite believe her. Jessica hadn't gone out with Bill since.

Not returning to school until the beginning of February, Jessica had missed Michael Olson's last days at Tabb. Sara remembered how Jessica's face fell when she had heard Michael was gone. To this day, however, Jessica denied they were close or that she cared one way or the other about him.

'She's doing real good,' Sara continued. 'She should be here any minute. Why don't you wait for her?'

He looked doubtful. 'I have a lot to do today.'

17

'But you're coming to the ceremony this afternoon,' aren't you? I heard you're valedictorian?'

He smiled faintly at the mention of the word. 'Yeah, it looks like I am. I have to give a speech.'

'You're not the only one. Well, that's great. I'll get to introduce you. But I wish you could stay now. She should be here any sec. I know she'd love to see you.'

He glanced down at the closed yearbook in his hands. 'I really can't wait. But say hello to her for me.'

'I will.' She was trying to get rid of the habit of talking people into stuff. Russ had told her – before they had locked him up – that it was one of her least desirable personality traits. On the other hand, she didn't believe Michael couldn't wait a few minutes, any more than she believed Jessica when she had said it was no big deal that Michael had left school early. 'She's as pretty as ever,' she added.

Michael smiled politely. 'I don't doubt it.' He turned to leave. 'I'll be back this afternoon for the ceremony.'

'Hey, hold on. Let me sign your yearbook.'

'Sure.' He handed it over. 'Where's yours?'

'I've been so busy with everybody else's, I haven't had a chance to look for my own. You can sign it later on the boat. You're coming to the all-night party, aren't you?'

He hesitated, spoke under his breath. 'If need be.'

'Huh?'

'I don't know. I didn't buy a ticket.'

She pulled a ticket from her back pocket and gave it to him. 'It's on the house. The party won't be complete without our class genius.' She clicked out her ballpoint pen and turned to one of the blank pages at the back of his yearbook. 'I promise not to write anything disgusting,' she said.

'Don't let me stop you,' he remarked, stuffing the

18

ticket into his back pocket and scanning the half-filled courtyard. Sara thought for a moment and then wrote.

Mike,
   Of all the people in the school, you're the only one I wish I knew better. All the rest, I wish I could forget. Just kidding! What I really mean is, I'll never forget you. You're so smart! Figure out how to be happy and then tell the rest of us miserable slobs. We're counting on you.

Luv, Sara

She returned his yearbook, saying, 'Read it later tonight, preferably when you're drunk.'

He nodded. 'Thanks for the free ticket.'

Sara hugged him briefly. 'I'm so glad you're here. I think we're going to have a wild time today.'

'I think so, too.'

Michael left and Sara returned to distributing the yearbooks at the snack-bar window. Bubba put in a typical annoying appearance ten minutes later. He didn't have to say or do anything. Just the sight of him irritated Sara. It had been Bubba who had talked her into renting the cruise ship for the all-night party, even when he had known it was way beyond their means. She was beginning to believe he was purposely prolonging her personal crisis with the school funds to keep her dependent on him. After the homecoming dance, he had continued to pay her creditors just enough to keep them from suing, but not enough to make them go away. Lately he had been hinting at a scheme that would clear up all her money worries. Of course he hadn't said what it was.

'Come for your book?' she asked wearily. The predicted temperature for the day was a muggy ninety-

19

five and Bubba had on an immaculate pair of light blue slacks, a navy-blue sports jacket and a red-and-white-striped tie. His choice of hat that day was a wide-brimmed straw sombrero. He looked positively ridiculous and was loving every minute of it.

'No, I've come for you to sign it,' he replied, lifting up his yearbook from beneath the counter. The silver name tag on the top read – in unusually big letters – BUBBA.

'Where did you get that?' she demanded. 'I didn't give you that.'

'I was sent an advance copy.' He produced a feathered quill pen. 'While you're signing mine, may I have the pleasure of brightening yours with a few words of love?'

'No. Go away, I'm busy.'

Bubba glanced at the line behind him, smiled. 'No time for Bubba on this, our last day of school? No time to share a precious moment to express our unspoken feeling for each other? Surely you must realise that an occasion such as this – '

'Stop it! I'll sign your stupid book. Lori, fetch my annual, and then do me a favour and take the window again. Thanks.'

She met Bubba outside in the same spot she had spoken to Michael and Clair. Before handing over her annual, she said, 'I talked the captain of the ship into taking a postdated cheque like you told me to. Now I want to know if the cheque will clear?'

'It should.'

'What? Two days ago you told me it definitely would!'

'I do not believe I used the word 'definite'. The only things definite in this world are death, taxes, and my good humour.'

'But my name's on that cheque!'

'Better your name than mine.'

'Why are you doing this to me? What have I ever done to you?'

Bubba chuckled. 'I've done nothing you haven't asked me to. You wanted a party the class wouldn't forget, and I told you how to give them one. I'm only here to serve, Sara.'

She started to yell at him again, but couldn't think of anything to say. To her immense horror, she realised it was because what he said was partially true. He'd had no trouble putting her out on another financial limb. All he'd had to do was dangle before her nose another way to impress the school with what a fantastic president Sara Cantrell was.

'How are you serving me this week?' she asked. 'Where's the school money?'

'I'd prefer not to say at this moment.'

'Why not?'

'I'd rather not make you more nervous than you already are.'

'What kind of answer is that? Where's the money?' Sara asked again.

'Do you like basketball?'

'Yeah, it's all right.'

'The seventh game of the NBA finals is tonight. The Lakers versus the Celtics. A classic matchup. I grew up with the Lakers. They're my team. I know them better than their own coach.'

'Wait a second. You didn't bet our money on a basketball game?'

'I was given excellent odds. We'll double our investment if we win.'

'What if we lose?' she screamed.

He shrugged. 'We'll still have our good looks.' He

21

held up his yearbook and offered her a regular ball point pen. 'You don't have to go overboard. A few paragraphs and a poem or two will suffice to let me know you care.'

Bubba came very close at that moment to losing whatever good looks he believed he might have. Sara almost poked his eyes out. Only because she was essentially a non-violent person did she grab his yearbook and pen instead. Inadvertently she let him get hold of her annual in the process. She plopped down on a nearby bench and began to scribble furiously on a back page.

Bubba,
    Words, even the filthiest, cannot convey what I think of you. You are a liar, a thief, and a pervert. You are also the most unattractive slob to ever abuse my eyesight. I consider it the greatest misfortune of my adolescence that I had a chance to get to know you. You will not go far. You will end up in the mud – where you belong – with the rest of the world's slime.

Get There As Soon As Possible,
Sara

When she looked up, Bubba had vanished. He reappeared a couple of minutes later, her annual in his hand, a beatific smile on his lips. She snapped her book back and tossed him his. He read her inscription with obvious pleasure.

'You have beautiful handwriting,' he said. 'Very sensual.'

'Go to hell.'

'Later.' He grinned as he walked away. 'Later, Sara.'

She was back inside the snack bar when she opened her yearbook. Her scream frightened everyone. Bubba had covered the entire inside cover with fat black marking-pen letters. There was no way to tear out the page. She shook as she read it.

My Dearest Sara,

My heart patters at the thought of us making love tonight above the deep ocean swells, our bodies locked in passion, the salty sweat on the burning flesh of our entangled limbs mingling like oil and wine, ready to burst into flaming ecstasy. My head swoons. Tonight, Sara, I promise you, will be our night. The gods will envy our joy.

But we mustn't be foolish. We mustn't forget, in our carnal hunger for each other, certain responsibilities. You would rather float on love-intoxicated perfumed clouds, I realise, ignoring the practical demands the world places upon us, only fantasising about the pleasure I will send throbbing through your body. Yet we have to be careful. We can have our cake and eat it, too, but only if we don't let the ice cream melt. We have to get some condoms.

As you have probably guessed, anything that will heighten our delight is fine with me. I prefer the natural to the artificial, the tight to the loose, blue to red. Keep this in mind when you visit the pharmacy, Sara, and you will be thanked a thousand times over when the time comes.

Love You Always,
In So Many Different Positions,
Bubba

P.S. Or, if you'd like, I can pick up something on the way to the boat?

'What is it?' Lori asked, standing beside her.

If the Lakers should win, would he keep the money if I don't come across?

Stupid question.

Sara slammed the book shut and answered Lori. 'Don't ask.'

CHAPTER TWO

Michael had never seen Clair so happy. As they walked the familiar hallways searching for Bubba, she kept glancing over at him and giggling.

'What is it?' he asked finally.

'I have a secret I want tell you, but I can't.'

'What if I promise to tell no one else?'

'I still can't tell you. Bubba would kill me.'

'He knows the secret?'

'He knows everything.' Clair giggled again and grabbed his arm. 'Everything!'

'How come he doesn't know we're looking for him?'

She smiled, her blue eyes clear and bright. 'Maybe he's trying to avoid us.'

'That's probably the truth. How's the modelling coming? Is Bubba really acting as your agent?'

'Yeah, and he's doing a great job. I'm shooting an ad for Nabisco next Monday, and on Wednesday I'm starring in a video with Killer Kids.'

'Is that a heavy metal group?'

'Punk. Their music stinks but the pay's great. I'm making so much money! Bubba's investing it for me.'

'Legally, I hope.'

She laughed easily, still holding on to him. He didn't understand why she liked him so much, unless it had to do with stuff Bubba had told her, which was hard to imagine. He regretted his initial low opinion of her. She was really very sweet.

'How about you?' she asked. 'I hear you're working at JPL?'

He had not planned to leave school in January. But after Maria's accident and Jessica's subsequent disappearance, he began to feel that Tabb High had lost whatever charm it had once possessed. From his freshman year on he had taken a heavy load. He had more than enough units to call it quits. Plus Mr Gregory, his MGM (Mentally Gifted Minors) adviser, had helped him land another workstudy position at Jet Propulsion Laboratory. The job was only twenty hours a week, so he hadn't quit his job at the 7-Eleven to take it – much to the relief of the store owners. The JPL job came with the impressive title aeronautics intern, but it amounted to little more than errand boy to the engineers. It was not that he wasn't learning. Often he was allowed to sit in on discussions relating to the design of future spacecraft, both manned and unmanned. The problem was, the experience was boring him.

Throughout his school days, he had seen himself as a budding scientist. Now he was finding out that the entire analytic approach to the universe left him feeling cold and unsatisfied. This was a critical discovery; it completely threw off his future plans. He no longer knew what he should study in college, or even *if* he should go to college. Looking around at the other kids in his class hanging out in the hallway, signing one another's yearbooks and gossiping about how loaded they were going to get on the ship, he wondered if he was the only one who felt confused. He often wondered that – why he felt so different from everybody else.

'Yeah. The rocket and space business is OK,' he

26

replied. 'But I've been thinking of starting my own rock-and-roll band. Would you like to front it for me?'

Clair was amused. 'I'm totally tone deaf.'

'But you can dance. That's all that matters.'

'You should get Jessie. She's got a great voice. She's singing at the ceremony this afternoon.' She stopped, obviously afraid she might have offended him somehow. 'I'm sorry, Mike.'

'No problem. That's neat, she'll be in the ceremony and all.'

Clair was watching him. 'You never talk to her any more, do you?'

He shrugged, feeling uncomfortable. Bubba must have told Clair how he felt about Jessica. 'I never see her.'

'You'll see her today.'

'I guess.'

'Look I'm being nosy.'

'No.'

'Well, then, talk to her today. Hey, I said a lot of nasty things about her before – and I still think she deserved them – but she *is* a classy chick. She really likes you.'

Curiosity got the best of him 'What makes you say that? You haven't seen her in six months.'

'I can tell.' She leaned closer. 'Do you want me to tell her?'

'Tell her what?'

Clair reconsidered. 'Nothing.'

'What?' he insisted.

She grinned mischievously. 'Nothing.'

'Clair.'

She shook her head. 'I won't say anything.' But she had to add, 'As long as you say something.'

'You've been hanging around Bubba too long. That sounds like a threat.'

She gave him a quick kiss on the cheek and began to bounce away. 'I've got to talk to my pals on the cheerleading squad. If you run into him before me, tell him I went to look for them in the gym. Think about what I said!'

'You remember what *I* said,' he called after her, embarrassed.

He continued to search for Bubba. The first period bell would ring in a few minutes, but he doubted that many kids would be heading to class. As usual on the last day of school, there was a party atmosphere all over campus. He observed it without feeling it. The hot weather contributed to his mood. He remembered how it had been hot the day he had met Jessica.

Am I looking for Bubba or trying to hide from Jessie?

He bumped into Nick Grutler next outside. They had kept in touch: regular telephone calls, occasional one-on-one basketball games. Tabb High had finished first in the league for the second straight year. Some people were saying Coach Seller was a genius. None of those people had been on the team. The title belonged to Nick. Come next fall, he would be attending U.C.L.A. on a full athletic scholarship. Michael was proud of him.

'Does the old school still look the same?' Nick asked.

'Hey, I haven't been gone that long.' Nick had been heading in the direction of the parking lot. 'Where you going?'

Nick averted his eyes. He had gained a great deal of confidence since he had stumbled stuttering into the 7-Eleven at the end of the first week of school, but when he was troubled, he reverted to his old habit and looked away. 'Maria's coming to the graduation ceremony,' he said. 'I'm picking her up at the rehabilitation clinic in San Diego.'

'How is she?' He knew Nick hadn't seen Maria since

28

she had been discharged from the hospital in February to the spinal injury clinic to begin rebuilding her body. But Nick had talked to her on the phone, although he wouldn't say what they talked about.

'I don't know,' Nick said.

'Does Jessie or Sara know she's coming?'

'No.'

'I wonder if someone should tell them?'

'I think Maria wants it to be a surprise.'

'Why?'

Nick shook his head. 'I guess none of us can know what it feels like to be suddenly crippled.'

Michael knew he was trying to make excuses for her ahead of time, and felt bad for him. 'Tell her I'm looking forward to seeing her again.'

Nick nodded. 'I will, Mike.' He glanced at his watch. He had one now – and a car. His dad had begun to let him hold on to his money, or else the college recruiters had been very generous. 'I better go.'

They exchanged goodbyes. Michael decided he might find Bubba in the computer room. He spotted Polly McCoy as he was on his way there. A talk with Polly was on his list of things to do.

She was sitting by herself on a bench outside on the far side of the girls' shower room. Her dark hair hung long, straighter than before. The weight she had lost following Alice's death had not returned; if anything, she was thinner. She glanced up as he approached, her eyes dark and uncertain. She had been studying her palm.

'Hi,' she said.

'Hi, Polly. How are you?'

'Fine . . .' The word trailed from her lips. Then she blinked. 'Mike, it's you. Where have you been?'

He sat beside her on the green wooden bench. Her

blue jeans were old, skintight, her white lace blouse, long and loose. She had bitten her nails down a fraction too far. The only makeup she wore was lipstick, thick and red.

'I finished school at the semester,' he said. 'Didn't you know?'

'Jessie didn't tell me. She never tells me anything.'

He forced a smile. 'I don't think *I* told Jessie. What are you doing way over here in the middle of nowhere?'

'I have a headache.'

'Oh, that's a shame. Is it bad?'

'No. It's long.'

'Long?' Mike asked.

'I've had it a couple of months.' She paused. 'I've missed seeing you. I'm glad you've come back to school.'

'She was outside when the gun went off. We're sure of that, aren't we?'

He had asked Jessica that question six months ago. The answer was still yes. That was a fact. But he still didn't trust Polly. 'Just for the day. You must be excited about graduating?'

'I'm glad it's almost over.' She glanced down at her hands and wove her fingers together. She answered his initial question again. 'I like to be alone.'

'Do you want me to go?'

'No. But why do you want to talk to me?'

'I like talking to you.'

'Did you find him?'

'Find who?' He knew who she was talking about.

'Clark.'

'No,' he lied. He had found him, he just hadn't spoken to him. He planned to do so today. 'Does he know I'm looking for him?' he asked carefully, his heartbeat accelerating.

30

'I think so,' she said, her expression dreamy.

'So you've seen him?'

'Not in a long time.'

'When was the last time, Polly?'

'A long time ago.'

'You don't remember?'

She jerked slightly, then frowned, concentrating. 'It was the night Aunty died. It was raining.'

The sun shone bright in their faces, rebounding off the light brown wall at their backs. Michael realised that he was sweating.

Her aunt had died the night of homecoming, but there had been no storm. And since then, Polly had been alone. The court had not appointed her another guardian; apparently she was over eighteen.

'What did he do?' Michael asked, referring to Clark.

'The doctor said she died of natural causes.'

'Your aunt?'

'You don't think he killed her, do you?' She could have been talking to herself. 'I know you think he killed Alice. That's why you're looking for him. But he says he didn't.'

'He told you that?' Michael asked.

'Yes.'

'Do you believe him?' She looked him straight in the eye. Her dreaminess lessened. Indeed, she seemed suddenly cautious. 'I do.'

'But was he there, the night of the party?'

'He said something about coming at the end.'

Michael could hardly contain his excitement. 'Was he up in the bedroom when Alice died?'

She became slightly annoyed. 'Why are you asking all these questions? I told you, I have a headache.'

'I'm sorry, I was sort of pushy. Let me ask just a couple more and then I'll help you find an aspirin.'

'I don't take aspirin. They make your stomach bleed. I have to save my blood to donate to the hospital.'

'Was Clark in the room with Alice just before she died?'

'No. He left when I left.' She put a hand to her temple – as she had done when he visited her last winter – and paled. 'I wish you'd stop. Please stop.'

It drove him nuts, to be so close and yet so far. 'I have to ask you, Polly, if I'm ever to clear Alice's name.'

'She's dead. She doesn't care about her name. The dead don't care about anything. The only one who cares is me.'

'That's not true. I care.'

She paused, surprised. 'You do?'

'I really do, Polly.'

She thought for a moment, then looked away. 'Don't go to the all-night party, Mike.'

'Why not?'

'Clark might come,' she answered.

'Did he tell you he was coming?'

'No.'

'Then why do you think he will?'

'I – I feel it. It's a bad feeling.'

'But I want to talk to him.'

Polly shook her head. 'He won't talk to you.'

'What will he do?'

'I don't know,' she said, standing, obviously upset. 'Excuse me, but I have to go to the bathroom.' She looked right and left, confused. 'I hate this school. I come here and Alice shoots herself and then Aunty chokes on a pillow. It's an awful place. It makes me want to throw up.'

'Polly,' he began.

'Just don't get too close,' she cried, running away.

32

Michael wondered if anything she had told him had been accurate.

Bubba appeared a minute later, dressed to kill, except for an oversize sombrero that bobbled around on his head. Michael had not seen him in over a month. Bubba had lost a few pounds. Must be Clair's doing. He sat beside Michael on the bench, a brown paper bag in his right hand, his yearbook in the left. Michael knew what was in the bag. He immediately glanced all around.

'We're alone,' Bubba said.

Michael nodded at the sack. 'You got it?'

'I got it. Are you sure you want it?'

'Where did you get it?'

'Kats,' Bubba said.

'Bubba! I told you no one is supposed to know.'

'You only gave me a few days. Besides, I fed Kats a good story. Don't worry.' Bubba glanced at the bag, appearing a tad worried himself. 'You know, Mike, you're a smart guy, but I know a lot of smart guys who have done stupid things with one of these.'

'I'll be fine.'

'If you'd tell me what you want it for, I might be able to give you some sage advice to keep you out of jail.'

Michael held out his hand. 'The less you know, the better for you.'

Bubba reluctantly gave him the package. 'Everything's inside. The keys, too.'

Earlier in the week Michael had asked Bubba to slip into Polly's school locker, borrow her purse, and make a copy of her house keys. Michael wanted another look at the bedroom where Alice had died, but wasn't fond of the idea of breaking into the McCoy residence. 'I appreciate it.'

'What are Bubbas for? I hear Maria's coming to the ceremony.'

'Did Nick tell you?'

'No. A confidential source. Do you have your speech ready?'

'I haven't given it a moment's thought. Hey, what am I doing as valedictorian anyway? What happened to Dale Jensen? Did he get a C in a class or what?'

'He got busted.'

'When? How?'

'Tuesday night. Remember that narc that was hassling Nick before Christmas? Randy Meisser?'

'Yeah. You said you were going to run him off campus.'

'I changed my mind. Thought he might come in useful. He busted Dale snorting coke in a bathroom.' Bubba took off his hat and fanned himself. 'We can't have an ill-mannered druggie giving any long-winded speeches graduation day. Not when it's hot like this.'

Michael sighed. 'You set Dale up.'

'I may have put the white powder beneath his nose, but I did not force him to inhale.'

'Were his parents able to bail him out?'

'Yes, and weren't they embarrassed. Relatives flying in from the Midwest and all. Would you like me to write your speech for you?'

'No, thank you.' Michael stood up, gripping the bag, testing its weight. 'Clair's in the gym. She wants to talk to you. You probably know that, right?'

'Of course.' Bubba got up, too, brushing off the seat of his trousers.

'She said she had a secret to tell me.'

Bubba raised an eyebrow. 'Did she tell you?'

'No.'

He nodded. 'She's a good girl. Did you know Kats will be receiving a diploma today?'

'He mentioned something like that once.'

34

'He's also coming with us on our cruise to Catalina.'

'Wonderful.'

Bubba smiled. 'He might surprise you. He might just be the life of the party.'

Michael had what he had come for. He had a great deal to accomplish before he returned to the campus at three. He bade Bubba goodbye and hurried towards the parking lot. Crossing the courtyard, extremely conscious of the sack in his hand, he spotted Jessica talking to Sara outside the snack bar. He practically dropped the sack. He stepped behind a tree, peeping around like a frightened lowlife.

'No. Don't touch me. Don't get near me. I'm no good, Michael. I'm not.'

Her brown hair and brown eyes. He always saw them first. Long and silky, big and round. Then would come her smile. Yet she was not smiling now. She was as pretty as ever, but it seemed to him, even at a glance, that she didn't smile as often as she had. She was no longer the young girl who had almost wept over the grape juice he had spilled on her sweater.

Her clothes were seductive now – as was her body. She had on a short green skirt and thin yellow blouse. Her legs were every bit as tanned as Clair's. He had dreamed about them the last few months, along with the rest of her body.

Love would not care. It should not care.

Yet Michael did not feel guilt over his sexual desire for Jessica. It was natural, he realised. He could not separate who she was from her body. He didn't want to.

I just want her.

But she did not want him. Bill came up to talk to her then. He put a hand on her shoulder. Now she smiled.

Michael left quickly for the parking lot. In his car he removed the gun from the brown paper bag and opened

35

the box of shells. Pressing the bullets into the clip of the automatic weapon, he wondered if maybe he should have waited for Jessica as Sara had suggested. If maybe Bubba was right, and he was stupid.

He put the loaded automatic in the glove compartment and drove away.

CHAPTER THREE

Jessica Hart was thinking of winning and losing. She had begun the year at Tabb optimistically. She had figured she would earn outstanding grades, be nominated homecoming queen, get accepted to Stanford, fall in love with a cute boy, and enjoy the respect and goodwill of all she met. She hadn't thought she was asking for more than her fair share.

And none of those things came to me. Not one.

She had received a C in chemistry, the same grade she would receive on her report card. She hadn't been able to find a lab partner after Maria got hurt. Her overall grade-point average for the year was a C-plus. In a class of four hundred and sixty-four, she was graduating somewhere in the mid-two hundreds. The ranking would have been lower if they'd averaged in her SAT score.

Her father had held back her application for Stanford. Maybe after a couple of years at a local junior college, he said. Junior college – it would be like going to summer camp after expecting to climb Mount Everest. Her father had been so disappointed in her. Sara was heading to Princeton.

She had found a boy she sort of liked – good old Bill. But he wasn't a real boyfriend. They'd only been out three times. She didn't love him and she seriously doubted he loved her. She was beginning to doubt there really was such a thing as love. Sex, yeah – she was as horny as anybody else. But where were the couples who cared more for each other than for themselves? She couldn't find them. All she saw around her were boys and girls struggling to boost their egos at the expense of those they supposedly adored. She despised it, particularly since she wanted to do the same thing.

The year died when Alice died. I should have written it off right then and quit.

'I love this material,' Jessica said to Bill, feeling the upper sleeve of his red shirt. 'It feels like silk.'

'It is,' he replied. 'My mother bought it for me.'

'For a graduation present?' she asked.

He nodded. 'Yeah, and I got a car. A Corvette.'

'I hope to God it matches your shirt,' Sara said. Sara had just given them each a copy of the new yearbook. Jessica had no desire to open it; she knew all too well what most of her photographs looked like. The yearbook club had been very disappointed in her. Had they not been so desperately short of football and basketball pictures, they probably would have trashed all her 'pre-glasses material'. She didn't care, she told herself, but it did bother her. So, maybe, she really did care. Letting go of Bill's shirt, she pushed her glasses back on her nose. She was never going to get used to wearing them. She hoped the sun burned out soon and everyone could walk around blind with her in the dark.

'It's black,' Bill said seriously. 'It goes with everything.'

Sara winked at Jessica and patted her hair. 'My colour coordinator says I absolutely should never be seen in a black car.'

'That's too bad,' Bill said.

'Our parents are sending us to Hawaii next week for

our graduation presents,' Jessica said, wanting to stop Sara before she got started. Because Polly was now off-limits, Sara got her kicks out of ridiculing Bill. Jessica hated it that he never even knew it was happening. 'Isn't that neat?'

'They've got great surfing there,' Bill said.

'It's the waves,' Sara said confidentially. 'Something to do with the waves.'

'Yeah, that has a lot to do with it,' Bill agreed.

'Bill, could you do me a favour?' Jessica said, clearing her throat and looking pointedly at Sara. 'Could you get me a book from my locker?'

'Sure. Did you want one in particular?'

No, any old book will do. Just make sure it has pages, a cover, words in it – the usual.

In reality, she didn't care what book he got. She just wanted to talk to Sara alone.

'My political science book,' she said.

'We handed those in to Mr Bark yesterday,' Sara said. 'Get her something else. Get her a brush.'

'Do you want a brush?' Bill asked, and now even he was beginning to wonder.

But Jessica kept a straight face. 'Yeah, I'd appreciate it,' she said.

When Bill was gone, Sara said, 'He's lucky he's so good-looking or we'd have to have him stuffed.'

'Leave him alone, he's all right.'

'Oh, I think he's great. I love him. I can see why you love him.'

'Right, my feelings go real deep.'

Sara laughed. 'Hope it goes plenty deep tonight.' She leaned close, her excitement barely concealed. 'You know how I told you the captain wanted the passenger suites on the ship kept locked and off limits? Well, last night I had a long talk with him and arranged for the use of couple of adjacent rooms. I've got the keys. Isn't that great? Everything's set.'

Jessica was not sure why she was doing this. She supposed that like anything else, virginity got old after a while and – like a hundred per cent of the young ladies in her present situation – she'd been a virgin since she was born. Once she had imagined that when she finally did give herself to a guy, it would be to someone she really cared about. She guessed hormones and biology had finally caught up with her. Now all she wanted was to have a good time.

It's all I can hope for at this point.

That was closer to the truth. She wanted a lot more than a roll in the hay, but she felt – until something better came along – that this would give her life spark. The flatness of each day was becoming almost unbearable.

Yet she hoped boredom was all there was to it. She hoped she wasn't attempting to seduce Bill in an effort to prove to herself beyond a shadow of a doubt that she really didn't care about anything.

That was a frightening thought.

And what was even more frightening was that she recognised her self-destructive streak, and its source, and still wasn't able to free herself from it. She had not killed Alice. She had not crippled Maria. She had not chased Michael from school. But somehow she felt as if she had *allowed* all those terrible things to happen. As if she should have known ahead of time. As if someone had been trying to warn her of the dangers and she had not been listening.

Someone . . .

'Everything's set like hell,' Jessica said, forcing her thoughts back to Sara and trying to shake off her melancholy mood. 'We don't even know if we've got ingredient A.'

'Russ will be down. Bill's coming to the party. What's the problem? You think we can't seduce two eighteen-year-old boys?'

Jessica remembered back to senior-prom night. Bill had kissed her long and hard in his car before dropping her off home, yet she couldn't have sworn they had been passionate kisses. He had made no move to grab her or even touch her. It had left her feeling frustrated and with all sorts of doubts about her own sexuality.

'I don't know if the shower routine is what we want,' Jessica said.

'What's wrong with it? We have every reason to be in the shower when they get to our rooms. People are dirty creatures – they're always taking showers. It won't look like a set-up. They'll see us naked, we'll squeal, and the rest will be history.'

'Don't give me that confident B.S. You're scared to death Russ will take one look at your bare ass and bust up laughing.'

Sara was insulted. 'What's wrong with my ass?'

'I don't know. I've never looked at it that closely. Christ, this is beginning to sound ridiculous. You would think we were hard up or something.'

'Yeah, isn't that a ridiculous thought.'

Then they laughed at how far past ridiculous they already were. Jessica began to feel a bit better. If nothing else, she had her best friend to share her misery with. Jessica nodded at Sara's yearbook.

'Let me sign it,' she said. 'And you can be the first person to sign mine.'

But Sara held her book back. 'Later. On the boat.'

'No, let's do it now.' Jessica reached out for it, and when Sara held it further away, Jessica naturally snapped it out of her hands. 'What's the problem with you. What's – ' She stopped. Sara's yearbook had a crudely

41

cut rectangle of brown paper pasted over the inside front cover. 'What is this?'

Sara grabbed her book back. 'I got a defective copy.'

'How can you get a defective yearbook for God sakes?'

'All of them are defective, Miss Fuzzy-Film Face.'

'Haven't you insulted me enough times about that already this year? I know what's wrong with your book. Somebody wrote something nasty in it.'

'Sure, yeah, who would do that?'

'Bubba. That's who. I know that's it.'

'I wouldn't let that slime touch my book if he didn't have any hands.'

'What did he write?'

'He didn't write anything!'

'Forget Russ and the shower. Bubba will do it with you no matter how many clothes you have on and no matter how flabby your ass is. What did he say?'

Sara sucked in a breath. 'I wish, Jessie, for the sake of our long and warm association that you would please change the goddamn subject.'

'OK. But you're right – the grease just sweats off that guy. Can you imagine why any girl would go to bed with him?'

'I try not to think about it.' Sara stared at the ground, thinking, chewing on her lower lip.

'What's the matter?'

'Nothing.'

'What?' Jessica persisted.

'I was wondering if I should tell you this.'

'Don't tell me. Play it safe. Keep it to yourself.'

'All right.'

'Sara?' she said, getting exasperated.

'Mike was here about half an hour ago.'

'Michael?' The strength went out of her. She had not

been thinking of winning and losing. Only of losing. 'Why didn't you tell me?'

'You just got here.'

'But where is he?' She quickly scanned the courtyard, almost afraid to find him. 'Where did he go?'

'I don't know,' Sara said.

'What do you mean, you don't know? Which direction was he heading when he left you?'

'He went after Clair.'

'Clair's here, too?'

'Yeah.'

She swallowed. 'I don't care.'

'Jessie, of course you care.'

'I don't. So she's got her stupid face on the cover of some stupid magazine?'

'We're talking about Mike. You might be able to find him if you go look.'

'First period's going to start in a minute. I don't have time.' She shielded her eyes from the bright sun – it was going to be a cooker of an afternoon – searching harder. 'Why was he here?'

'He came to pick up his yearbook. He's going to be at the ceremony. He's valedictorian.'

'*What?* When did this happen? What happened to Jensen?'

'All I know is Mike is going to be giving the speech.'

'Since when have you known this?' Jessica pressed.

'Since yesterday,' Sara said.

'Why didn't you tell me?'

'You didn't ask me.'

'Why should I have to ask you?'

'Because you keep telling me you don't care.'

'I don't care. I mean, what's there to care about? He

43

left school early. He didn't even say goodbye. I hardly knew him. How did he look?'

'Great.'

Jessica smiled. 'Did he?'

Sara smiled, too. 'Yeah. His hair's longer. He's got a tan.'

'I always wanted him to grow his hair.' She scratched her own hair. 'He wasn't with Clair, like in *with* her, was he?'

'No.'

Jessica bounced on her feet. 'I've got to find him. Talk to you later.'

'Good luck.'

Unfortunately, she had no luck at all. She was hurrying down the first hallway when she ran into Bubba. He had on a straw hat so huge it was causing traffic jams.

'Bubba, have you seen Michael?' she asked casually.

'He left already.'

'But he's coming back, right?'

Bubba showed a flicker of uncertainty. 'I hope so.' Then he grinned and reached out his hand. 'May I sign your yearbook, my dear?'

'Yeah.' She clasped it to her chest and looked at his fat ink-stained fingers. 'Later.'

CHAPTER FOUR

Ray Bradbury had written a short story called 'Rocket Man'. Michael had read it in junior high. It told of a man who piloted a rocket for a living. Most of the time he worked alone in space, but occasionally he returned home to earth. He had a wife and son, and although the story was largely told through the son's eyes, it was the wife's point of view that had stayed with Michael. It came to him as he stood in the cemetery at the foot of Alice McCoy's grave.

The wife always worried that her husband would crash into the moon, or die on Mars, or Venus, or on any other planet in the solar system. Then she would never again be able to look up when the moon was in the sky, or when the particular planet was close to the earth. For that reason, she tried to keep distance between herself and her husband. She knew that one day she would lose him, and that from then on there would always be a light in the heavens to remind her of him, and break her heart.

Of course the husband's rocket fell into the sun. It had been a sad story. Yet the Western custom of pumping dead people's veins with preserving fluids, Michael realised, and sealing the bodies in airtight coffins to bury them in concrete-lined holes, affected him in much the same way. One of the reasons he couldn't get over Alice, no matter how often he told himself her soul was free, was that her decaying body was always, in a sense, beneath his feet. He wished they'd had her cremated and thrown her ashes into the ocean, or tossed them on to the wind.

At the same time, he wondered if it would have made any difference.

He had not intended to visit the cemetery. He had many things to do. He had to question the coroner who had performed Alice's autopsy, examine the bedroom again, speak to Clark, and give that silly speech. The fact that he had so many things to investigate all on one day caused him to wonder about his convictions. He could have made his appointment with the coroner months ago. He could have had Bubba duplicate Polly's keys any time. And he had found Clark three weeks ago, but still hadn't approached him. There was really no two ways about it – he had postponed the investigation. The question was, had he done it because he was afraid to discover a fact that proved she had pulled the trigger?

But why would she kill herself?

Even Jessica had not attempted to address that point. Maybe Clark would. Michael glanced back towards his car and the gun safely stowed there. More questions came to mind. Why had he postponed his investigation until this particular day, the last day of school? And why did he feel he could no longer postpone it?

'I feel it. It's a bad feeling.'

It was hard to stand beside her grave, but harder still to leave it. He wished he had brought flowers. This was the first time he had been to the cemetery since the funeral. He glanced at the two graves on either side of Alice: Martha McCoy and Philip Bart, Alice's aunt and an employee of McCoy Construction who had died from an on-site accident. The grass was not quite as green around their tombstones. They had been in the ground

46

less time, but perhaps it would always be greenest near Alice.

It was just a thought. He turned and left the cemetery.

Michael had obtained his appointment with Dr Gin Kawati under false pretences. He had called the doctor the previous week and explained he was an assistant editor at a local paper in need of technical information on modern forensic techniques for an article his boss was doing on how modern murders were sometimes solved. Michael had given the doctor the impression the name Dr Kawati would figure prominently in the article if he would help him out. The doctor had sounded interested.

Michael drove to downtown Los Angeles and parked across the street from the ARC Medical Group. This was his first visit to the office, but Bubba had been there before when he swiped certain codes from the physician's secretary. It was those codes that had allowed Bubba and Michael to dump the medical group's files on to Tabb High's computers homecoming day.

The receptionist showed him directly into the doctor's office. Dr Kawati was of Japanese descent which was no big surprise given his last name – short and moustached. He was not old – thirty-five at most – and appeared at first glance to be friendly. He gave Michael a firm handshake and offered him a seat beside his cluttered desk. But Michael couldn't help glancing at the man's hands and thinking to himself that here were hands that spent their days dissecting people. Michael couldn't understand how anyone could willingly go into such a gruesome field.

'I wear gloves,' Dr Kawati said. Michael glanced up.

'Pardon?'

'I wear gloves when I perform an autopsy.' The doctor smiled. 'I have yet to be at a party or any social occasion

47

and not have someone stare at my hands. Don't be embarrassed, I am proud of what I do.'

'You read minds?' Michael asked, shaken at his own transparency.

'I read mysteries. The human body is the most mysterious of all God's creations, and when it ceases to work, for whatever reason, it often leaves behind a puzzle more complex than anything you can find in a movie or a book.' He nodded towards the tape player Michael had brought. 'That would be a fine opening for your piece. You might want to turn on your cassette machine.'

On the spur of the moment, Michael decided to take a big chance. Perhaps the doctor's obviously keen perception gave him the inspiration. 'I lied,' he said. 'I don't work for a paper.'

The doctor raised an eyebrow, not fazed. 'I'm intrigued. What is your real name and why are you here?'

'My name *is* Mike, and I wanted to question you about an autopsy you performed last fall on a friend of mine. Her name was Alice McCoy.' He added, 'I realise I deserve to be kicked out, but I really would like to talk to you.'

'This Alice – she was a close friend of yours?'

Michael nodded. 'Yes.'

Dr Kawati turned to the computer on his desk. 'M – C – C – O – Y?'

'Yes.'

Kawati called up a file menu, then typed in the name. A moment later an autopsy report appeared on the screen. Michael recognised it; he had, after all, read it a dozen times. Kawati frowned. 'I remembered the name McCoy when you said it. A most interesting case.'

'Why?' Michael asked.

'A minute, please,' the doctor said, taking several

minutes to read the report from start to finish. When he was done, he looked over at Michael. 'I believe you are a friend of hers, but why are you concerned about the results of her autopsy?'

'I have serious doubts about the police's investigation into her death.'

'Please be more specific.'

'I think Alice McCoy was murdered.'

'Why?'

Michael hesitated. 'I've read your report.'

'Did the police show it to you?'

'Not exactly.' The doctor smiled. 'You *are* an intriguing young man. I won't ask you how you managed that. I don't believe I want to know.' He glanced at the screen, frowned again. Michael spoke quickly.

'She didn't break her nose falling to the floor after firing the gun. She was sitting when she was shot. None of us rolled her body over when we found it.'

'You can't be certain she was sitting,' Kawati said.

'It is likely when you take into account where and at what angle the slug hit the wall. Also, she had the gun in her mouth, with her hand around it, when we found her. How could she fall and break her nose with that in the way?'

'How could someone have got close enough to put the gun in her mouth, wrap her fingers around the handle, and then pull the trigger?'

'Before I answer that, why did you remember the name? What was so interesting about the case?'

'What you mentioned – the fracture to her nasal cartilage.'

'Then you don't think it was caused by a fall?'

'I didn't say that,' the doctor replied.

'How else could she have broken her nose?'

49

'Any number of ways. She could have been struck across the face, or rather, struck directly on the nose. There were no scratches on her cheeks, nor any other signs that she had been in a struggle.' Kawati paused, intent upon the details, apparently not minding the exchange. 'You still have not answered my question.'

'In your report you mentioned brain haemorrhage that appeared unconnected to the path of the bullet.'

'It *may* have been unconnected. The bullet followed a twisted route before exiting at the back of the skull. The brain was in extremely poor condition. What are you getting at?'

'I have thought about this a great deal. I was there the night of the party.'

'Go on.'

Michael remembered back to another night, to homecoming, to the moment before the varsity tree toppled and destroyed the snack bar. The idea had begun to form in his mind even then. 'I think she was dead before she was shot,' he said.

The doctor thought a moment. 'It's possible.'

'Is it?' Michael asked, realising he had been holding his breath waiting to hear those exact words.

'Possible, but unlikely,' Kawati quickly added. 'Why would someone quietly and effectively kill her with a blow to the nose and then put a gun in her mouth and fire a shot that alerted everyone in the house?'

'To give the impression it had not been a murder, but a suicide.'

'Why?'

'To give the police an excuse not to investigate, which is precisely what has happened. They threw the file on the shelf and closed the case before they opened it.'

'You sound angry.'

Michael felt a tightness in his throat. 'She was very

dear to me.' He started to get up. 'You've told me what I wanted to know. Thank you, doctor.'

Kawati glanced at the screen a last time. 'There is one other thing you might want to consider. If someone did strike her, cracking her nasal cartilage and giving her a cerebral haemorrhage in the process, then he must have done it with a baseball bat. Either that or he was a strong devil.' Kawati put a hand to his chin, nodded thoughtfully. 'Incredibly strong.'

CHAPTER FIVE

Nick Grutler drove fast down the coast, reaching San Diego in less than two hours. He had never been to the rehabilitation clinic before, but Maria's directions were precise and he found the huge modern, two storey building without difficulty. Since her discharge from the local hospital three months ago, Nick had spoken to her on the phone every couple of weeks. Each time, *he* had called her. Each time, she had sounded much the same, quiet and withdrawn. Yet the bitterness that had unexpectedly arisen after her accident still remained. It had faded, true; nevertheless, it tore him apart to catch hints of it in her voice. Sometimes he felt as if he were talking to a stranger, that he was in love with someone who no longer existed.

She was sitting outside, waiting for him as he walked towards the front stairs. She had a red wool blanket over her legs and a battered suitcase by her side. Only she wasn't simply sitting; she was sitting in a wheelchair.

Oh, Jesus, please heal her.

He had prayed the same prayer a thousand times since last winter. Jesus was either keeping him in suspense or else He had already given him his answer. Nick was a big, strong young man but he almost broke down and cried at that moment.

'Hi, Maria,' he said. She had cut her hair, her beautiful hair. There was hardly any of it left. It was probably easier to take care of shorter, he reasoned. She smiled briefly, and rolled towards him. He wondered if it would be OK to hug her, if he would hurt her.

'Hello, Nick,' she said, glancing up at him before quickly looking down to make sure of her hold on the wheelchair handles. She still seemed to be learning how to get around. 'Thanks for coming.'

He stood above her, afraid to move. 'It was no problem. It's good to see you again.'

'It's good to see you.' She nodded to her bag. 'I'm already checked out. We can go.'

He stepped past her and picked up the suitcase. He knew it was all she had to her name. After the accident, her parents had been exposed as illegal aliens in the United States. They had subsequently been deported to El Salvador. Maria's status was still questionable. As long as she needed medical attention that only the United States could provide, she was allowed to stay. She might be deported now that she was leaving the rehab clinic. Michael had helped Nick write a letter to their local congressman pleading her case. So far, there had been no reply.

Nick helped her into the front seat of his car – he could have picked her up with one hand, she was so light – and folded the wheelchair and put it in the trunk. It was a tight fit but he was able to close the lid. He climbed in beside her and started the engine.

'Nice car,' she said.

'Thanks. The Rock sold it to me cheap.'

'The Rock – I remember him.'

'I bumped into him in the parking lot when I was leaving school this morning. He told me to tell you he'd like to see you. Mike also said he was looking forward to seeing you again.'

'Good old Mike. Is he still searching for a murderer?'

There was an edge to her question, but not of sarcasm; she really wanted to know. 'He doesn't talk to me about it,' he said, feeling uncomfortable. He wanted to touch her, kiss her, and comfort her, but he could have made the trip for nothing. She was still a hundred miles away, wrapped in a cool protective shell.

'I bet he is,' she said.

'Are you?' He hadn't shifted the car into gear yet. He hadn't intended to ask that question. Maria looked over at him. He noticed a faint two-inch scar near her right eye. She'd had some plastic surgery; she'd need more.

'Yes.'

'And you want me to help you find the murderer?'

'You'll help me,' she said, implying with her tone that he didn't understand what she was talking about, which was true.

'How?'

She smiled, slow and calculating. 'You'll know when the time comes.'

CHAPTER SIX

Sara hated L.A.'s downtown bus station, located in one of the worst parts of town. She always felt relieved to get in and out of it without being molested. The whole world was full of perverts. Society was sick. It still infuriated her how the courts locked Russ away for a crime he had not committed. She wished she'd sent him an aeroplane ticket. Then she could have driven to Los Angeles airport instead. She had suggested the idea in her last letter, but he hadn't answered her last letter, so that had been the end of that.

He didn't answer my letter before that, either.

It didn't matter. He wasn't into writing letters. She couldn't stand writing them herself. The only reason she had sent him so many was that she'd had nothing else to do – only get good grades, keep her mother and father from killing each other, and run the whole school. Actually, she was going to give him hell for not answering her – immediately after she determined if he still liked her. She was worried he might have found someone else.

In a juvenile hall full of boys?

One could never tell. They probably had a buxom secretary or two working in the warden's office. She'd always had the impression Russ could go for an older woman, or a teenybopper for that matter. God help him if he had been unfaithful to her.

He was supposed to be on the one o'clock from

Sacramento. She was on time and waiting at the right gate, but when all the people had passed by, there was no Russ. She couldn't believe it. The bastard had missed his bus and hadn't had the decency to call her house and leave word that he'd be on the next one arriving at – she glanced up at the schedule board three o'clock. Three o'clock! She couldn't wait till then. She was ASB president and this was her last and most important day on the job. That insensitive son of a bitch had dragged her all the way down here *after* getting himself thrown in jail where she couldn't see him at all, and now he had stood her up.

She reached in her bag for her handkerchief. Life sucked. She hated this trying not to care when all she felt like doing was crying. She dabbed at her eyes. Well, that was the end of that. Jessica would get Bill tonight, and there would be no one there to save poor Sara from being raped by Bubba.

Sara blew her nose and headed for the exit. If she'd known for sure he'd be on the next bus, she would have waited, her important speech notwithstanding. But he had decided not to come, she realised, because he didn't want to see her. God, she hated him!

She ran into him the second she stepped outside. He was crouched on the kerb feeding a pigeon a piece of chocolate doughnut, his duffel bag propped against a nearby fire hydrant. They had cut his hair short. They must have been keeping him inside; he had lost his bronze sheen. It didn't matter. He looked incredible, simply incredible.

'Where have you been?' he asked, glancing up.

'Where have I been? You were supposed to be on that bus that just came in. You had me standing there waiting for you like some lost bag lady. You have a lot of nerve asking me where I've been.'

56

He gave the bird the remainder of the doughnut and checked his watch. 'It's five past one and you only got here. I've been waiting around a couple of hours. I told you I was coming in at eleven.'

'No, you didn't.' She pulled his last letter from her bag – it was little more than a slip of paper – practically ripping the envelope in the process. 'See, it says one o'clock. You wrote it yourself.'

He stood and studied the paper. 'There're two ones there.'

'What? No, that's not another one. It's just a scratch.'

'No, I made it. It's a one.'

Now that he mentioned it, the scratch did bear a faint resemblance to a one. 'Why didn't you call, then?' she asked.

'I didn't have your number.'

'Why not? What did you do with it?'

'I didn't do anything with it. I never had it memorised.'

'Is that why you haven't called me since you left?'

'I couldn't afford it.'

'You could have called collect,' she began to yell.

He stared at her a moment. 'You look great.'

'What do you mean? Do you mean my body or my face?'

He shook his head. 'Never mind.'

She pouted. 'How come you're not being nice to me?'

'How come you're yelling at me?'

'I'm not.' She wanted to reach over and brush a hair from his eyes as she used to, but she couldn't see any hair long enough to give her an excuse. 'I'm sorry if I am.'

'It's all right.' He paused. 'Your body's all right.'

'It's not great?'

'No.'

57

She started to sock him, but he grabbed her hands and gave her a quick kiss on the lips. A little too quick. She had been hoping for a lot more. As he stepped back and picked up his duffel bag, he averted his eyes. He didn't want to talk, not about why he had been out drinking homecoming night at a bar he couldn't remember. She had the feeling he didn't really want to talk about what he thought of her, either.

'The car's over here,' she said. She wished she understood him better.

CHAPTER SEVEN

The keys opened the door. Michael knew they would. Bubba was a master when it came to secretive preparations. Glancing down the McCoys' long driveway to make sure no one was watching, Michael quickly slipped into the house and reclosed the door.

I could get arrested for doing this.

That would be a joke. He could share the same cell with Dale Jensen and the local paper could do an article on the shortage of good valedictorians this year. In reality, he wasn't concerned about getting caught. The chances were against it, and even if someone did call the cops and he was carted down to the station, he didn't care. It would give him an excuse not to go to graduation. He still hadn't thought about what he was going to say. Not having gone to the rehearsal a couple of days earlier – he hadn't been valedictorian back then – he didn't even know when he was supposed to speak: first, last, or what.

He had hit traffic returning from the coroner's office and was running behind schedule. He would have to go to Clark's house after the ceremony.

The house was silent in the manner empty houses are prone to be. Yet it was not a comforting silence. It reminded him of the silence that hung in the air following a major argument or an explosion. It seemed to him that acts of violence somehow transcended time. He remembered when he was a boy going with his mother to a bank where there had previously been a hold-up and a fatal shooting. He told his mother it was a 'bad place' before she had told him what had happened there. The McCoy house now felt like a 'bad place'.

He paused for a moment at the foot of the stairs, looking towards the kitchen. Standing in this spot, Nick had seen Bill with his head bent over the sink. Bill never explained why he had been standing there upset, before the gun went off.

Michael decided to retrace Nick's steps to the room where Alice had died. He climbed the double flight of stairs and paused at the first door on the left. It had been locked the night of the party, the room beyond silent, and it was the same now. The next door on the left led to the bathroom. The Rock had been there, showering and flushing out his chlorined eyes.

Michael opened the sole door on the right and peeped out on to the second-storey porch, where Kats had been getting a breath of fresh air and admiring the stars. It seemed to clear Michael's mind, going through this ritual. This hallway had one more door on the left. Nick had paused there, too, and listened at the door and heard snoring. Russ said he had been asleep inside. Then again, Russ couldn't remember where he had been when the varsity tree had toppled to the ground, or whether it had been Polly or Sara who had taken his axe away the first week of school.

The hallway turned to the right. There were two doors on the left. The first swung open easily, revealing a spacious bedroom with an adjoining bathroom. But it had been locked when Nick tried it, and there had been moans coming from inside. Bubba said he didn't know anything about it. No one seemed to know anything.

Michael came to the last room. The door was closed,

and as he opened it, the hinges creaked loudly, doing wonders for his nerves. The room was bare except for an aluminium ladder set beside the closet. He remembered the ladder from his last inspection the day of the funeral.

The starkness of the wooden floor struck him, as it had before. Every room in the house had carpeting except this one. He found the fact disturbing, although he wasn't sure why. He stepped inside.

The blinds on the windows – those facing east and south – were down. He raised them, letting in more light. The bullet hole in the wall beneath the east windows had not been plastered over. As he knelt beside it, his conviction that she had not broken her nose falling strengthened. It was less than three feet above the floor and straight as an arrow into plaster.

Yet all this was old news. He searched the room and the adjoining bathroom, and discovered nothing significant. The screens on the windows were all screwed down. There were no trapdoors, as Jessica had once pointed out. There was only one entrance into the room, one exit.

If she was dead before she was shot, was she dead long?

He found himself standing at the east windows, which faced the McCoy garden – as opposed to the south windows, which overlooked the pool – pondering what the coroner had said about the strength of her assailant. Clark had been thin, thin as a rail. In a fight, Michael figured he could have taken him easily.

Then he looked up and noticed the broken shingle at the overhang of the eaves outside the east window. It appeared to Michael as it had before, as if someone had been on the roof and stepped too close to the edge and broken off a couple of inches of the dark brown wood with the heel of his shoe. When he thought about how steep the east slant of the roof appeared from the front, however, he began to doubt that the damage could have been caused by a misplaced foot. Only the original roofers, with the help of safety lines, would have been able to stand that close to the edge. Why wouldn't they have repaired the damage? It was the only shingle on the entire side of the house that was broken.

Michael wanted to have a closer look at it. But he didn't bother undoing the screws on the screens. The overhang was too far for him to reach, even if he were to hang out the window. He hurried downstairs to the garage instead, where he found a tall ladder. After assorted jostling and banging noises – and, thank God, Polly's nearest neighbours were more than a hundred yards away – he had the ladder situated beneath the bedroom window. Unfortunately, it wasn't tall enough for him to reach the shingle.

He had come down the ladder and was returning it to the garage, walking past the pool where Nick had almost drowned The Rock and beside the covered patio attached to the rear of the house, when he spotted the piece of yellowed paper lying in the grass next to the bushes. He set the ladder down and picked it up.

It was the permission form he had given Polly to have her aunt sign so that he could examine Alice's autopsy report. Polly had never returned it to him. It looked as if it had been sitting outside in the elements since that day. He stuffed it in his pocket.

He wasn't crazy about his next plan. He almost hoped, as he searched the garage after replacing the ladder on its hooks, that Polly didn't have any rope. Then he'd have an excuse not to play Mr Roofer. But in a cabinet above the workbench, he soon found a fifty-foot coil of one-inch cord.

He didn't return to the bedroom, but took the second-storey hallway door on to the porch that overlooked the backyard. The shingles came directly down on to the tar floor of the porch, giving him easy access to the roof. Climbing up towards the peak of the house, Michael felt the hot sun on the back of his head, the slickness of the wood beneath his feet. He was glad he had chosen to wear his tennis shoes that morning.

If I slip and break my neck, people will say I committed suicide.

At the ridge, he tied one end of the rope to the sturdiest vent he could find, the other end around his waist. With the life insurance in hand, creeping down towards the broken shingle was not nearly so intimidating as he had imagined it would be. He actually found it quite exhilarating. He wasn't even worried about the neighbours. Not many crooks climbed on to a victim's roof in the middle of the day and performed gymnastics.

A moment later he was kneeling beside the shingle, forty feet above the spot where Alice and he had had their last talk over the hot coals of the barbecue. He felt the damaged edge and was immediately taken by its smoothness. There were splinters, yes, but they –

They were turned *upwards*

Strange, very strange. Did the roofers break the shingle while it was lying upside down on the ground, and then install it? He found that hard to believe.

It was fortunate that he had a safety line. His next discovery almost sent him reeling. Placing his head inches from the finely splintered edge, he noticed a number of tiny round metal pellets embedded in the wood. He dug them out with his nail, studied them in his palm.

They were from a shotgun blast.

CHAPTER EIGHT

The stadium stands were packed, and the football field was jammed with grey folding chairs and blue-robed seniors. The ceremony would start in minutes. Sara still hadn't finished rewriting her speech. Jessica hadn't decided which song to sing. It was hot and getting hotter.

'Should I bring up the state of the environment?' Sara asked. 'People are always talking about pollution. Maybe I could work it into my overall theme.'

'What is your overall theme?' Jessica ask.

Sara glanced at her notes. 'Isn't it obvious from what I've told you so far?' she asked anxiously.

'No.'

'Jessie!'

'Well, I'm hardly listening to you. I have problems of my own. I can't sing the Beatles song I rehearsed.'

'Why not?'

'Mr Bark says it's too racist.'

' 'All You Need Is Love' is racist?'

'That's what he says. He wants a song with more of a political message, like 'Back in the U.S.S.R.' or something.' She took off her cap and glasses and wiped the sweat from her forehead. Her tassel was blue. Sara had a gold one. Both their parents were in the stands. The six of them were supposed to go for an early dinner to an expensive restaurant afterwards. Big thrill.

'What if I bring up the space programme?' Sara asked. 'Everyone likes astronauts.'

'What if I sang Bowie's 'Starman'? I know the chords.'

'That's ridiculous. You can't sing about spacemen at my graduation.'

'Then you can't talk about astronauts at mine.' Jessica replaced her glasses and scanned the crowd for Michael. 'When is he going to speak?'

'After Mr Bark.'

'I forget, when do I sing?'

'After Mike speaks,' Sara said. 'It's all there in your programme.'

'Michael's not even listed in the programme.'

'Dale Jensen is. You know he's taking his place.'

'Yeah, you told me – as of this morning.'

'What are you complaining about? I can't even have notes with me when I go up there.'

'Why not?'

'I have no place to put them.'

'What's wrong with the podium?' Jessica asked, pointing to the stage in front of the folding chairs.

'It's been fixed.' Sara smiled suddenly. 'You'll see. Mr Bark wants to talk before me. He thinks he does. What grade did he give you?'

'A B-minus,' Jessica said angrily.

'He gave me an A-minus.'

'That's so unfair. You fell asleep the first day I was back.'

'Well, then, I was obviously most improved.'

'You are beginning to bore me. I think I'll leave.'

Jessica had another reason for splitting. She wanted to check out the piano – how it had been miked. She was a fair pianist; she'd had lessons since she was six years old and could play most popular songs if she had

65

the music in front of her. She knew dozens of Beatle tunes by heart. Although many people complimented her on her voice, she didn't think of herself as a vocalist. Her voice was too similar to her speaking voice which had always bothered her for some strange reason.

The school piano had a single microphone rigged above it – that was all. Yet the sound appeared to carry fine when she tapped out a few chords. She wondered if it would offend the older members of the audience if she played Alice Cooper's 'School's Out for Summer'. It annoyed her, being censored by Mr Bark, especially when he considered himself so liberal.

'Don't worry,' The Rock said, coming up at her side, a green plastic trash bag in his hand. 'The chance of there being a record producer in the audience is five hundred to one.'

She smiled. 'I'm not here to get signed. I just want my diploma. What's with the bag?'

She knew it without asking. Being a Big Brother wasn't enough for The Rock. A couple of weeks ago he had joined the Keep America Clean Society. He took his membership seriously. Tabb High was now the cleanest school in Orange County, or it should have been. Bubba had organised a counterorganisation; It's Biodegradable. Bubba had a lot of friends. The Rock could regularly be seen at break and lunch picking up half-eaten apples and banana peels. Nothing irritated Bubba like a social conscience.

'The gang's getting started early,' The Rock said. 'I've already collected a hundred beer cans at school today.' He sighed and shook his head. 'I hope no one falls overboard tonight.' He patted her on the shoulder. 'Stay sober.'

'I'll try.' Either that or she was going to get stinking drunk.

She was heading towards the stands to ask her mother for a throat lozenge – she wanted to keep her vocal chords well lubricated – when she caught sight of Michael standing alone by the equipment shed on the far end of the stadium. He had his head down and appeared deep in thought. She hesitated to disturb him. As Sara had mentioned earlier, his hair was a lot longer, and he looked so damn good to her that she felt her eyes water. She found herself jogging towards him before she knew what she was doing.

He did not see her coming. She trembled inside as she came to a halt a few feet from him and spoke his name. 'Michael?'

He glanced up with a start. Then he smiled. 'Jessie. I love your glasses.'

She laughed. She could have cried. She spread her arms wide and gave him a big hug. It might have been the best moment of her life when he hugged her back. Except he had to let her go. What a mush she had become.

'It's good to see you again,' he said casually.

'It's good to see you. Oh, God, these glasses. I hate them.'

'Why? You look like a scholar in them.'

'I do?' He was being serious. She should have worn them all along. She giggled, shaking on the outside as well as the inside. No one in the world made her feel this way. She hated it, but only because she knew, like his hug, that it would not last. He would go away again. He always did. 'So, how have you been? You look great. I hear you're building a spaceship at JPL?'

'Not exactly. I'm doing janitorial work.'

'Really? No! You're kidding. I know you. Our chemistry teacher told us one day he'd never had a student like you. He said you invented the carbon bond!'

He chuckled. 'Now I'm responsible for all the life on this planet. What a reputation. What have you been up to?'

She shrugged. 'Oh, the usual. I sleep all day in a velvet-lined coffin and then prowl the streets at night. Hey, Sara told me you're valedictorian. Congratulations! Your mom must be real proud.'

Michael nodded past her shoulder. 'Here she comes. You've never met her, have you?'

Oh, no, she's going to hate me. Mothers always hate me.

His mom was massively pregnant; she waddled as she walked. Jessica hadn't even known she was married. Michael indicated that they should meet her halfway. Jessica could not believe how nervous she was. One would think she was Michael's fiancée.

'She's due in a couple of weeks,' Michael remarked as they walked towards her. 'Did you know I have a stepfather now?'

'That's neat.'

'I never see him. They spend most of their time at his place by the beach. I'm still at the old house.'

That was not news to Jessica. She had driven by his place a couple of times and parked down the street to wait for him to come home. But each time he appeared, her nerve had failed and she'd driven away.

His mother had his black hair and dark eyes, but little or none of his seriousness. Jessica spotted that the moment she spoke; her voice was light, happy. Jessica could tell at a glance she was looking forward to the baby.

'Mom, this is Jessie. You remember her, don't you?'

'Sure, I do.' She offered her hand. 'I spoke to you on the phone once. Nice meeting you, Jessie.'

'Thank you. Nice meeting you.'

The lady turned to her son, handing him a letter. 'This

68

came from the observatory this morning. Is it what I think it is?'

'Probably,' Michael said, slipping the envelope into his gown pocket.

'Aren't you going to open it?' his mother asked, slightly exasperated.

'Later. We know what it says.'

'What is it?' Jessica asked, curious.

'Nothing,' Michael said quickly, catching his mom's eye.

'All right,' the lady said. 'Be that way. Be rude.' She nodded to Jessica and laughed at Michael. 'She's pretty.'

'I know,' he said quietly.

Jessica quickly pulled off her glasses, embarrassed. 'I have to wear these stupid things all the time.'

'You look wonderful with them on,' his mother said.

'Like a philosopher,' Michael said.

'A professional woman,' the mother said, reaching out and fixing Jessica's cap.

'I don't even have a gold tassel,' Jessica muttered, trembling worse. The lady brushed a hair from her cheek, then took the glasses from her hands and checked the lenses for dust.

'These are strong,' she remarked. 'You *do* have to wear them.'

'Come on, Mom,' Michael said. 'Give her a break.'

'I know,' Jessica said. The lady wiped them on her green dress and then carefully fixed them back on Jessica's nose, momentarily staring into her eyes.

She's checking me out.

'I hope we get to meet another time, Jessie.'

'So do I,' Jessica replied, a bit confused. Michael's mother turned back to him.

69

'Daniel and I are sitting near the bottom on the far right,' she said. 'In case you wanted to know. Be sure to thank your mother in your speech for being so wonderful.'

'I'll mention it several times,' he promised. She hugged him briefly, and then to Jessica's surprise gave her a hug, too. When she left, Michael tugged gently on Jessica's tassel.

'Would you like to trade caps?' he asked. 'I know you would have got an A in chemistry if I'd done a better job structuring the universe.'

'Yes, it's all your fault.' She added softly, 'No thanks.'

'I didn't mean – '

'No, it's me.' She shrugged. 'I really messed up this year. It was my own fault.' She smiled quickly. 'Your mom's neat.'

'I'm glad you like her. I'll have to meet your parents.'

'That's right. You didn't see them when we went out.'

Hint. Hint. Hint. Ask me out again.

Of course he hadn't asked her out in the first place. He never had in all the time they had spent together. She must be crazy to think he liked her.

In the hospital, however, the morning after Maria's accident, he had begun to say something that had since given her cause to wonder.

'I know how you feel. You're not a bad person. If you were, I wouldn't care about you the way . . .'

She had been crying because Maria had been bitter to her. He had probably been trying to cheer her up. She would never know. She had run away from him. She would run away again. She didn't deserve him. She was going to seduce the football quarterback tonight. It was all she was good for.

70

She suddenly felt as if she were going to cry. Here it was her last day of school, a beautiful summer day. She had everything: rich and understanding parents, perfect health, a bright future. Yet she had nothing. She had no love. Alice was gone. Michael was going. And Maria hated her.

It was at that precise moment that she saw Maria. Had that not happened, she might have been able to push aside her self-recriminations long enough to invite Michael and his parents to have dinner with her and her family after the ceremony. It was an idea, a good idea. But Nick guiding Maria across the track and on to the football field was bitter reality. She froze in midstride. Michael glanced at her face, then followed her eyes.

'I was going to tell you,' he said.

'I haven't spoken to her since that morning.' Jessica swallowed thickly. 'She's in a wheelchair.'

'It was a terrible accident.' He laid emphasis on the last word. She found that strange. He had always given her the impression that he didn't believe in accidents. He was trying to dispel her guilt. He might as well have tried to convince her she would gladly have traded places with Maria. But she wouldn't have, not for the world, and so her guilt remained.

'I'll talk to you later, OK?' she mumbled. 'I have to get in line.'

She walked off the field and hid in the crowd. Maria had asked Jessica never to make her see her again. It was the least she could do for her crippled friend, Jessica thought.

The ceremony began shortly afterwards. The huge audience had been seated when the chatty senior class marched in and took their seats. Mr Smith, Tabb's elderly principal, was the first speaker. Dressed in the same blue robe as the rest of them, he thanked the many parents, relatives, and friends for coming, and then proceeded to praise the group of graduates as the most dynamic in his long academic career. Jessica found his choice of the word 'dynamic' appropriately vague. Hitler had been dynamic. Of course, she realised, it had not been a bad year for everyone.

The diplomas were to be presented alphabetically; for that reason, the seating followed roughly that order. But Jessica Hart had switched with someone so she could sit next to Polly McCoy rather than Larry Hay. Larry not only had a weird name, he also had such consistently bad breath that Sara once remarked that if at the end of his life he donated his body to medical science, he would probably be found posthumously guilty of involuntary manslaughter when the medic students cut open his cadaver and choked to death.

Jessica also wanted to be with her old friend at this special time. Polly had suffered far more than any of them, and Jessica had courageously helped her the last few months by avoiding her. Not entirely, naturally; they continued to talk at lunch and stuff. But they no longer hung out as real friends do. The reason was simple. They were both down, and Jessica had discovered that the truism that the depressed seek out the company of other depressed people to be entirely false. Being around Polly only made her feel worse.

Yet seeing Maria again made Jessica want to atone for her cowardly approach to the situation. Sitting to the far right of the stage, in the back row – twenty rows behind Maria's front-row wheelchair – Jessica leaned over to Polly as Mr Smith completed his talk.

'He's such a nice man,' she said.

'He must be to have put up with Sara all year,' Polly said.

'Who's that he's introducing?'

'A car company executive. He's here to inspire us to go out into the big wide world and get rich.' Polly winced slightly, took off her cap, and put her hand to her temple. 'I'm already rich.'

'Do you have a headache?'

'Yeah.'

Jessica wiped the sweat from her bow. 'It's this sun.'

'It's sunny every day.' Polly searched the stands.

'Looking for somebody?'

'No, nobody.'

The guest speaker did turn out to be a strong believer in capitalism. His name was James Vern and ten years ago he had swiped – his actual phrase was 'drew from the research of' – an invention that improved the efficiency of transmissions in large trucks, parlayed it into millions. He laughed when he recounted the lies he had told to get financing for his company. Jessica wondered if he knew what a jerk he was. He talked for forty-five long minutes.

Sara came next. People giggled as she made her way to the microphone. Jessica tossed around in her head the idea of singing 'Hey Jude'.

'Thank you, Mr Vern, for your enlightening words,' Sara said, the tiniest hint of tension in her voice as she adjusted the mike down to her height. 'The world of modern business really sounds like a jungle. But I suppose even a snake needs a place to live.'

The audience chuckled uneasily. The senior class cheered appreciatively. Sara smiled and went on more confidently, not using any notes. Jessica noticed for the first time that the top of the podium had been removed. As Sara had mentioned, there was no place to put papers.

'I have written several speeches this last week,' Sara said. 'I have one on this country's need to remain competitive in the world marketplace. I put a lot of time into it. Then I thought, haven't we been number one long enough? Shouldn't we give someone else a chance? I decided it was all a question of whether we want to be greedy or cool about it. I also had this speech on *our* future. It is my understanding that ASB presidents across the country talk about this subject graduation day. I really got into the idea myself – for a while. Then I realised that the best minds on Wall Street can't tell if the Dow Jones average is going to go up or down a couple of lousy points tomorrow, never mind where it's going to be ten years from now. The earth could get smashed by a huge meteorite this instant and vaporise us all, and then what would we do? Why worry about it? Why talk about it? I'm certainly not going to. Then, finally, I had this speech on the problems facing the youth of America: overindulgence in alcohol, lack of ambition, sexual promiscuity. But I had to ask myself, Are these things really that bad? Think about it for a second.' Sara turned to the class and raised her voice. 'Do we really want to give them up?'

The class let out a resounding *no*! Then it burst out altogether. The audience – full of real-life parents – didn't know what to think. In the end, though, the crowd joined those on the field, and applauded Sara. She loved it.

'You know what I finally decided?' she said. 'Not even to give a speech. Let's get this thing over with as quickly as possible and get to the party.' She cleared her throat and glanced to the side as the class clapped and hooted. 'With that in mind, please welcome our senior faculty adviser, the wonderful Mr Bark!'

Their political science teacher, wearing a blue graduation gown and a dyed fringe of hair that was supposed to take ten years off his age, strode confidently to the microphone. Sara remained on the stage. Jessica leaned forward in anticipation.

'Mr Bark and I have had our disagreements this year,' Sara said pleasantly as the teacher stood nearby. 'But I like to think our trials have brought us closer together. I think, especially in the last month, I have only begun to understand his commitment to social causes, particularly his concern over the arms race.'

Mr Bark leaned forward and spoke into the mike. 'I am happy to hear that, Sara. It means a great deal to me.'

'I wanted to show you how much it means to me,' Sara said, nudging herself back behind the mike. 'I bought you a present, a very special present.' She gestured to someone on the left side of the stage. Jessica was surprised when Russ Desmond – Sara had not said a word about the progress of *the* relationship since she had picked him up at the bus station, and Jessica had been hesitant to ask – stood up and strode on to the stage, a small white package in his hands. He gave it to Sara, then hastily retreated. Sara presented it to Mr Bark.

'Open it,' she said.

Mr Bark beamed. 'This is so thoughtful of you, Sara.' He began to peel away the paper. 'I wonder what it could – ' The crowd murmured expectantly. It took a minute to get through all the wrapping. When he had, he was left holding what appeared to be – from Jessica's admittedly poor vantage point – a black rectangular stone. 'Sara?' he said, uncertain.

'It's a paperweight,' Sara explained.

'Oh.' He grinned as he weighed it in his palm. 'It feels like it should be able to handle the job. Thank you.'

'Thank *you*, Mr Bark.' Sara muttered the next line

75

under her breath as she turned away, but the mike caught it. 'It's a uranium paperweight.'

It was perfect. He obviously had a long speech prepared. Undoubtedly it was to be every bit as long as Mr Vern's. He would talk about how much he loved working with the kids this year, how sad he was to see them all leave, but how happy he was to know they were going on to bigger and greater things. Then he would bring up the nukes, the goddamn nukes that could destroy all of them at the push of a button.

Yet he had a uranium paperweight in his hand, and though he probably understood intellectually that the level of radiation it was emitting was extremely small – probably one thousandth or one millionth of what he would absorb if he had a chest X-ray – he would not be able to stop thinking about it. Jessica watched as he began to speak and then glanced down at the thing in his hand and fidgeted. There was no place to put it, except on the ground. And he couldn't do that. No, that would be rude. He clearly didn't want to be rude.

'I am very happy to be here this afternoon with all you fine people,' he began uneasily. 'It is always an honour for me when I am given a chance to speak to – fine people.'

He paused and glanced again at the paperweight. For a moment, it appeared that he might actually drop it. Jessica could practically read his mind. He was thinking of gamma rays, beta rays, and those always terrible cosmic rays – all those mean nasty things he read about every night in his literature about the mean nasty military industrialists.

'It's always a sad day, graduation day,' he mumbled. 'And a happy day.'

His voice faltered. He moved the paperweight from

76

his right hand to his left, then moved it back. He was probably imagining the different rays penetrating his flesh, Jessica thought, mutating the DNA in his cells, setting him up for a hideous case of cancer five years down the line. His fear practically screamed out at the crowd.

This rock is killing me!

He couldn't take it any more. He took a step away, realised what he was doing, and then leaned back and spoke hastily into the mike. 'And all I'd like to say is, good luck, good luck to all of you kids. Thank you.'

He left the stage in a hurry, pausing at his seat only long enough to get rid of Sara's present, then strode toward the end of the folding chairs and off the football field. The audience watched quietly, reacting little. The class members whispered among themselves, relieved to have been spared another speech. Sara returned to the microphone.

'Our next speaker is the rarest of people,' Sara said seriously. 'He is the smartest individual I have ever met, and the nicest. He is Michael Olson, our class valedictorian.'

'You should have gone out with him instead of Bill,' Polly whispered as Michael stood up and walked to the microphone. The welcoming applause was the loudest of the afternoon.

'I know.' Jessica sighed. 'Do you think it's too late?'

'Yes.'

'Thank you, Sara, for the kind introduction,' Michael said, standing perfectly straight, his hands clasped in front of his gown below his waist, not as relaxed as he could have been but nevertheless in control of the situation. 'And thank you, ladies and gentlemen and fellow classmates, for inviting me to speak on this occasion. Like Sara, I will try to keep my talk brief. I, too, have written and discarded several speeches in the last couple of hours. None of the topics I chose seemed right. I suppose that is the problem with selecting any topic. It can only be about one thing, while our lives are about so many things. I finally decided I would simply talk about what is important to me as I prepare to graduate from school.'

He glanced down at a small white card he held in his hand, and Jessica looked down at her shiny white high heels, and the grass beneath them. She was sitting on the forty-yard line, directly above the hash mark. She remembered the first Tabb High football game she had attended, how the team had tried for a first down on this part of the field and failed. Bill had fumbled the ball. She had a picture of the fumble in her files at home. She smiled at the memory, especially at how Michael had inadvertently helped her take the picture when he was demonstrating to her how to fit the telephoto lens on to her camera.

But that had been a long time ago.

Polly's right. It's too late.

'In a way I'm five months late with my speech,' Michael went on. 'I left school in January, and today is my first day back. Since I've been gone, I've been rather busy, working and stuff. But I've often looked back and thought abut what I learned at Tabb. The obvious thing that comes to mind is the science and maths and history I absorbed. The teachers here are really great, some of the best, and now, I think, would be a good time to thank them for their patience and dedication. They always praised me and gave me confidence. But maybe they did too good a job. One of the problems with people thinking you're smart is that you eventually begin to believe it. I remember all the times in class – how restless I would be for the teacher to get on with the lesson. I've grasped the concept, I used to think, why haven't the rest of the kids? What I didn't realise then is that learning something doesn't just mean figuring it out. It's also the pleasure you get from the knowledge. I didn't appreciate that the teacher would sometimes dwell on a particular subject because he or she loved it. I got mostly As but now I wish I'd had more fun doing it. I hope this is one lesson I won't forget.'

Michael paused and looked over the audience. When he spoke next, it was in a lower voice, and Jessica found herself leaning forward, afraid she might miss something.

She knew he was going to bring up Alice.

'But there is something else high school taught me,' he said. 'Something I did not know until I was no longer here on a daily basis. Like everybody, I suppose, I knew certain people at school that I didn't really like. They bugged me for one reason or another, and I used to think I'd be glad when I didn't have to see them any more. Then again, I had friends I loved to be around, people that made it easy for me to get up in the morning and drive here. But the strange thing I've discovered since I've been gone is that I miss both groups of people. And I like to think I've been missed by both groups. I like to think we're all good friends. Maybe I've learned the importance of friendship. Mr Bark was right – today is a happy day, but it's also sad. We'll all promise to keep in touch, but realistically, many of us will never see one another again. Today is supposed to be the day we grow up, yet in a way, it's a shame any of us have to. Your high school friends – I think they're your best friends.'

Your final friends.

Jessica didn't know why she thought that. There was life after high school. There would be other boys besides Michael. There was only one problem. She didn't want any other boy.

Michael coughed once and looked down. 'In closing I would like to pay tribute to the memory of a very special friend who had her life taken suddenly from her. If possible, I would like her remembered with a minute of silence. Her name was Alice McCoy. She would have graduated in a couple of years.'

Michael lowered his head. Most of those present did the same. Jessica closed her eyes and felt a tear slide over her warm cheek. Just one tear. The minute lasted an eternity. Sara's voice made her sit up with a start.

'And now Jessica Hart will close the ceremony with a song.'

Jessica stood and glanced at Polly, who in turn stared up at her.

'Was he right about us not having any more friends?' Polly asked sadly. Jessica squeezed her shoulder.

'We'll always be friends, Polly.'

Jessica found the piano and sat down. The silence persisted, but a faint breeze had begun to cross the stadium. She felt it in her hair and on her damp cheek. She had no music before her; she had to choose a Beatles song. That was OK. They had composed the perfect one for the occasion, especially since Michael had forgotten to thank his wonderful mother for having given birth to him.

Jessica began to sing.

'When I find myself in times of trouble, Mother Mary comes to me, speaking words of wisdom, let it be. And in my hour of darkness, she is standing right in front of me, speaking words of wisdom, let it be. Let it be, let it be, let it be, let it be, whisper words of wisdom, let it be . . .'

She went through the song alone, and when she came to the final chorus, no one in the stands or on the field joined her. That was OK, too. She may not have sung it as beautifully as Paul McCartney, but she sang it as if it were important to her, which it was. When she finished, the silence returned, deeper than before and just for a moment. Then the applause poured down upon her from all sides and she smiled. It was the first time she had felt good all day.

The diplomas were handed out, one by one, with Mr Smith shaking everybody's hand and wishing each one well. When that was done, Sara squealed something ridiculous into the mike and the class sprang to its feet and cheered. Then five hundred caps sailed into the air, the largest of which was Bubba's huge straw sombrero, complete with gold tassel.

Jessica hugged Polly. They had made it. School was over, and if they wanted, it could be over for good. Sara burst through the crowd and embraced them both. And then they laughed and insulted one another, and it was just as it always had been between them and, she hoped, always would be. Michael didn't know everything after all. Jessica meant it when she had told Polly they would be friends for ever.

Jessica didn't find Michael in the crowd, though she looked long and hard. He seemed to have disappeared.

Michael had indeed left the school, but Carl Barber, better known as Kats, had not. He stood in the middle of the joyous crowd, watching everybody hug and kiss, a wide grin on his face, but a scowl in his heart. Nothing really changed, he thought bitterly. He had his diploma. He had earned it attending hours of tedious night classes. He was as good as the rest of them. But how many of them wanted to shake his hand? As many as had shaken his hand last June when he had failed to graduate because of a few lousy grades. Nobody cared about him. Nobody ever had and nobody ever would.

After tonight, though, they would remember him, if they remembered anything at all. Almost the entire senior class would be on that cruise ship when it left the dock for Catalina. But if he had his way – and he would, he swore it – not a single one of them would be on board when it reached its destination. That ship would be a ghost ship.

CHAPTER NINE

Michael parked down the street from Clark Halley's house and removed the gun from the glove compartment. Checking again to be sure it was fully loaded, he stuffed it inside his sports jacket pocket. Clark's huge black Harley-Davidson sat at the end of the crumbling asphalt driveway, fuming in the boiling sun from recent exertion. Clark was home. If the place could be called a home. It looked more like a chicken coop, out at the far east end of San Bernardino Valley, where the desert began and the rents plummeted. The place stank, yet when Michael had finally located the house a month earlier – after a great deal of effort and an equal amount of luck – he had celebrated.

And then I did nothing but watch and wait.

A last name is not the same as an address. Michael discovered that soon after he had found Clark's ugly picture and full name in the Temple High yearbook. The Monday after Maria's accident, he had revisited Temple High and asked to speak to Clark Halley. Turned out the guy no longer went there. He should have been in the middle of his senior year, but he had unexpectedly dropped out at the beginning of October. He had, in fact, disappeared just after Alice had died.

No sweat to find him, Michael had figured. He would get Clark's family address and catch up with him there. Easier said than done. Clark didn't have a family. He lived alone. He was an orphan or his parents had died or something; the secretary at Temple High wasn't sure what the situation was. Using the best of his charm, and a couple of tricks Bubba had taught him, Michael was able to obtain from the secretary – the same woman who had given him the yearbook during his original visit – the address Clark had had his mail sent to while at the school. It proved to be phoney – a closed Laundromat.

Michael went back to Temple High at lunchtime, again and again. He mingled, made friends, asked questions, and listened. He led the other kids to be believe he went to Temple. He began to build up a picture of Clark Halley, and it matched the one he already had – the guy was a creep.

Clark had kept mostly to himself, but when he did speak up, it had usually been to insult somebody. One girl recalled how he'd asked to sign her cast after she'd had a skiing accident. He'd drawn a tasteless sketch of her stepping into a bear trap, her foot being sliced off at the ankle and bleeding all over the ground. That was one thing everyone seemed to agree on – the dude could draw. He had talent. He might even be a genius.

What he didn't have, and what Michael desperately needed to find, was a friend. Clark didn't seem to have a single one. No one knew where he lived. No one had his phone number. He had attended the school for three years and no one could provide Michael with a single fact about his personal life. Did he have a job? Did he have any brothers or sisters? Did he have a favourite place to eat? Michael heard the same answer repeatedly – I don't know. At one point he began to feel he was chasing a phantom.

Then in mid-March he got a lead. He was on something like his twentieth visit to Temple High and talking to a guy who had gone motorcycle riding with Clark a couple of times. The guy's name was Fred Galanger, and although he appeared to be a pretty tough son-of-a-bitch – he carried thick biceps and lurid tattoos beneath his biker jacket – he spoke of Clark reluctantly, as if he were afraid Clark's ghost might suddenly appear and rake him over with a steel chain. Fred probably knew Clark better than anyone at Temple, which, of course, was not saying much. Michael had cultivated his acquaintance carefully. Then he had tired of the game and offered Fred twenty bucks for a single slice of useful memory. Fred's brain cells had lit up.

'We were out that afternoon I told you about before,' Fred said carefully, sliding the crisp bill into his pocket and keeping his hand wrapped around it in case it somehow vanished while he spoke of the mysterious rider. 'We were hotdogging these turns in the foothills down from Big Bear. That's a dangerous place to be riding hard, but Clark, he'd have a smile on his face heading into the bonnet of an oncoming truck, if it came to that. He was crazy. It took guts to keep up with him. I was one of the few guys who could.

'Anyway, we came around this one turn near the bottom of the mountain and there was an oil spill on the road. Clark's front wheel caught the edge of it and he went flying, right off the embankment and into this ravine. I figured he'd bought it right then. But he didn't even have a scratch. Don't ask me how. He was already pushing his bike back up the hill and on to the road before I could get to him. He thought it was the funniest thing in the world. But his leather coat was torn to shreds and he'd crashed his shift lever. It was weird; I went to help him bend the lever back so we could get home, but he wouldn't let me touch it. He said he didn't let anyone near his bike except this Indian who works at a station

85

in Sunnymead. He wouldn't even work on it himself, like it was sacred to him or something dumb like that.'

'What's the name of the station?' Michael interrupted.

'I don't know. It's an independent, right off the freeway, I think at Branch. Yeah, it's on Branch. We crawled there at ten miles an hour, Clark's bike stuck in first gear the whole way. The Indian's a mechanic at the station. I don't remember his name – Birdbeak or Crowfoot or something. He must have been in his nineties. You shouldn't have any trouble finding him. They seemed like old friends. He'll probably know where Clark lives.'

'Anything else?' Michael asked.

'No. Except if you do find him, don't mention my name. I mean it.'

'Why not?'

Fred Galanger wouldn't tell him why. He didn't have to. He was obviously afraid of Clark.

Fred was right about one thing – Michael did find the station without difficulty. He also met the Indian mechanic. His real name was Stormwatcher, and although he didn't have Clark's strange pale eyes, he had a similar otherworldly stare that made Michael uncomfortable. Michael figured it would be a mistake to approach him directly for Clark's address. He suspected that Clark was somehow involved with the occult, that he was in fact an apprentice of the Indian. The old guy might warn Clark he was being hunted.

It was the perfect time to go to the police. Michael didn't have the time or the inclination to stake out the station day after day, hoping Clark would show up. The police could demand that the Indian tell them what he knew of Clark. But Michael did not trust the police; in particular, he did not trust Lieutenant Keller's detective skills. Keller would question Clark, Clark would tell him about Alice's instability, and Keller would go away satisfied, confident he got what he had come for.

A month later Michael was still debating how to make friends with one of the teenagers who worked part-time at the station – someone who could alert him by phone if Clark should arrive – when he got another big break. He was getting petrol at the station when Clark drove up.

Clark didn't see him – Michael was pretty sure of that. He was off again quickly after exchanging a few words with the old Indian. Michael followed him carefully, but not too closely. Clark drove very fast. Yet he didn't go far before he pulled into the driveway of a broken-down house in a decrepit neighbourhood.

And this was the same house Michael found himself sitting outside an hour after he had graduated valedictorian, a gun in his pocket, doubt in his mind. Yet he had sat here before – without a gun but with the same doubts – and he had done nothing.

Clark could say one word, and smash everything I believe.

Michael did not fear Clark so much as he feared Alice – feared who she might have been. When he got right down to it, he hadn't known her that long.

He got out of his car, the sweat sticking to him like a layer of deceit; surely Clark would be suspicious about his wearing a coat on such a hot day. Yet Michael had no intention of lying to Clark about the purpose of his visit.

A cat ran across Michael's path as he walked towards the door. It was brown, not black, but it had green eyes. Most cats did, he supposed. He wondered if he was going to die in the next few minutes.

Michael knocked on the door. Clark answered quickly. He had on a grey T-shirt and black trousers. His red hair was shorter than it had been last autumn, neater and he was not nearly so bony or pale. Indeed, Michael wondered briefly if he had the right house. He remembered Clark as fish dug from a foul swamp. This guy was not unattractive. The eyes gave him away, however; they could have been plucked from the cat that had just crossed the yard. And the southern twang was still there.

'Can I help you?' he asked, standing behind a torn screen door.

'Maybe. I don't know if you remember me. My name's Mike. I met you at a football game at Tabb High? You were with Alice.'

'What do you want?' His voice was cautious, but not hostile.

'I'd like to come in and talk to you about Alice. If that would be all right?'

Clark considered a moment. 'All right.' He held open the screen door. 'The place is a mess. It always is.'

It was messy only because it was crammed with paintings and artistic paraphernalia: recently stretched canvases, tubes of oils, stained rags, dozens of brushes in sizes and shapes standing upright in tin cans. Except for the supplies, the house, though claustrophobic, was not bad. There were no half-finished TV dinners or overfilled ashtrays. Clark was not a slob. His place was, in fact, neater than Alice's studio had been.

Michael had part of an answer to one of his questions even before he sat down on a stool beside the narrow kitchen counter. Art had been at the core of Alice's life. Michael remembered how her bright blue eyes had constantly darted about wherever she was, as if she were eternally starved for visual input, of the beautiful or the unusual kind. Here, in Clark's place, she could have drunk up images to her heart's content. Maybe that, and that alone, had drawn her to Clark. The room was the inside of an LSD-gorged brain cell, despite the fact that the bulk of Clark's work was black-and-white sketches and not psychedelic paintings. Michael didn't know how he filled the colourless with colour. It was as if he used magic; the mind saw something the eye did not.

A phantom.

The subject matter of the sketches consisted largely of women and *creatures* relaxing together on barren desert scenes. The women were always beautiful. More than a few looked like Alice. The creatures had insect and reptile qualities. They smiled a lot. They obviously liked their women.

'Want a beer?' Clark asked, picking up a can of Coors from the floor beside his chair. Clark appeared to have been reading when Michael had knocked. The book lay face down on the thin green carpet, a hardback. Michael couldn't make out the title.

'No, thank you,' Michael said.

Clark sat down and crossed his long legs at the ankles. 'You were a friend of Alice's, weren't you?'

'Yeah. Do you remember me? We met at that football game I mentioned.'

'Sort of. I wasn't feeling so hot that night, if you know what I mean.'

'You seemed stoned,' Michael said. Clark didn't look stoned now. He appeared very alert. He was definitely watching Michael closely. Michael pulled his coat tighter, conscious of the weight of the automatic pistol in his inside pocket.

'I might have been. What did you want to ask me about Alice?'

'Well, she's dead, you know.'

'Yeah, I know,' Clark said, betraying no signs of grief. 'I read about it in the papers.'

'Did you come to the party that night?'

'No. Alice didn't invite me. Were you there?'

'Yeah. Why didn't Alice invite you?'

'I don't know. She was mad at me.'

'Why?'

Clark took a gulp of beer and set down the can. 'What is this?'

'What's what?'

'Why are you here? Who gave you my address?'

'I discovered your address by accident. As to your other question – I have doubts about how she died. The police say it was suicide. I think they might be wrong.'

'You think she was murdered?'

'I think it's a possibility.'

Clark thought a moment. His eyes never left Michael. 'Go on,' he said finally.

'Do you think she killed herself?'

'I wasn't there.'

'But you were her boyfriend. Did she show any signs she was about to commit suicide?'

'No. When I read about it, I was surprised.'

'How come you didn't come to the funeral?'

'I don't believe in funerals.'

'That's not much of an answer.'

'I wasn't invited.' Clark stood slowly and moved towards the kitchen, stopping beside the wall, standing above Michael. 'Sure you don't want a beer?' he asked.

'I'll take one,' Michael said. Clark stepped into the kitchen, opened the refrigerator, and handed him a can of Coors. Clark had left his own beer on the floor beside his chair. He returned to his seat beside the wall, only a few feet from Michael's stool. Michael opened the can and took a sip. 'It's cold,' he said.

I wish he wasn't so close.

'Tell me more about Alice's party,' Clark said, staring.

'It was big, with lots of people coming and going.' Michael felt uncomfortable under Clark's scrutinising gaze. The boy's eyes were not only bright, but penetrating; naturally an artist as talented as he would be visually perceptive. Michael wondered what he was giving away to Clark. He was getting nothing back from him. Clark was impossible to read. His expression – if it could be called that – was as flat as a dead man's.

'Yeah?' Clark said. He didn't appear overly interested in the details of the party.

'But there were only a few people there when Alice died.'

A painting sitting on the floor next to Clark caught Michael's attention. There was a creature and there was a girl – the usual. But this one was in a house, an ordinary room. It looked like an empty bedroom. The girl looked like Polly. The creature was a manfly. It was kissing the girl on the neck, probably sucking her blood. There was a real fly buzzing around the room. It landed on the wall near Clark's head. He took no notice of it.

I'm on fire.

The temperature inside the house had to be over a hundred. Michael was dying to remove his jacket. He thought of the gun, why he had brought it. He wasn't going to kill Clark. He had meant only to scare him into telling the truth. Now he was beginning to feel scared. He took another gulp of beer.

'Have you been to the McCoy house much?' Michael asked.

'No.'

'Have you been there lately?'

'No.'

'Oh.' The fly leaped on to the shoulder of Clark's grey T-shirt. Clark continued to ignore it. Michael felt off balance. He had plotted too long against Clark in his own mind. The physical presence of the guy was intimidating the hell out of him. And that stupid fly. He had always hated flies. 'Have you been to see Polly since Alice died?' he asked.

'No.'

'But I spoke to Polly this morning. She says you were at her house the night her aunt died.'

'She's wrong.'

The fly crawled towards Clark's neck, pausing beneath his Adam's apple. He mustn't be able to feel it. Or else he liked flies.

Of course he likes flies. He's always painting them.

'Polly also thought you were there the night of the party.' Michael said.

'She wanted me to come at the end, but I didn't.'

'So you were invited?'

'Why are you asking me all these questions?'

Michael desperately wanted to move. He wanted to brush away the fly from Clark's neck, and then put more space between the two of them. He also wanted to pull his coat closed tighter. Clark was staring at Michael's coat pocket now, the way it hung down slightly. Michael could feel the eyes of every creature in every sketch in the room watching him. He felt – knowing full well it was a hysterical thought – as if they were Clark's allies.

'I told you why,' Michael said.

'The paper I read said Alice died with a gun in her mouth?'

'That's right.'

'That doesn't sound like murder to me.'

'The gun in her mouth didn't kill her,' Michael said, straining to keep his voice steady. The fly crawled around the back of Clark's head and disappeared. But Michael knew it was still there. He could feel it as if it were

92

crawling along the base of his own skull. 'She was killed by a blow to the nose.'

Clark showed a flicker of interest. He stood away from the wall, moving closer to Michael. 'Go on.'

He was committed. He would throw everything at Clark that he knew or suspected and see what happened.

He saw plenty happen, quicker than he thought he would.

'It was some kind of setup,' he began. 'We were downstairs in the living room when we heard this shot. But the shot – '

The fly suddenly buzzed from behind Clark and went straight for Michael. It had chosen a bad time. Michael was in the middle of trying to readjust his coat. The fly made him jerk slightly, as if he were going for something *inside* his coat. Then again, maybe the fly made no difference. Clark obviously suspected Michael was carrying a weapon. Sooner or later, he would probably have lashed out.

Clark snapped his right foot up. He had on heavy black boots. The tip caught Michael in the lower right side of his rib cage, sending him and the stool he was sitting on toppling backwards. Michael hardly had a chance to react. Pain flared across his side. The back of his skull hit the wall hard. He fell to the floor at an awkward angle.

Oh, man this is bad.

Clark loomed above, the manfly painting in his hands. This time Michael definitely reached for the gun. He had his fingers on the handle and was pulling it out when the canvas came crashing down on him. The frame tore into the top of his scalp, the canvas ripping down over his face. He felt the gun slip from his hand. Then another hand – this one had thick numbing fingers – reached inside his brain. He momentarily blacked out. The next

93

thing he knew, Clark was leaning over him, the barrel of the automatic pressed to his cheek. Clark's hair seemed suddenly much redder. Then Michael realised he was seeing him through the film of his own blood.

'I didn't kill her, dude,' he hissed, showing some emotion at last. 'She was my girl. Maybe it was you who killed her. Maybe I should kill you and bury you in the backyard. What do you say to that, Mr Mike?'

'Go to hell,' Michael whispered.

Clark chuckled. Then he drew back the hand that held the gun and a freight train hit the side of Michael's head.

He came to an hour later. The fly was crawling around his ears. He waved it away, feeling nauseated. His hair and shirt were a mess with sticky, wet blood. Clark was gone. So was the gun. He sat up and groaned, the room spinning at odd angles. He suspected he had concussion. He noticed Clark's book still face down on the floor. He crawled towards it, throwing off the painting wrapped around his neck. *Shakespeare's Collected Works*. Clark had been reading *Romeo and Juliet*.

Michael stumbled outside on to the cracked drive. The Harley-Davidson had gone for a ride. He checked his watch. The sun would be setting soon.

'Don't come to the all-night party, Mike.'

Michael climbed into his car. He had to get down to the dock.

CHAPTER TEN

Jessica and Sara stopped at the first drugstore they saw when they got off the freeway in San Pedro not far from Los Angeles Harbour. It was after six. The boat was set to sail at precisely seven. They had little time to purchase the contraceptives.

'So what are we going to get?' Sara asked as Jessica turned off the engine.

'Ask the pharmacist for his recommendation.'

'No way. I'd be too embarrassed.'

'What's the big deal?' Jessica asked. 'They're professionals.' She added, 'I'll wait for you here.'

'Hold on a second, sister. I'm not going in there alone. You go in.'

'Why me?' Jessica asked. 'You look more innocent.'

'All the more reason you should do it.' She grinned. 'You slut.'

Dinner with the parents had been far more enjoyable than Jessica had anticipated. First of all the food had been fantastic. Both Sara and she'd had lobster. Then her mom and dad had been in good spirits. They hadn't brought up her future once. The conversation had revolved mainly around the ceremony. Mr and Mrs Cantrell had loved her song. Sara's various improvisations had been tactfully forgotten. Jessica's mom had fallen in love with Michael.

'He seems such a nice boy. How come you only went out with him one time, Jessie?'

One sticky spot during the entire meal wasn't bad. Russ and Bill were riding down to the boat with their buddies. Make that two different sets of buddies. Nobody on the football team would speak to Russ. He had, after all, supposedly wiped out their varsity tree. The situation didn't seem to bother him. During the brief time Jessica had spent talking to Russ after the ceremony, he'd appeared removed from the whole situation. Perhaps that was what came from being locked up too long. Sara and Russ had looked stiff together. Sara still wasn't talking about it.

Jessica's mood had continued to brighten since the applause for her song. But it could have been hormonal. The idea of a sleazy encounter on the high seas no longer depressed her. Indeed, she was now looking forward to it.

'I wish I had more slut in me,' Sara said, jolting Jessica back to the present situation.

'Is someone having second thoughts?'

'No,' Sara sad quickly. 'I was just wondering, you know, if it will hurt. I've heard that it can. Have you heard that?'

Jessica nodded solemnly. 'I read about this one girl – the first time she had sex, she bled so much she had to have a transfusion.'

Sara snorted. 'Get out of here.'

'Don't worry. I honestly believe we'll find it a deeply moving and fulfilling experience.'

'I hope not. I just want to have some fun. So what are we going to get?'

'What are our choices?' Jessica asked.

'In a drugstore, there're condoms, foam, and sponges.'

'Guys aren't supposed to like to wear condoms.'

'I heard that, too,' Sara said. 'But they're safer.'

'You think Russ caught something at juvenile hall?'

'The place is full of guys.'

'That's worse,' Jessica teased.

'Please, we just ate.'

'Why don't we get all three? None of it can cost much.' Not to mention the fact that she wasn't hurting financially. Less than an hour ago, her father had given her an envelope stashed with ten crisp one hundred-dollar bills. The cash was supposed to be spending money for next week in Hawaii, but she was going shopping this week. Boy, was she going shopping.

'Great,' Sara said. 'And have Bill put on a wet suit while you're at it.'

'We just have to buy the stuff. We don't have to use it all at once. Come on, I'll go with you.'

The drugstore was empty except for the pharmacist and a helper. Unfortunately, the pharmacist appeared preoccupied in the back making up prescriptions. Worse, his sole employee was a total babe of around nineteen years old. He smiled as they entered.

'Can I help you find something?' he asked.

'No,' they said in unison, looking at each other. Jessica leaned over and whispered in Sara's ear, 'Let's go somewhere else!'

'We don't have time!' Sara whispered back.

'This is totally humiliating. I'd rather have a baby.'

'You're coming to the counter with me.'

'I'm just here to get a toothbrush.'

'Jessie!'

'Shh! Tell him our names why don't you.'

They huddled into a back row and inspected the store's G.I. Joes and Gumbies. Sara idly picked up a package of pink balloons. 'Those won't fit,' Jessica warned.

Sara threw the balloons down in disgust. 'I'm

supposed to be the first one to the ship. I have to talk to the captain about a cheque I gave him.' She glanced towards the counter. 'I think I see them.'

'Where?'

'Near the cash register.'

'All right, here's what we'll do,' Jessica said. 'I'll call the guy over and get him to help me pick out a toy. You grab the stuff, get the pharmacist's attention, and we'll be on our way.'

'Why can't I get help with the toy?'

'Because I thought of it first. Now get away from me.'

Sara sulked over to the laxative section. Jessica smiled and waved her hand. The guy saw her and hurried to her side. He had blond hair like Bill's, but was taller and thinner than Bill. She could tell he liked her, glasses and all.

I hope to God he doesn't ask me for my number.

'Looking for something?' he asked.

'Yeah,' she said, picking up a brown plastic horse. 'I wanted to ask you about this toy.'

'Yes?'

'Ah – how much is it?'

He checked the price, which was clearly marked on the side. 'Two twenty-five.'

'Oh,' she said. Sara had reached the proper area and was quickly examining the boxes on the shelves. 'What kind of horse is it?' Jessica asked. He took it from her hands and fiddled with the cheap tiny hatch on the underbelly.

'It looks like the Trojan horse.'

'Trojans?' she whispered. *How did he know?* Then she realised he was *not* – thank God – referring to the popular brand of condoms. She giggled loudly. 'Yeah, that's what it is.'

He smiled uncertainly. 'Buying it for a nephew?'

'Yeah.'

'What's his name?'

'Michele.'

'Your nephew?'

'I mean Michael.'

Oh, no, no, no!

Sara had finished making her selection – it apparently didn't take long when one was willing to take everything the store had to offer – and signalled the pharmacist. Unfortunately, someone else had entered the store. No, not another person. An all-seeing, greasy butterball.

'Do you live around here?' the guy asked Jessica.

'Sara, my darling!' Bubba exclaimed, sauntering up to the counter, still wearing his ridiculous gold-tasselled sombrero and blue graduation gown. He must have stolen it.

Sara turned a distinctly unhealthy shade of green and threw Jessica a look of pure misery. She wanted help, Jessica knew. But Jessica wasn't about to give it to her. Bubba hadn't seen her so far and Jessica had no intention of letting him see her. She pulled the young man with her towards the corner, using him as a shield.

'I'd really like to know more about this horse,' she said.

'What are you doing here?' Bubba asked, picking up one of the boxes. Devilish delight filled his face. 'Sponges! A girl who thinks more of her man's pleasure than her own. Bravo, Sara! Bravo!'

'How old is your nephew?' the guy asked.

'Who cares?' Jessica asked. 'I mean, what?'

'I was just wondering if another gift might be more appropriate,' the guy replied, not put off by her rudeness.

'Is this all?' the pharmacist asked Sara. Sara nodded

stiffly, not looking at Bubba, even though she was obviously trying to dematerialise him by the sheer power of her thoughts. Bubba raised a hand.

'Wait,' he said. 'We would like a bottle of baby oil.' Bubba spoke to Sara. 'Usually, after exerting myself in lovemaking, I enjoy a full body massage. It restores my vital energies that much quicker.'

The pharmacist somehow kept a straight face, but it was clear it was only because he had been a pharmacist for many years. 'Would you like the oil?' he asked Sara.

'No,' she said curtly.

'Is that guy hassling your friend?' the handsome young man asked Jessica.

'I don't know her,' Jessica said.

Bubba put his arm lovingly around Sara and spoke to the pharmacist. 'This is all new to her. She's embarrassed. Look, she's blushing. Give us the largest bottle of oil you carry.'

'My name's Dave,' the guy said to Jessica. 'What's yours?'

'Why?' she asked, terribly distracted.

'I don't want the oil,' Sara said, pushing forward her money. 'But I'll pay for this other stuff *now*.'

'I won't hear of it,' Bubba said, reaching for his wallet.

'I was just wondering if maybe we could get together later?' the handsome young man asked Jessica.

'I can't,' she said.

'Why not?'

'I'm busy,' Jessica said. 'I'm married.'

Sara kept shoving her own money on the pharmacist. He finally showed mercy on her and took it, ringing up the three different boxes of contraceptives, minus the oil. Bubba moved back a step.

'Modern women,' he told the pharmacist, shaking his head, not overly displeased. 'They think they know what they want, when they haven't a clue what they *need*.'

'Thank you,' Sara told the pharmacist, grabbing the bag and hurrying for the door. Bubba watched her leave, then turned towards the rear of the store. Jessica tried to duck behind Dave. Too late.

'Give my regards to Bill, Jessie,' Bubba called. 'But if I were you, I'd keep Sara's receipt.'

Jessica gave the Trojan horse back to Dave and chased after Sara. When they were back in the front seat of the car, trying to breathe and not groan at the same time, Sara glanced over at Jessica and remarked, 'That wasn't so bad.'

Jessica stuck the keys in the ignition, her hand trembling. 'We handled it like mature adults,' she agreed.

CHAPTER ELEVEN

Wrong and right. Dark and light. Polly was confused. She did not know what to do. The flowers in her hands were dying. She had just bought them. Roses – the day they bloomed they began to wilt. She didn't suppose it mattered. Alice wouldn't care.

Polly knelt beside the grave, the grass thick and wet beneath her bare knees. Her headache had returned. The voice at her back didn't surprise her. She'd heard the motorcycle approaching from far off.

'So she really is dead,' Clark said.

Polly turned. Clark was all in black. She couldn't remember when she had last seen him in the sunlight. It could have been the day they had met. It didn't make much difference, the time of day; he brought the night with him. He was the only guy she knew who stood in his own shadow. She had not seen him since the night her aunt had died.

'Hi,' she said.

'Hello.'

'Did you think I lied to you about her?' she asked.

'You lie to me all the time.' He turned back to the tombstone, annoyed. Alice Ann McCoy. Polly could have sworn Ann was her own middle name. 'Go away.'

'You're not happy to see me?'

'No,' Polly said.

'Then why did you call?'

'I didn't call.'

'Then why am I here?' Clark asked.

'I don't know.'

Clark stepped on to the neighbouring grave, her aunt's. He grinned as he looked down, and she thought that he might spit. A green canvas bag hung by a strap over his shoulder. 'She finally choked to death, I see,' he said.

'The doctor said she went peacefully in her sleep.'

'But doctors lie.'

'Did you smother her?' she asked angrily.

Clark shrugged. 'She was old and ugly.'

'I hate you.'

He chuckled. 'You hated her. You hated taking care of her.'

'That's not true! Get out of here and leave me alone!'

Clark circled Alice's grave. He did so carefully, almost as if he feared the spot. He moved to Philip Bart's grave. A rock from a dynamite blast had put him in the ground. Polly had donated the plot to his family. It was supposed to have been her own plot.

Clark slipped the bag from his shoulder and set the strap over Philip's tombstone. His middle name had been Michael. Her father's name had been Michael. But neither her father nor mother was buried in this cemetery. There hadn't been enough of them left to fill a coffin. Their car had burned for ever. Ashes and smoke. If she closed her eyes, Polly could still smell it, and hear her father shouting at her to behave in the backseat – right before he had driven off the road.

Polly liked the name Michael. It brought back warm memories. But she still hoped Michael Olson didn't come to the party. Clark knelt beside his bag and began to unzip it.

'I'm not leaving,' he said. 'Today's your last day of school. It's our last chance.'

'For what?'

'To even the score.'

'You're not doing anything. They won't let you on the boat.'

'You can get me on board.'

'Why should I?' she asked.

He let go of the bag. Anger filled his face. 'You're sitting on your why.'

'They didn't kill her! She killed herself!'

'That's a lie. You're lying to me again.'

'Then you killed her.'

His anger left suddenly. He grinned. He had ugly lips, like a fish. It made her sick to remember all the times they had kissed. 'Closer to the truth, Polly. But not close enough. Go on.'

'What?'

'Tell me how I killed Alice.'

She stared down at her roses. They'd scraped away the thorns at the florist; nevertheless, she felt a sharp prick – a band of thorns wrapped around her head like the crown of thorns Jesus wore. Bloody red roses. Funeral flowers. A waste of money. Her vision wavered at Clark's question. 'I was outside in the backyard,' she said.

'All right.' He appeared to sigh. He'd wanted her to say something else. He went back to his bag, pulling out a tiny metal clock, black and red wires, and a lump of what could have been orange Play-Doh. 'We'll say the party killed her. If there hadn't been a party, there would still be an Alice.'

Polly nodded wearily. 'Yeah.'

'Most of the kids who were at the party will be on the boat.'

'What is that stuff?'

Clark tapped the tombstone at his back. 'Mr Bart could tell you.'

'You're not going to blow up the boat!'

'Of course not.'

'You better not.'

He laughed. 'I'm just going to put a hole in it.' He crawled towards her, his leather-clad legs slithering over the grass like twin snakes. She thought he was going to grab her, kiss her – she didn't want him to kiss her, not that much – but he halted, shy of Alice's grave.

'You remember the party? All the kiddies were in the pool. They know how to swim.'

'Not all of them,' Polly said.

'Who doesn't know?' he asked gleefully.

'Jessie.' That was a fact. Jessica had grown up with a pool in her backyard and was going to Hawaii next week, but she had never learned to swim. She had almost drowned as a child. She was terrified of the water.

'Who talked you into the party?' Clark asked.

'Jessie. And Sara.'

Clark glanced at his bag. There was something black and muddy inside that he had not unpacked. 'Sara never did like you.'

Polly put her hand to her head. She could feel the blood pounding beneath the skin. She had given blood all year – to different hospitals, more times than she was supposed to – and there was still so much pressure inside. Sometimes she honestly felt the only real way to let it all out would be to take a gun and put a hole in her skull the way Alice had.

'How did you know Jessie couldn't swim?' she whispered.

Clark reached over with his bony left hand – he was left-handed, as Alice had been – and touched Polly's lips with the nail of his index finger. He touched her teeth. He probably would have stuck his finger inside her if she had let him. He was trying to get inside her. He had been trying from the beginning, though he had never wanted to make love to her. She had never been able to understand that. He was one way, and he was another way. She imagined his finger would have felt the same way the cold hard barrel of a gun would have felt inside her mouth. She knew it would have been just as deadly. But that might not be such a bad thing, not if it stopped the pain. Her head was killing her!

'If I tell you that,' he said. 'I will tell you everything.'

He was asking for her permission. 'No,' she said.

'Are you sure?'

'No.'

'I'll kill them. I'll kill them all.'

She set the roses down. *For my sister.* 'He'll stop you.'

'Who?'

'Michael.'

'I very much doubt it.' Clark stood and put the explosives back in his bag. He held out his left hand. 'Come along, Polly. It's time.'

She went with him.

CHAPTER TWELVE

Haven was her name, and she was at the end of a long and fun-filled career. In the sixties and seventies, she had been a popular choice for vacationers looking for an intimate cruise ship to take to Mexico's Mazatlán, La Paz, or Acapulco. But that had been before a new generation of vessels – larger and more sophisticated – had pushed *Haven* into an uneconomic no-man's-land; she was too plush to haul cargo, and she was too plain and small to attract parties of the rich and pretty. When Bubba had come to Sara in the spring with the idea of renting *Haven* for Tabb High's all-night senior party, he had never spoken so truthfully as he did when he said it was the chance of a lifetime. Her captain had just decided to rent her out as a party boat, making the trip between Catalina and the mainland. This class party was to be one of his first short cruises.

Bubba had caught Sara at an anxious moment. She had been thinking hard and without success for a way to blow everybody's extracurricular mind one last time, and thus for ever ensure their fond memories of her leadership skills. Because neither side was aware of how desperate the other was, the negotiations between the captain of the *Haven* and Sara proceeded with remarkable smoothness. The captain didn't even mind a postdated cheque.

Yet the cost for the all-night party was unusually high

107

– forty dollars per student, and that didn't include a hotel room to recover in on Catalina. But you only graduated from high school once, Sara had thought. She figured the class should be able to stay awake until *Haven* returned them to the mainland the next evening. From the beginning, the idea of the class bumming around together on the island all day had struck her as the best part of the plan. When she had announced the extravaganza, practically every senior had bought a ticket.

It was only because Sara had taken extra pains to keep the price as low as it was that she found herself in desperate need of an L.A. Lakers victory over the Boston Celtics.

Jessica, however, was blissfully unaware of the financial complications surrounding the evening as she sat on the edge of the bed in 'her' cabin and watched as Sara split their drugstore bounty. It was just as well. Jessica already had plenty on her mind, not the least of which was the fact that, although *Haven* was still anchored to the dock, she was no longer on dry ground.

They don't have icebergs this far south, Jessica told herself. *The Titanic was one in a million.*

Maria's accident had been one in a million. It had been that kind of year. Jessica wished they had gone to Disneyland as a normal school class would. She was afraid to hold her breath and stick her head underwater in her own bath. The floor beneath her feet was swaying now, ever so slightly.

'I think we should put the stuff in the bathroom cabinets,' Sara said, dumping everything out of their boxes and on to the bed.

'Are you giving me the condoms and taking the foam or what?' Jessica asked.

'No, you take some of each.'

108

'Then I don't think we should put it in the cabinets. Imagine how Bill or Russ will feel if he sees we have a selection. We should make it look like we just happen to have something with us.'

'That's a good idea.'

'Another thing, don't throw away the boxes. I want to read the directions.'

'The stuff is pretty self-explanatory, don't you think?'

'I don't know. I've never seen it before. Have you?'

'No.'

Jessica picked up the roll of condom packets. 'Let's look at one.'

Sara stopped her. 'No, we shouldn't waste any.'

'We won't waste it opening the corner and peeping inside.'

'Yeah, we will. Then it will be contaminated.'

'So what? We can just throw it out. What do we have here? A dozen. That's six each,' Jessica said.

'Is that a lot? I mean, how many times do people usually have sex when they have sex?'

Jessica laughed. 'What a stupid question.' Then she thought a moment. 'I'm not sure.'

'I don't think we should waste any.'

'All right. You know what just occurred to me?'

'What?'

'That we don't know what the hell we're doing.'

'Do you think they will?' Sara asked, serious.

'Oh, yeah. Bill and Russ have been around. Hasn't Russ?'

'I never asked him. Have you asked Bill?'

'No,' Jessica said.

'But you figure he did it with Clair, right?'

'What an awful thing to say! Now you have me worrying how I'll match up.'

'Sorry,' Sara said. Something outside the cabin's tiny round porthole caught her attention. 'Oh, no. Don't look.'

'What?'

'Nick's just appeared, and he's got Maria with him.' Jessica stood up from the bed and reached the window in one step. The dimensions of the cabin were going to take some getting used to. The whole room was not much larger than her walk-in cupboard at home. She could feel her heart pounding as she pressed her face to the circle of glass.

'She'll have trouble getting around the ship in that chair,' Jessica said. *Haven* sat between the dock and the western sky, throwing a deep shadow over the boarding ramp and the boardwalk beyond. Despite the fact that they were to set sail within minutes, a surprising number of kids continued to mill about the dock. Nick was having no trouble wheeling Maria's chair up the ramp. Jessica had forgotten how small she was.

Her lovely long hair. She cut it all off.

Hair meant nothing next to an injured spinal cord, and yet its loss deeply troubled Jessica.

'Not as long as she stays on deck,' Sara said, also peering out the window.

'I didn't know she was coming to the party.'

'Who did?'

'Well, she must have bought a ticket,' Jessica said in a slightly accusatory tone. She still hadn't forgiven Sara for not telling her Michael was to be valedictorian when Sara must have known way in advance. Jessica had been anxiously awaiting Michael's arrival. Sara swore she had *given* him a ticket.

'The tickets are tickets. They don't have names written on them.' Sara paused. 'You won't be able to avoid her all night.'

The ramp carried Nick and Maria out of sight around the curve of the ship. Jessica came to a decision. 'I'm not going to try.' She stood back from the window. 'Come on. We'll talk to her now, get it over with.'

'Whatever you say,' Sara replied without enthusiasm. She picked up the contraceptives on the bed and stuffed most of them under Jessica's pillow. Except for Polly, they were the only students who had rooms. Theirs were located towards the stern, adjacent to each other, but unconnected by a door. Jessica wasn't sure where Polly's was. Polly had asked when she had come on board if Sara could get her a place to crash. Sara had been quick to oblige; the evening had yet to begin and Polly already looked wasted.

The remainder of the passenger rooms were locked tight, and would remain so the whole night. Kids who wanted to sleep before they reached Catalina would have to do so outside on the top deck or on the floor in one of the main rooms.

'We'll take care of the stuff later,' Jessica said as Sara continued to stare at the label on one of the boxes.

'Do you think he was right?' Sara asked.

'Who?'

'Bubba. About using a sponge and a man's pleasure and all that?'

'Ask him. What did he write in your yearbook, anyway?'

Sara hid the box under Jessica's top sheet. 'Shut up.'

The corridor to the stairway, or companionway, was narrow. Jessica detected a faint odour of diesel in the air. No nuclear power aboard this vessel. Mr Bark would have been pleased. Too bad he was going to be unable to chaperon the party. Word had it that he had developed a sudden unbearable rash on his hands. Miss Fenway, a secretary in the administration building, was to take his place.

A bell rang as they climbed on to the upper deck. The kids loitering on the dock began to walk up the boarding plank. The temperature was still warm, but Jessica could feel it dropping. Cool air over warm water – the fog would roll for sure. She hoped the captain didn't accidentally miss Catalina on the way out to sea.

'Aren't you going to check people's tickets?' Jessica asked, making a brief futile scan for Michael.

'Nope,' Sara said. 'If someone wants to come that bad, I ain't going to turn them away.'

Nick had parked Maria's chair near the bow of the ship. He was pointing out something of interest on a nearby tanker. Maria appeared to be listening closely.

Promise me I will never have to see you again.

'Do you want me to come with you?' Sara asked, watching her.

'Yeah,' Jessica said.

Nick noticed their approach and alerted Maria. Jessica saw one thing had not changed. Maria's eyes were still dark, still solemn. Yet a smile seemed to touch her lips as their eyes met. Jessica reach out both her hands. Maria took them after a slight hesitation. Their fingers squeezed together briefly, lightly.

'I'm glad you're here,' Jessica said.

'Thank you,' she said, her eyes fixed on Jessica's face.

'Hi, Maria,' Sara said, leaning over and giving her a quick hug and kiss. Jessica wished she had done the same. Maria gently returned Sara's embrace.

'I liked your speech,' Maria said.

'I'm having it copyrighted,' Sara said. 'How are you?'

'Fine.'

'You look good.'

'Thank you.'

It was all too formal. Maria continued to watch Jessica with her dark eyes, and even though Jessica didn't detect a hint of hostility in them, the tension between them was still there.

Why can't we just talk?

A silly question. She could walk and Maria couldn't.

'You got us a big enough ship here, Sara,' Nick said.

'Hey, Nicky,' Jessica said.

'Hey, Jessie,' he replied, chuckling.

Sara moved to his side and wrapped an arm around his waist, saying, 'There is one thing I haven't told anybody about this boat.'

'What?' Nick asked.

Sara poked his powerful biceps. 'How are you at rowing?'

Sara went on flirting with Nick, and Jessica thought it was cute and everything, but she couldn't help wondering why Sara wasn't spending every available minute with Russ. He would be heading back up north come Sunday morning.

Jessica lightly squeezed Maria's hands again and asked if they could talk later. Maria hesitated before nodding. Jessica left her to go and stand by the boarding plank, and repeatedly checked her watch. A second bell rang. The last of the people on the dock boarded.

Please be here, Michael. Please God.

'Should be a fun night,' Bill said, appearing suddenly by her side. He had on a yellow turtleneck sweater, and shiny black shoes. He looked good. He always looked good. The boxes of condoms and foam popped into her mind. She pushed them away. She tried instead to imagine the thrill of having his naked body lying beside

113

hers. The picture wouldn't come. A third bell rang. One of the few crewmen appeared and began to withdraw the plank.

'Yeah, it's going to be great,' she said, her heart sinking.

'Is Michael here?' Bill asked.

'Who?'

'Olson?'

'No.' She spoke to the crewman. 'We're expecting someone.' The sailor went right on pulling in the plank. The end clanged off the dock and hung out limply from the faded white hull. 'That's a shame,' he said. '

'Could I sign your yearbook?' Bill asked.

'Later,' Jessica said sadly. Then she spotted a figure striding briskly around a wall of stacked pallets. She almost lost her glasses jumping to her toes. 'He's here! He's here! Sir, our friend's come. Put down the plank, please, sir. Thank you. He's here.'

Michael was on board a minute later, his yearbook in his hand. Bill gave him a warm slap on the back and complimented him on his valedictorian speech. Jessica felt more than a little awkward welcoming Michael with Bill at her side. Michael didn't seem to mind. Her joy at his arrival surprised even her. Once she had thought she was in love with him. Now she knew she was.

Before the night is over, I have to tell him.

Michael shook her hand and thanked her for holding the boat for him. He seemed to have just taken a shower. His hair looked damp. He moved on to speak with Nick after talking to her for less than a minute.

Jessica left Bill a moment later to be alone at the stern of the boat. A breeze came up from the north and a fine mist rose up over the flat ocean. The anchor was lifted and the ship slipped away, the lights of the harbour

114

blurring in the mist, growing fainter. The western sky went from orange to purple to black. The party kicked into high gear. Jessica felt little inclination to join in. She shivered, looking at the dark water beneath her feet. She had always had nightmares of drowning.

CHAPTER THIRTEEN

Although he had been in a hurry to reach the harbour when he left Clark's house, Michael soon realised he could not board the ship with his hair and clothes full of blood. He made a quick stop at his house to wash and change. Fortunately, his mother and Daniel were not there to see what a mess he was. They had been disappointed when he hadn't let them take him out for a celebration meal after the ceremony. He had given them some feeble excuse about work he had to finish at JPL.

Michael was worried his mother would have the baby early. She hadn't said anything, but he noticed after the ceremony that her breathing was irregular, as if she were having pain. If he hadn't felt so close to solving the mystery of Alice's death, he wouldn't have left her.

Close does not count in life and death. Only in horseshoes.

When had the shotgun been fired that had torn away part of the shingle outside the bedroom window? What did that shot have to do with the one that had been fired into Alice's head? Who had broken Alice's nose? Had Clark really been at the party? Why would Polly lie to him?

The endless stream of questions didn't frighten Michael as it might have another investigator. He, in fact, felt as if he had almost enough pieces of information to solve the puzzle; he simply had to arrange them properly and the picture would make sense. But as with a child's puzzle, he knew that one more piece – preferably a big corner piece – would help speed up the process immensely.

Showering at home, Michael had begun to take Polly's warning more seriously. He began to worry that if he didn't return from the all-night party, his efforts on Alice's behalf would be wasted. Cursing his shortage of time, he took a piece of paper and quickly jotted down everything he had discovered, including half a dozen different scenarios that might cover the facts. The problem was, all of his scenarios had at least one major hole.

But he *was* able to print Clark's full name and address on the bottom of the paper. If nothing else, Lieutenant Keller could follow up that lead.

Sealing his information in an envelope, he took it to the station. The lieutenant happened to be in his office.

'What can I do for you, Mike?' he asked politely, offering him a seat. Michael was not fooled by the seriousness with which the officer welcomed him. Keller may have respected his intelligence and persistence, but he also had doubts about his emotional stability. Michael did not take the offered seat.

'I'm sorry, I'm in a hurry,' he said, handing the policeman the envelope. 'I want you to hold this for me until next Monday. If I don't return for it by then, I want you to open it.'

Keller glanced from the envelope to Michael's face a couple of times and Michael could see the lieutenant's doubts about Young Mr Olson's stability being replaced by something far worse – pity.

'What's inside?' Keller asked.

'Information.'

'About Alice McCoy's death?'

'Yes.'

Keller stood uneasily. Perhaps he was worried Young Mr Olson was going to follow in Alice McCoy's footsteps and go out with a bang. 'Why wouldn't you be back to pick it up?'

Michael smiled to put him at ease. 'Who knows? I just graduated today. I might find a girl tonight and elope.' Then he got serious. 'Please hold it for me. And if, by chance, you still have it Monday, give what I had to say some thought.'

'But where are you going tonight?' he asked.

'To our all-night senior party.'

The lieutenant relaxed slightly. 'Sounds like fun.'

'I think it's going to be a wild party,' Michael agreed.

Now he stood at the edge of the party and above the ocean. They were an hour out of dock and he had already searched *Haven* from the bow to the stern. Clark didn't appear to be on board. Yet Michael was far from convinced he wasn't there. He had been unable to persuade the captain to let him look in the thirty locked passenger rooms. Granted, if he couldn't get into the rooms, Clark shouldn't be able to. But with so many places to hide, Michael had to wonder. Even without access to the rooms, a sufficiently determined individual could probably have found some hidden corner to tuck into. It was a big ship. Michael was debating whether or not to give *Haven* another going-over when Nick came out of the main lounge and joined him by the rail.

'The game's going to start in a couple of minutes,' Nick said.

'I'll watch the second half,' Michael said.

Nick stared out over the calm water. The rise and fall of the ship was almost non-existent. The fog continued to gather. The coast was already invisible and their path

118

through the night seemed to be taking them into a land of clouds.

'It's peaceful out here,' Nick said.

'You like the water?' Michael asked.

'I didn't know how much until tonight. Did you know, Mike, when I was growing up in the barrio, I never saw the ocean once?'

'That's amazing.'

Nick leaned on the rail. 'I hear they have a sailing class at U.C.L.A. I think I might sign up for it.' He laughed softly at the thought. 'Imagine me on a yacht?'

'Who knows, with the salaries they pay in the NBA, you might be able to afford one some day.'

Nick shook his head. 'That's a one-in-a-million shot. I'll never play pro ball.'

Michael leaned on the rail beside him. He wondered how deep the water was. The thought nagged at him. He wasn't able to relax. 'Yeah, you'd be better off concentrating on your education. You sprain your ankle or twist your knee and you're out. But they can't take your degree away from you.'

'The day I get it, I'll have you to thank for it.'

'You get what you deserve. Good things are going to come to you.'

'I read that last book you gave me,' Nick said.

'Which one was that?'

'The *Hound of the Baskervilles* – Sherlock Holmes. It was great.'

'I'm glad you enjoyed it. I'll give you another one.'

'You remind me of him.'

'Me? I don't smoke a pipe.'

Nick looked at him closely. 'What's wrong?'

'Nothing.'

'You look kind of down.'

'I'm all right,' Michael said.

119

'Have you talked to Jessie today?'

'Not really. How's Maria?'

Nick frowned. 'Very quiet.'

'Has she told you why she wanted to come tonight?'

'No.'

'Has she threatened you again like she did at the hospital?'

'No, nothing like that. But she's got something on her mind. She seems to be *waiting*.'

Michael glanced about, feeling he couldn't wait. He tapped Nick on the shoulder. 'I'll catch up with you later, buddy.'

Above the main lounge, where the bulk of the class had gathered in front of the large screen TV to watch the final game of the NBA play-offs, sat *Haven*'s bridge. Michael looked up and spotted the helmsman – lit a faint blue and red by rows of luminescent dials – turning the wheel several degrees to port. That was another place the captain hadn't let him inspect.

Am I searching for Clark or Jessie?

He found Polly instead. She stood alone against the entrance to *Haven*'s galley. Michael could hear kids laughing and carrying on inside. Few were walking the deck. The temperature had dropped steadily since they had pulled out of the harbour. The salty breeze, however, continued to blow soft and easy.

'Is your headache better?' he asked cheerfully.

She jumped slightly at the sound of his voice. She had on a short-sleeved white blouse, a thin red skirt. Gooseflesh covered her arms. 'I'm all right,' she said.

He had told Nick the same thing a minute ago. He had lied. His head was throbbing from Clark's blow. Worse, his vision continued to blur off and on. It blurred now as he looked at Polly. She went back to playing with her dark hair, watching the fog.

'I'm sorry I ganged up on you this morning,' he said.

'That's OK.'

'Having fun?'

'I'm cold.'

'Why don't you go inside and have a hot drink? I'll have one with you.'

She stared at him. 'He likes me cold.'

'Come again?'

'He told me: 'Stay alive babe and stay cold. It's the only way for the likes of us.' That's what he said. He's weird.'

'I saw him today.'

It didn't surprise her. 'At the cemetery?' she asked.

'No, I went to his house. Did you see him at the cemetery?'

She nodded. 'Before I came to the harbour.'

'When was that?'

'Five o'clock, six o'clock?'

Clark must have gone straight to the cemetery after knocking him out. 'Did he have a gun with him?' Michael asked.

'I didn't see everything in his bag.' She chewed on her lower lip, looking exhausted.

'Is he on board?' he asked.

'Yes.'

He moved a step closer. 'Are you sure?'

'Yes.'

'Where?'

'I don't know.'

'You must have some idea?'

'I don't. He comes and goes, like lightning.'

The simile made him pause. Polly was the only one who even indirectly supported his belief that Alice hadn't committed suicide, and yet, whenever he spoke to her, he didn't believe her. 'Why is he here?' he asked.

'I can't tell you.'

'Why not?'

'He'll kill me.'

'Does he intend to kill me?'

'If you get in his way.'

She was doing it to him again – confusing him. He remembered the weather-beaten paper he had found in her backyard. 'Polly, back in November, I gave you a form for your aunt to sign. What did you do with it?'

'I gave it to Clark.'

'Why?'

'He wanted it.'

'Where and when did you give it to him?'

'In my backyard, during the storm.' She shivered. 'I have to take a warm bath now before it gets any later, Mike. I don't care what he says. I have to warm my blood.'

'I'll see you around,' he muttered, distracted, hardly caring how or where she would take her bath. As Polly turned and walked away, for an instant, everything in his immediate surroundings seemed to jump into the air, and land in reverse. He put his hand to his head and took it away and found blood on his fingers. No, it was not concussion that was making reality dance. She had given him the answer! For an instant, he'd had the entire solution to the night of the party, to the whole crazy year, in seed form in his mind. Not the details of the truth, but the essence of it. Unfortunately, it had gone as quickly it had come, leaving him more confused than ever; leaving him cold, too, almost as if he had just fallen overboard.

It will come back.

CHAPTER FOURTEEN

Either one person had sneaked fifty gallons of alcohol on board or else a fair percentage of the class had ignored the prohibition against mixing ocean cruises and intoxicating substances and had brought enough good cheer on to *Haven* to give themselves and their closest friends a respectable buzz. The air in the main lounge literally stank of booze. Sara was getting drunk just breathing. Unfortunately, the basketball game on the tube was keeping her more sober than she wold have liked. Half-time had just begun and the Lakers were down by eight points.

'The Lakers are a great second-half team, aren't they?' she asked Nick, who, along with Maria, was sitting with her in the rear of the lounge. Maria appeared to be enjoying the game, although she hadn't said more than five words since it had begun.

'They are, yeah,' Nick said.

'That's good,' Sara said.

'But so are the Celtics,' Nick added.

A faint creaking sound went through the lounge as the floor dropped a few inches. It was a rare sign that they were far out at sea. The lounge could have been in a bar on the west side of town. It was loud enough.

'But an eight-point lead,' Sara said. 'That's nothing in a basketball game, is it?'

Nick nodded. 'It can disappear in a couple of minutes.'

'If you were to put money on this game right now, who would you bet on?' she asked.

'You'd have to be crazy to put money down on the Lakers versus the Celtics. It's always close.'

'But just suppose? Who do you think is going to win.'

'The Celtics.'

'What? I thought you were a Lakers fan?'

Nick smiled. 'Yeah, but you're talking about money.'

He was not very reassuring. Sara stood. 'I've got to find somebody,' she said.

Bubba was sitting on the bar on the far side of the room. Most of the kids who were drinking were doing so from brown-bagged pints barely hidden in their coat pockets. Bubba had a fifth of Jack Daniel's riding his left knee. Every time the Lakers scored, he toasted the room and the basket and took a chug. It really pissed her off that he was having such a good time.

Clair stood by his side. She was not drinking. In fact, she didn't seem all that happy about his flagrant consumption. She was trying to take the bottle away from him. She was a little late; the thing was three-quarters empty. Then again, it was always said that Bubba could drink a crew of sailors under the table.

Why are people always saying good things about this jackass?

'You've had enough,' Clair said, unwrapping one finger from the neck of the bottle only to see the finger before it wrap back around the neck. 'It's still early and you're already loaded.'

'I'm not loaded,' Bubba said, slurring his speech. 'I'm merely giving a few of my brain cells a much needed vacation.'

'You're going to end up falling overboard,' Clair said,

getting annoyed. She gave up trying to be gentle about it and yanked the bottle from his hand. He laughed uproariously.

'That's why I've got to get my drinking done now!'

Sara poked him in the side. 'I need to talk to you.'

He turned, his jovial smile rolling around his fat face like a goldfish in a bowl. 'Sara, how come you've left your post? Who's steering the ship?'

Clair gave her a sympathetic look. 'He's impossible when he's like this.'

Bubba reached out and grabbed Clair, putting his arm around her, snuggling the side of his head up to her smooth tanned cheek. 'But nothing is impossible when we're together, darling,' he said.

Sara half expected her to shove him away; he was, for all intents and purposes, slobbering on her. But Clair did nothing of the kind. She put her arm around him instead and hugged him back, blushing red and laughing as he turned and whispered something in her ear.

Sara just couldn't understand how such beauty could be attracted to such disgust.

Clair gave him a quick kiss on the forehead as she broke free a moment later, the bottle still in her hand. She began to walk towards the rear exit. 'I'm still dumping this poison, Bubba,' she called over her shoulder.

'There's plenty where that came from!' he called after her, giggling. He turned back to Sara. 'Isn't she wonderful?'

'The Lakers are losing,' she said flatly.

He sat back in mock surprise. 'No.'

'They're down by eight points. Nick says they're going to lose.'

'Does Nick want to play?'

'Huh.'

Bubba clapped his hands together. 'Yeah! The coach should put Nick in. He's a homegrown boy. It'll be legal.' Bubba went to jump off the bar. 'I'll radio for a helicopter.'

Sara grabbed his arm, keeping him on the bar. 'Stop carrying on like a lunatic. We've got a serious problem here.'

He eyed her as best he could with his eyes rolling around in a multitude of directions. 'We can't have a problem until the game's over.'

'But what if they lose?' she cried.

He leaned closer, his breath enough to anaesthetise a tubfull of clams, and raised a fat finger close to her nose. 'You know what your problem is, Sara?'

She paused. 'What?'

'You don't know how to dress.'

'What's wrong with the way I dress?'

He gestured to her orange dress. 'You're always in autumn colours.'

'So what?'

He turned his head and sneezed. She felt the spray. He went on in a confidential tone. 'Autumn is a rotten time of year. School starts in autumn. Leaves fall off the trees in autumn. People hate autumn. They hate people who remind them of it.'

She sneered. 'Get off it.'

He belched loudly. 'It's a fact. You send out depressing vibes. Look at me. A minute ago, I was finishing my bottle and singing. Then you showed up.' He wiped at his eyes. 'Now I'm beginning to feel sad.'

'What are you sad about?'

'I feel so unhappy.'

'No, you don't.'

'I do. I can't bear it.'

'Well, what do you want me to do about it?'

126

He thought for a moment, looking as miserable as he would have her believe he was. Then a wild gleam entered his eyes, and he suddenly reached for her with his grubby paws. 'I want you to take your clothes off!'

She dodged him easily. He fell from the bar stool and landed on his face. She kick him while he was down. He sat up and rubbed his head. 'Bubba, you're drunk,' she said, disgusted.

He rolled his eyes upwards and grinned. 'No, Sara. I'm just happy.'

She decided she would give him to the end of the game – then she would kill him. She left him giggling on the floor.

Russ was bothering her as much as the game. He was acting like a stranger. No, stranger was too strong a word. He was being friendly and all – but that was the problem. He wasn't supposed to be her friend. He was supposed to be her boyfriend. At least that was her understanding. But she wondered if he knew. He had kissed her. He had told her he liked her. He had let her bail him out of jail. He had written to her while he was away; not so often as she might have wished, but a letter and a postcard should count for something. Yet they had never made any promises to each other. When she thought about it, they had never even *talked*, not really, not for any length of time. And now they were supposed to make love before the sun came up.

What the hell have I talked myself into?

It was a lonely thing, to suddenly realise that maybe she had been suckered all along, not by Russ, but by her own imagination.

He was watching the game with 'the boys'. That was fair enough. He hadn't seen his pals from the cross-country team since December. She didn't require every blessed second of his time. But eyeing him from across the room as he was sitting on the arm of a couch and laughing at some fool joke, a beer can in his hand, obviously having more fun than she was, she thought of all the trouble she had gone through to pick him up at the bus station. He owed her something. She strode up to him.

'Hi,' she said.

'Hi,' he said, glancing over briefly, before continuing with his wild tale of mystery and intrigue at the state's most exotic juvenile hall. 'Then I said to him, I said, 'You hide that knife under my pillow again during a shakedown and I'll use it to shred every piece of clothing you've got.' He called my bluff, the idiot. And a month later he was walking around with his – '

'Excuse me,' Sara interrupted. 'Russ?'

He looked at her again. 'What, Sara?'

She smiled. 'How are you doing?'

He glanced at the beer in his hand. The rest of his buddies were waiting for him to continue. 'I'm fine,' he said. 'What's wrong?'

'Nothing's wrong. I just wanted to, you know, say hi.'

'How about we talk in a few minutes?'

'The game starts in a few minutes.'

'Then we'll talk after the game. Would that be all right?'

'Sure. Yeah.'

He went to give the punch line of his story, then noticed she had made no move to leave. He smiled uneasily. 'I don't know if you want to hear this, Sara.'

'Why not?'

'It's kind of disgusting.'

'OK. Thanks. I'll take that as a compliment, being told to bug off because I'm not disgusting enough to listen to you.' She spun on her heel and stalked away. He called to her, but she didn't slow down till she was standing outside in the damp darkness beside the rail. The fog kept getting thicker. She kept getting more tense. She hadn't wanted to fight with him. She had promised herself she wouldn't. But whenever she was around him, she just wanted to strangle him!

Or kiss him. Why didn't he even kiss me after the ceremony when everybody was kissing everybody else?

She stood there for several minutes, catching her breath and trying to tell herself she was too cool to get upset about a boy. After a bit she began to notice her surroundings. It was a bizarre night. She could hear the splash of the water against the hull, could even smell it. But she could not see the ocean in any direction. *Haven* could have been ploughing through the sky above a storm.

'Hi,' a nearby voice said. It was that weird dude who worked at the petrol station, the one with the greasy hair and moustache, the guy who had owned the gun that had killed Alice. He had come up so quietly that he had startled her.

'Hi,' she said.

He grinned. He had incredibly crooked teeth. 'You don't remember my name, do you?'

'No.'

'You're Sara, right?'

'Yeah. You go by a nickname – Rats?'

'Kats.'

'Yeah. Sorry. How are you doing?'

'Couldn't be better. How are you?'

'Fine.' He wasn't someone she would have chosen for a late-night ocean-cruise partner. The way he kept grinning at her – it was as if he was thinking about doing things to her she preferred not to know. His next question did not exactly put her at ease.

'Can you swim, Sara?'

'Yeah. Can you?'

He leaned over the rail and spat into the fog. How disgusting! Sara thought she heard the splash of the spit in the water. He must have grime in his saliva glands. 'I don't have to,' he said. 'I know how to float.'

'I think I'll go back inside.'

She heard him laughing to himself as she re-entered the lounge.

CHAPTER FIFTEEN

Haven did not ordinarily require an entire night to reach Catalina. Usually the trip took only a couple of hours, but the captain was cruising slowly for the party; the engines were operating at only quarter power. Standing near the diesel-driven turbines, Michael was surprised at how quiet they were, especially since they must have been close to thirty years old. Michael always had a special admiration for machinery that performed its function year in and year out, and for the men who built it.

Clark was not in engineering. Michael had serious doubts that he was on board.

Haven's chief engineer had explained the fundamentals of the propulsion system to Michael earlier. He was now in the crew's galley having a cup of coffee. Michael had the engine room to himself. There was no wasted space. The turbines were housed in huge, twin white-steel tunnels, out of which sprang a complex array of pipes that stretched about thirty feet to the ceiling and walls before disappearing into a massive black fuel tank. The tank was set in the middle of the floor; it neatly divided the rear of the ship's lowest deck from the front. It was amazing the amount of fuel a vessel like *Haven* consumed. Michael estimated the tank's capacity at over a thousand gallons. If fire ever got to it, the whole ship would blow.

Following the narrow passageway to the right of the

tank, Michael left the rhythmic drone of the engines and headed for the storage area. He had been through the place once already, but decided to have another quick inspection before he headed topside.

The crew for the cruise was at a minimum; besides the captain, there were only eight men on duty. It was probably plenty. Although the ship seemed large to most of the class members, he knew it would be dwarfed by a modern cruise ship. Also, the trip out to Catalina was little more than a warm-up for *Haven*. Michael saw no one as he went through the various sections: the janitorial supply area, the linen department, the food stores, finishing with the machine shop. The latter was small but uncluttered. It occurred to him the place might be ideal for the meeting he was hoping to have later in the night.

Another invitation to Alice's party.

He surfaced into the night air at the ship's stern. He was surprised to find Jessica standing alone and staring back the way they had come, staring into nothing; the fog had cut visibility to practically zero. Thank God for radar. *Haven*'s horn blared once from the bridge, sounding lost as it faded and died over the invisible waters. Michael wondered why Jessica had been spending all her time by herself. He tactfully cleared his throat, and she turned around.

'Hi, Michael,' she said, smiling, quickly removing her glasses and slipping them in her back pocket.

He climbed the last treads of the companionway and stepped on to the deck. 'You should have a jacket on. It's getting chilly.' He moved up beside her, the water softly churning beneath their feet. Despite his remark, he liked the way she was dressed – in tight white trousers and a light blue sweater, her long brown hair reaching almost to her waist. He supposed she could have had on a canvas sack and he still would have found her perfectly presentable. She tugged at the arm of her sweater and looked at him expectantly.

'I had to wear this tonight,' she said. 'It's the last day of school.'

'Oh?'

'I had this same sweater with me my first day at Tabb. Don't you remember?'

'I do now, yeah. I still don't see how you got the grape juice out. I think you flew over to Switzerland and bought another one just so I wouldn't feel guilty.'

Her eyes lingered on him. 'Maybe I did.'

He laughed softly, feeling uneasy and happy. He was used to the contradictions she inspired in him. 'Why aren't you watching the game?' he asked.

'Why aren't you?'

'Not fair. I asked first.'

'It's so loud inside. It was giving me a headache.'

He nodded. 'I'm not a great party person myself.'

'I thought you weren't going to come. You cut it pretty tight.'

'Yeah, I had some business to take care of.'

'What was it?'

'Ah, nothing. Just stuff.'

They had a big wooden lifeboat and dull yellow light at their backs. Jessica was staring at his head strangely. She reached out to touch his hair. He stopped her. He knew his head was still bleeding. He wished he'd had time to get it stitched. He couldn't very well bandage it now. He had already wiped it several times with toilet paper.

'Your hair was wet when you came aboard, too,' she said, pulling her hand back, her face falling slightly. 'You're the one who's going to catch cold. I should find you a towel.'

He could just imagine the colour he would turn the towel. Fortunately, in his black hair, the blood was hardly recognisable for what it really was, even under better lighting. No one else on board had even said anything about it.

Clark had struck him a nasty blow. Michael was looking forward to repaying the favour. He was still annoyed with himself for having been caught so easily. 'Don't bother,' he said.

'It's no bother.' She turned. 'Really, you must dry it.'

He stopped her again, this time grabbing her arm, perhaps a shade too hard. He released her quickly when he saw her startled expression. 'I know where a towel is, Jessie,' he said.

'OK.' She forced a smile. 'So, what's new? I loved your speech. It touched me.'

'I'm just glad I got to give it before you sang. You stole the show. How come you never told me you could sing like that?'

'You really like my voice?'

'I do. Have you ever thought of doing anything with it? Like getting in a band?'

She smiled, pleased. 'When I was younger, I used to fantasise about being on stage and having everyone chanting my name. Alice used to . . .' She paused. 'Alice used to encourage me to do something with it.'

'You should think about it.'

'Yeah? I don't know. I'll see.' An awkward silence followed, during which a disturbing warmth began to spread over the right side of Michael's scalp. He knew what it was. Jessica finally spoke. 'I broke the ice with Maria.'

'How was it?'

She sighed. 'Not horrible, not good. We only talked

for a minute. But I felt like – this is going to sound weird – she'd like to talk more, but not yet.'

Nick had made a similar comment. Maria was waiting. Interesting. 'Give her time. The fact that she's here says a lot.'

'I hope you're right.' Jessica shook her head.

'What is it?'

'I was just thinking of that morning at the hospital. It was awful. I couldn't talk to her.' She peeped over at him. 'I couldn't talk to you.'

'You can always talk to me, Jessie,' he said, feeling a drop of blood trickle into his right ear. This was getting serious. He turned his head away from the water. He had better get to a bathroom. Jessica shook her head again.

'How? I never see you. You're never at school any more.'

'Well, from now on, you won't be at school, either.' Here came another drop. He was lucky Clark hadn't done a lobotomy while he was at it.

'That's what's bothering me,' she said. 'We're together long enough to become friends, then we have to go our separate ways.'

'You'll meet a lot of people at Stanford.'

She chuckled sadly at the remark and brushed away a hair. 'I'm not going to Stanford.'

The blood was a distraction. He had momentarily forgotten the SAT disaster. She never had told him her scores. 'They didn't accept you?'

'There was no sense in even sending in my application.'

'I'm sorry,' he muttered.

'It's not your fault. I didn't mean to give you that impression. I shouldn't have brought it up.'

'I should have known they used different tests.'

135

She was getting upset at him. 'That's ridiculous. How could you . . .' She paused, staring. 'Are you bleeding?'

He practically leaped away from the rail. 'I scratched my ear. I think I'll go clean it up. It's nothing big. I'll talk to you later.'

'OK. Let's do that. Are you sure you're all right?'

'I'm fine, really.'

'I have to sign your yearbook.'

'Great.' He cupped his hand to his ear and backed away from her over the slippery deck. He had a regular vein pumping over his scalp from the feel of it.

'Michael?'

He stopped, for a second, caught by her eyes. She had the biggest eyes on the whole boat; he could have sworn it. 'What?'

She thought a moment. 'Nothing.'

The cramped and dimly lit bathroom behind the galley was empty. He was lucky, none of the blood had got on to the collar of his coat. Locking the door, he grabbed a whole roll of toilet paper and pressed it to the side of his head. The wound was deep and ragged. If he washed his hair in the sink, the bleeding would only worsen. When he had showered at home, the bath had been red as ketchup. He needed a hat. Maybe Bubba would lend him his.

Michael had stopped the bleeding and cleaned up as best he could when another spell of dizziness struck. He grabbed the edge of the sink, fighting to steady himself, his reflection in the mirror splitting into two. Before he could force his eyes back into focus, he thought he saw – in the mottled glass – Clark standing behind him. Not the Clark of this afternoon, but the one from last autumn, pale and drugged, arrogant and frightening. Michael jerked around frantically, his heart racing, then

136

shook himself for being so foolish. Of course there was no one there.

The lounge was noisy as Jessica had said it would be. The fourth quarter had just begun. Celtics 82, Lakers 78. Ordinarily Michael would have enjoyed such a game, but tonight was far from ordinary. He was beginning to think the ship was haunted.

Bubba was standing on top of the bar, a half-empty bottle of Seagram 7 in his right hand, cheering on a Lakers comeback. Michael had once seen Bubba down a case of beer and a fifth of rum and an hour later ski off the top of Mammoth's most dangerous slope. Michael suspected that that was not Bubba's first bottle. Bubba was waving his sombrero around as if it were a pompom. Michael tapped him on the knee.

'You're going to kill yourself up there,' he said.

'Worry not for the royal Bubba, my dear Mike,' he said. 'If he should by chance fall, he will surely bounce.' Then he let out a howl and thrust his bottle into the air – spilling a few stinging drops of whisky over the top of Michael's head in the process – as Lakers cut their deficit to two. 'My men!'

'I have to talk to you.'

'What?'

'I have to talk to you!'

'Go talk to Sara! She likes to talk!'

'Bubba.'

Michael probably would have got nowhere with him if the Celtics had not chosen that moment to call a time-out. Bubba apparently had a full bladder. As the players walked to the sidelines, he leaped off the bar, shouting, 'Show me to the captain's toilet!'

Michael led him to the bathroom he had used a moment ago. Bubba was not inside long, and when he came out, Michael grabbed him by the arm and dragged

137

him into the galley, to a quiet table in the corner. The lighting in the dining area was low. There was no TV and few people were present. Bubba looked around in a daze.

'Where're my men in purple?' he asked.

'Give me two minutes and I'll let you get back to your game.'

'Where's my bottle?'

Michael had taken it from him on the way to the bathroom and thrown it into a garbage can. 'I'll get you a fresh one in a minute.'

Bubba pounded the table with his fist, satisfied. 'A kingly deal! Speak, Mike, and may your words be inspired.'

'I wanted to ask you about the night of Alice's party.'

Bubba's joyful demeanour faded. Michael also knew from experience that, although Bubba could drink like a sink, alcohol often brought out a hidden sensitivity. Bubba shook his head sadly. 'That poor girl. She was so beautiful. Had she lived, she might have got to know me better.' Then he paused and eyed Michael. 'You don't think I killed her?'

'Of course not.'

Bubba nodded, relaxing. 'That is good. The Bubba can be nasty, but he only wants to have fun.' He burped. 'I consider the killing of a beautiful girl to be a sin against the gods and the boys.' He glanced about. 'What's the score?'

'It hasn't changed. I have a problem about that night, Bubba. I want you to help me with it. The bedroom next to the one where Alice died – who was in there?'

'Was it not the exalted Bubba himself?'

'Was it?'

Bubba hesitated. 'Is this a trick question?'

'Were you in the room just before the shot was fired?'

138

He spoke reluctantly. 'It was me.'

'Were you with Clair?'

'The Bubba is well known for his discretion and his silence. This is a delicate subject.'

'Please, Bubba, I have to know the truth. I have to cross that room out of the equation before I can go on. Was Clair in there with you or not?'

'Yes.'

'How about anyone else?'

'No. Yes.'

'What does that mean?'

'Bill was in there before I got there.'

'With Clair?'

'Yes.'

'What were they doing?'

'Nothing. Absolutely nothing.'

'And then you entered the room? Right after Bill left?'

'Yes.'

'Why didn't you tell me this six months ago? Why did you lie to me?'

'The Bubba is well known for his –'

'Cut the crap.'

Bubba lowered his head and took a breath, a breath that seemed to sober him considerably. 'I was trying to protect Clair's reputation.'

Michael had to laugh. 'But you bragged in the car on the way to the party, in front of both Nick and me, how many condoms you used on her before you even went out with her.'

'I didn't.'

'Yes, you did.'

'No. I didn't have sex with Clair on our first date.'

'Why did you say you did?'

'At the time I thought the topic made for stimulating conversation.'

'If you didn't have sex with her, how did you keep her from killing you when she found out you didn't have any U2 tickets?'

'I gave her a gold necklace,' he admitted sheepishly.

'You bought her off?'

'I wouldn't put it in precisely those terms.'

'All right, back to the night of the party. How did you just happen to be upstairs and see Bill leaving the bedroom?'

'I was standing outside the bedroom door.'

'How's that?' Michael asked.

'I followed Bill up the stairs.'

'What were you doing outside the bedroom?'

'Listening.'

'Listening to what?'

'To what was going on inside,' Bubba said.

'And what was that?'

'Absolutely nothing.'

'That's the second time you've said that. What does it mean?' Michael insisted.

'I don't know. Nothing.'

'Did Bill see you when he left the room?'

'He bumped into me.'

'Was he mad at you?'

'He was upset.'

'At you?'' Michael asked.

'No.'

'What was he upset about?'

'Clair and he weren't getting along.' He shrugged. 'I went inside to see how she was. I guess it was good timing on my part.'

Michael felt as if he were missing something obvious. 'Were you and Clair having sex when the gun was fired?'

'Mike! That is a very personal question. I do not feel legally or morally bound to answer it.'

'Did you hear anything coming from the adjacent room before the shot was fired?'

'No.'

'Are you sure?'

'Absolutely.'

'Dammit, Bubba.'

'Clair was moaning in my ear,' he admitted.

'You were having sex.'

'I didn't say that.'

'You two were having sex for the first time,' Michael said, finally understanding at least a part of the puzzle. 'And after doing it, you started to fall for her and feel protective of her.'

'Is there something wrong with that?'

'Not unless you have a huge stud reputation to maintain.'

Bubba sighed. 'It does demand a great deal of my energy.'

'Did you have condoms with you?'

'That's none of your business,' he snapped, showing a rare flash of anger. Then he showed something more rare, perhaps an emotion he had not displayed since before he had mastered the art of 'attitude' at the age of two. His face sagged into lines of deep pain. 'I didn't,' he said softly. 'I was careless.'

Michael leaned closer. 'She got pregnant?'

'Yes.'

'Well, that's all behind you now.'

'No, it's not.' Bubba took another deep breath; he was obviously struggling with intense feelings. 'She had an abortion, Mike. I talked her into it.'

Michael's instinctive distaste for the procedure rose up. He had to remind himself his views were not everybody's views. 'It must have been a difficult decision for both of you.'

'For Clair it was. For me it was just another problem to be handled.' The transformation was remarkable – he was close to tears. Michael thought an argument could be made for the beneficial effect of periodic alcoholic binges on Bubba's character. Bubba buried his head in his hands. 'But I couldn't forget what I'd done. The more I fell in love with Clair, the more I thought about the baby I'd killed.'

Fell in love?

'You made a mistake. Everybody makes mistakes.'

Bubba looked at him with red eyes. 'I murdered my son.'

'How do you know it was a boy?'

'Of course it was a boy,' he said, insulted. 'I would not have a female for a firstborn.'

Despite the serious nature of the discussion, Michael couldn't help but laugh. Bubba had finally begun to accept girls as people, but he was a long way from accepting them as equals. 'Bubba, promise me one thing. Ten years from now, when you're ruling the world, please try to remember that it was a woman who brought you into the world.'

Bubba was confused. 'What about Baby Bubba?'

'What about Clair?'

He brightened suddenly. 'We're getting married.'

Michael almost fell out of his chair. That was the big secret Clair had been afraid to tell him. '*What?*'

Bubba nodded solemnly. 'It's time I settled down. She's a good woman. She understands me.' He touched Michael's hand. 'I want you to do me a favour, Mike?'

'Anything.'

'I want you to be my maid of honour.'

'Your best man?'

'Yes. I want you to stand beside me on Sunday.'

'You're getting married this Sunday?'

'In Las Vegas.' Bubba sat back. 'I've thought about this a long time, Mike. It's nothing Clair has talked me into. I've made up my own mind.'

'I believe you.' Michael offered his hand. 'Congratulations.'

Bubba beamed. 'You're not going to try to talk me out of it?'

'Why should I? Like you said, she's a good girl. I hope you don't drive her crazy. You better not cheat on her.'

Bubba waved his hand. 'I've cancelled my subscription to *Playboy*, that's how serious I am about this.'

'Great. I suppose you want to get back to your game now?'

Bubba nodded enthusiastically, then furrowed his brow in concentration, worried. 'I haven't told you anything I wouldn't have ordinarily, have I?'

'You've been fine. Oh, there is one other thing. Now that school's over, how often did you use the computer codes to change stuff?'

Bubba scratched his head. 'I can't remember.'

'Did you make Sara president?'

'No, not that. Sara got elected by a landslide. But I did make Clair vice-president. Don't tell her, though. She doesn't know.'

'What about homecoming?'

Bubba looked unhappy. 'I don't know if I should talk about that.'

'Did Jessie get elected queen?'

He hesitated. 'Yes.'

'Why did you choose Maria?'

'I couldn't put in Clair. People were too down on her because of the abortion talk. And Clair wouldn't stand for Jessie being queen. Maria was neutral.'

'But Jessica should have been queen,' Michael insisted.

'Nah. Clair should have been queen.'

'Maybe, maybe not.'

'I'm glad neither of them won. They're both bigger than Maria. The float probably would have collapsed on them in the middle of the dance.'

Did someone tamper with the float thinking it would be Jessie?

'But what about Maria?' Michael asked.

He shrugged. 'What can I say? I'm only Bubba; I'm not God.'

'At least we've made some progress tonight.'

Michael accompanied Bubba back to the lounge. It was good that he did. Along the way, Bubba tried to tightrope-dance on the top of the rail. Had he fallen the wrong way, he would have disappeared into a hazy soup, probably disappeared for good.

Michael just couldn't get into the game, even though the score was close and the end was near. He went out to search for Polly. But he couldn't find her anywhere.

CHAPTER SIXTEEN

Polly lay soaking in the steaming bath, staring at her naked body. Her figure was fabulous. She had large firm breasts, a narrow waist, smooth wrinkle-free thighs, and soft creamy skin. Any normal guy, she thought miserably, would have been happy to climb into the tub with her.

The door to the bathroom lay wide open. Clark prowled the room beyond. In the last half hour, he hadn't so much as peeped in. She didn't understand it.

Polly was, however, grateful for the room. Sara had done her a good turn in that regard for once. Polly didn't know if she could have stood a whole night partying with people who didn't like her. She knew they didn't. She'd known it all along, actually, although she had never understood that, either. She wasn't a bad person. She had been sort of fat once, but now she had a nice body. You'd think they'd want to talk to her more often. The last few months at school, hardly anyone had talked to her. They'd avoided her as if she'd had the plague. She'd had bad luck, true, but a lot of people had bad luck. She wasn't alone in that respect. In fact, a lot of people on this stupid boat were unlucky.

They couldn't have imagined how unlucky they were.

Polly had left the hot water in the bath running a trickle. A drain prevented the water from overflowing. It was an old trick; it kept the water always hot. She liked it that way, so hot her skin turned cardinal red whenever she took a bath. She'd first learned the trick in a book she had read on the Mafia. It seemed that whenever a mob member got thrown in jail for life, his buddies on the outside would provide for his family if he'd take a hot bath and slit his wrists. Those mob guys were always afraid that anybody in jail would eventually break down and talk. The hot water was important; supposedly when you bled to death, you got real cold, and then nauseated. A good bath made the whole experience much more comfortable. Leaving the water trickling was the key; if you sat all night in a tub with the hot water faucet turned on a little and your wrists slit, in the morning most of the blood would be gone. No vomit, no blood, and naked as a babe. When Polly thought about it, she imagined it wasn't such a bad way to go. Much better than, say, being trapped in a room overflowing with icy sea water.

An open razor blade rested on the soap tray next to Polly's head. She picked it up and let the overhead light reflect off the sharp edge into her eyes. White light, star bright. Sitting up, she transferred the blade into her left hand. Like Alice, she was left-handed. Some things ran in the family.

Like bad luck.

'You should have got the paper cups when I told you the first time,' Polly whispered, taking the blade and pressing the tip into her right wrist. For a second nothing happened, and she wondered if she had a dull blade. Then a drop of blood drew a line down the pink flesh of her inner arm, dripping off her bent elbow into the clear water. It was interesting to watch how the red dissipated when it hit the water, how quickly her blood was lost. Maybe when she was through bleeding, her body would dissolve, too; it would be

146

as if she had never been. She started to push the blade deeper.

'Polly,' Clark said. He stood outside the bathroom, a lamp at his back; she could clearly see his shadow on the bathroom door.

'What?' She set down the blade.

'What are you doing?'

'Nothing. What are you doing?'

'I'm waiting for you.'

'I'll be out in a few minutes.'

Clark thought a moment. 'Why are you taking so long?'

She had been hoping he would come in and join her, make love to her before he killed them all. It had really hurt her feelings that he'd had her pose nude all those times and not once stopped painting to touch her. The drops of her blood continued to drip off the end of her elbow. 'I don't know,' she said.

'I don't believe you.'

'Go, do what you're going to do without me. I want to stay here.'

'I can't do that.'

'Why not?'

'You know why.'

She felt a stab of pain across her temple. 'I'm not going.'

'If you don't come, Alice will have died for nothing.'

'I don't care about Alice.'

He entered the bathroom. At first she thought he was bleeding, too – from the head. His red hair was ablaze, as were his eyes. But it was only hate. 'And where do you think you're going?'

She crossed her arms over her breasts, trying to hide her wrist. The red spilled over her nipples. 'I accidentally cut myself.'

147

He strode to the tub and leaned over, grabbing the razor blade and holding it inches from her face. 'I'll show you an accident. I'll cut your eyes out.'

'No,' she cried, suddenly terrified.

'I'll cut your tongue, make you eat it. Then you can bleed all you want.'

'I won't do it again, I swear. Stop it, Clark!'

He stood and threw the blade aside. Then he picked up her hair dryer and flipped it on. 'You're getting out of that water this instant. It's too hot for a bitch as cold as you.'

He threw the hair drier into the tub. The electric shock hit Polly's brain like a fistful of exploding dynamite, just as it had when she had been in the hospital as a child. She began to scream.

CHAPTER SEVENTEEN

The Lakers had called a time-out. There were ten seconds left on the clock. They had the ball. They were down by two points. Never in her wildest imagination could Sara have dreamed a stupid basketball game could make her feel so miserable.

'What if they don't make it?' she asked Nick, who stood beside her. With the exception of Maria, the whole room was standing. On the screen, the Lakers' coach drew diagrams on a big white sheet of paper while the players huddled in a semicircle at his back and nodded their exhausted, sweaty heads. On the left side of the lounge, Bubba paced along the top of the bar, shouting out encouragement.

'My men!'

'If they miss and don't rebound the ball, they're dead,' Nick said.

'But they don't get any points for a rebound, do they?' Sara asked.

'No. They'd have to put up another shot quick. And it would have to go in.'

Sara clasped her hands together. 'I'm going to kill him.'

'Who?' Nick asked.

'You'll know when you see the body.'

The time-out came to an end. Both teams walked on to the court. The noise in the Fabulous Forum and the lounge of *Haven* settled down. Sara bit her lower lip. The referee handed the ball to a Laker player and blew his whistle. Immediately the players of both teams scattered across half the court. A second went by, two seconds. The guy wasn't going to have time to inbound the ball!

'Shoot!' Sara yelled.

'He can't shoot from out of bounds,' Nick said.

The player inbounded the ball to a teammate at the top of the key. The guy fed to the right, dribbled to the left. Then he leaped; it was a magnificent leap. He floated through the air towards the basket. Green uniforms sprang up to block his way. Sara thought they were too late. The time on the corner of the screen went to six seconds.

'Shoot!' Sara yelled.

'He doesn't have the ball,' Nick said.

Nick was right. The player had passed the ball to a teammate in the left corner. The guy was all alone, far from the basket. He was going for a three-pointer! If he made it, the game would be over! There would be no need for an overtime!

'Shoot!' Sara yelled.

The clock went to three seconds.

He shot it. The ball sailed high through the air. It had beautiful arc, seemingly perfect touch.

'No!' Sara screamed along with the rest of the room.

It missed. A Celtic grabbed the rebound. The Lakers tried frantically to foul him. They were too late. Time expired. Sara collapsed into the chair behind her.

I will not kill him. He is fat and slimy, but he has a working heart, functional kidneys. I will force him to sell his organs to pay off the debt.

'Excuse me,' Sara said to Nick and Maria, standing and making her way through the crowd to the bar. The mood of the lounge was gloomy, but compared to Sara's

150

mood, the place was in seventh heaven. Yet Sara wasn't exactly angry. The pure fullness of her anger had transformed it into something quite the opposite, into an almost perverse joy. Bubba no longer had a hold over her. She could say what she wanted to him, do what she wanted. There were so many things she would do to him.

Bubba sat on top of the bar, his head bowed in misery, an empty bottle loosely clasped in his chubby fingers. Clair was not around.

'Bubba,' she said sweetly. He looked up, rubbed his red eyes.

'It's you again?'

She nodded. 'Outside.'

He did not protest. They exited the lounge and stood on the deck. A lot of kids had just come out for a breath of fresh air, however, and Sara decided their 'talk' would go better in private. She steered Bubba down a companionway and into a deserted hall. The locked passenger staterooms stretched the length of the boat away from them on either side. Bubba slumped to the floor and leaned against a wall. Sara stood above him, her hands on her hips.

'They should have gone for the tie,' Bubba said sadly. He looked up at her as though he expected her to offer him comfort. 'I should be coaching that team.'

'I don't care about the Lakers.'

He was shocked. He was even more drunk than before. 'I've followed them since I was a little Bubba.'

She knelt in front of him. 'Bubba, do you know how close you are to having terrible things happen to you?'

He was interested. 'How close?'

She held her thumb and index finger up a quarter of an inch apart. Then she squeezed them together. 'This close.'

He was *very* interested. 'What are you going to do?'

151

She leaned closer. 'I *need* the money you promised me. I *need* you to get it for me. I don't care *where* you get it. Do you understand me?'

Now he was disappointed. He brushed off her remark with a sloppy wave of his hand. 'I bet your money on the Celtics.'

'What?' Sara fell back on her butt. 'I don't believe you.'

'You can have all the money you need tomorrow evening.' Bubba wasn't much interested in the discussion. He clenched his fist and pounded his knee. 'They should have gone for two points.'

'Why would you bet against the Lakers? They're your team. You just said it – you grew up with them.'

He nodded. 'I knew in my heart it was time for them to take a fall.'

Sara laughed. Then she did something that could have ruined her reputation for all time had there been anyone around to see it. She gave Bubba a big hug. 'I never will understand you.'

'My true nature is unfathomable,' he agreed.

Sara suddenly remembered the bargain she'd made. She quickly sat back. 'I suppose now you'll expect me to put out for you?'

He hesitated. 'Does it mean that much to you, Sara?'

'My body?'

He spoke in a regretful tone. 'I suppose I could make love to you, give you a night you could carry happily to your grave, but I'd hate to do that to Clair. Faith and trust and not screwing around mean so much to her. Do you understand, Sara?'

'Are you saying you *don't* want to have sex with me?'

'It's not you personally.'

Her usual distaste for him returned. 'But you've been dying to sleep with me all year? Or was that just an act?'

152

'Well . . .'

'You don't find me attractive?'

'Now I didn't say that.'

Sara leaped to her feet and paced in front of him. 'What about me don't you like? Is it my face? Is it my legs? Come on, don't worry about my feelings. I don't care what you say.'

He studied her a moment. 'I've never liked the way you walked.'

She stopped. 'I walk just like any other girl. Just like Clair does.'

He shook his head. 'No, you walk like you're in a hurry. A lady is never in a hurry. Good things come to a lady. She doesn't have to chase after them.'

'What else?'

'Your clothes – '

'You said that earlier. I'm getting new clothes for the summer. What else is wrong with my body?'

'Nothing. Your body's fine.'

'Fine? China and silk are fine. Come on, what don't you like? Is it my ass?'

'I'd have to see you naked before I would be willing to express an opinion in that area.'

'Hold it right there, slimeball. I'm not taking my clothes off for you. No way you're going to trick me into that.'

'All right.'

'What do you mean, all right? You don't want to see it?'

'Not at the moment.'

She sagged against the wall, feeling totally unwanted. 'You really don't think I'm very sexy, do you?'

Bubba gathered himself off the floor and put his arm around her shoulder, the odour of half a dozen of the world's most famous distilleries on his breath. 'Sara, if

I had met you before I met Clair, I honestly believe things would have been different between us. Of course I think you're sexy. You have a great ass. A few private lessons and I'm sure you could have made me very happy.'

She realised he was feeding her a crock of pure BS. It was amazing – not to mention ridiculous – how much it meant to her. She kissed him on the cheek. 'I bet you're still a virgin.'

He reached around and pinched her butt. 'If I am, I was born with incredible natural talents.'

CHAPTER EIGHTEEN

If Nick had been told in his first week at Tabb High that he would end the school year as perhaps the most popular person on campus, he would have laughed. Yet, when the basketball game was over and the class gathered in groups to discuss it, the biggest group gathered around Nick. It was true, of course, they were talking about a subject he was an acknowledged master of; nevertheless, had they just watched a war movie, he still would have drawn the most people to him. He knew this without understanding it.

He was the best athlete in the school – he had no qualms about accepting *that* distinction – and he was no longer the shy mumbling ghetto exile he had been last September. He was, however, still soft-spoken and hesitant to express his opinion on any subject, including basketball. Also, his fearsome appearance had not changed with Tabb's capture of the league basketball title. But perhaps Michael had explained Nick's popularity best when he had said that Nick was the only one in the school who even vaguely fitted the definition of a hero.

'And people are always searching for a hero, Nick. Just look at who's big in Hollywood. It's usually the actor who can rescue the most prisoners of war in two hours or less. Enjoy it while it lasts. Someone's sure to come along soon and take your place.'

Nick did enjoy the adulation, although he found

himself shying away from it at the same time. A few
minutes of attention from a big group gave him a
pleasant high. More than that made him anxious. As
soon as was politely possible – after saying for the tenth
time that he didn't like second-guessing the Lakers' coach
for going for the win instead of the tie – he excused
himself from the lounge and wheeled Maria on to the
deck. Here there were fewer people; it was now cold and
the fog had gone beyond thick to frightening. Nick had
once seen a television show on the Bermuda Triangle
– a place in the Atlantic Ocean where many ships had
disappeared. Had those ships ended up in another
dimension, he imagined, it might have resembled *Haven*'s
present environment. Complete darkness would have
seemed more natural. The damp greyness was spooky.

'Are you cold?' he asked Maria, parking her chair
near the rail. The splash of the ocean against the hull
could be heard beneath the fog. Maria pulled her shawl
tighter.

'No.' She looked up at him. 'Are you?'

'The fresh air feels good.'

A period of silence went by. There had been a lot of
those between them since he had picked her up at the
rehabilitation clinic. 'They like you,' she said finally.

'I guess. They like my jump shot, that's for sure.'

'I wish I had got to see you play again.'

The remark warmed his spirits somewhat. Maybe she
did still care about him. She had given few signs one
way or the other. 'It was a fun season. Making the CIF
playoffs was exciting. Track was fun, too. I ran the
quarter mile and did the long jump.'

'I was told they gave you a trophy at the awards
banquet?'

He nodded. 'It's for having done well in more than
one sport.' Coach Campbell had presented the award,

the same man who had almost expelled him the first week of school when he had floored The Rock in the weight room. Coach Campbell had given him a big smile and a slap on the back with the trophy, but still no apology. Nick didn't feel any resentment. It was easy to forgive when you were winning. His father had been at the banquet. He had been the first one to stand and clap. The rest of the school had followed suit. Nick had never received a standing ovation before.

'Trophies, fans, scholarships,' she said. 'You must be happy?'

He looked down at her white tennis shoes lying still on the wheelchair's metal footrests. 'I'm not happy, Maria.'

'Why not?'

He turned away. 'Isn't it obvious?'

Another spell of silence. *Haven*'s foghorn broke this one. Maria touched his leg. 'Don't worry about me, Nick.'

He chuckled, staring into nothing. 'Sure. I'll just wheel you all over the place and forget that you used to walk. How can you tell me not to worry?'

'I don't want you to. I don't know why you do.'

A note of anger entered his voice. 'You know why.'

She took her hand back. 'I don't.'

He turned on her. 'How would you like it if *I* got crippled that night? What if I had gone up for a rebound and came down wrong and broke my neck? Would you even – ' He stopped, realised what he was saying. Awful as it was for him to see her paralysed, it was nothing compared to *being* paralysed. She answered his unfinished question.

'I would care.'

'I'm sorry,' he said quickly. His apology had a strange effect on her. She seemed to take up his shame. She

157

turned her chair as if about to leave, as if she were embarrassed to be with him.

'Nick, you don't have to – ' she began, getting upset. 'I can take care of myself. Really I can.'

He touched the handle of her wheelchair instead of her arm, holding on to her just the same; the chair was a part of her now. 'What do you want me to do?' he asked, afraid she would respond by telling him to go away. He didn't understand till right then how much he loved her. Maria composed herself and looked in the direction of the lounge.

'Later, when things slow down,' she said, 'I want you to talk to everybody who was still at the party when Alice died: Bubba, Clair, Bill, The Rock, Kats, Russ, Sara, Polly, Michael, and Jessica. I want you to gather them below, where we can be alone.'

'Why?'

'You'll see.'

CHAPTER NINETEEN

The night went on. The air grew colder. The fog grew thicker. Around midnight, *Haven* encountered four foot swells and began to rock uneasily, her hull softly groaning with each rise and fall, the stomachs of many of her passengers doing likewise. A few kids lost their dinners over the ship's rail. Yet the rough waters did little to slow the momentum of the party. Time took care of that. No matter that for many it was the most exciting night of their lives – passing the three o'clock hour, the bulk of the senior class could be found lying curled up in the lounge or the games room on sheets of foam someone had been thoughtful enough to provide. Those who were resting were smart. They would be fresh for the upcoming day on Catalina.

If they lived that long.

Once again, Jessica and Sara were in Jessica's cabin, trying to decide about the contraceptives. Jessica was not enjoying the pitch and roll of the ship. It made it impossible for her to pretend – as she had done most of the night – that she was still on dry land. The way *Haven*'s hull kept creaking was particularly disturbing. Sara's reassurances that the sound was natural didn't ease Jessica's mind in the slightest. Sara knew as much about boats as she did, which was precisely nothing.

'I don't see how you can be worried about drowning

at a time like this,' Sara said, the bottle of foam in her hand. 'You should be worrying about how you look.'

'Excuse me, but I've heard that when you drown it can affect your appearance,' Jessica said, sitting on the bed beside Sara. Jessica had already changed into her bathrobe. Sara was going to have to pop next door in a minute and get ready. Ten minutes ago they had told Bill and Russ – Jessica had told Bill and Sara had told Russ, to be precise – to meet them in their rooms in exactly twenty minutes. Bill and Russ thought they were being invited to a private party.

Just our luck they'll bring their buddies with them.

But it seemed unlikely. Jessica and Sara had both made it clear that they were to come alone.

'I don't think I like the ingredients in this stuff,' Sara said, studying the foam label. 'Nonoxynol nine, potassium hydroxide, benzoic acid – does that sound like something you want inside your body?'

'It sounds like it'll work.'

Sara handed her the foam. 'You take it then. If you explode, don't blame me.'

'Thanks,' Jessica muttered sarcastically. The room had a lamp hanging from a corner of the ceiling. The motion of the boat made it swing back and forth, sending shadows chasing its light, giving Jessica a headache.

'You don't look very excited.'

Jessica shrugged. 'I'll get excited when Bill gets here.'

Sara nodded, thoughtful, chewing on her lower lip. 'Can I ask you something, Jessie?'

'As long as it's not about your ass.'

'Well, I've been getting a lot of complaints about it lately. Come on, you've taken showers with me in PE.'

Jessica groaned. 'I just cannot believe you are asking me this. Who's complained about it?'

'Bubba.'

160

'Bubba! Bubba's screwed half the girls in the school.'

'Yeah. So he's a goddamn expert on the subject.'

'What did he say?'

'It's not what he said. It's what he didn't want to – Look, I'm asking for a vote of confidence here.'

'You have a great ass, Sara.'

'You're just saying that.'

'Please don't make me say it again. I'm changing the subject. How much light should we leave on?'

'I'm turning off all the lights.'

'You'll be in the shower when Russ gets there. How can you have all the lights off?'

Sara looked worried. 'I guess it would seem strange.'

Jessica realised Sara was more scared than she was. Actually, Jessica was surprised at her own lack of fear. She felt more resigned to the event than anything else. One thing had become clear: she was not giving up her virginity in joy. She just wanted to get it over with.

'How are you getting on with Russ?' she asked gently.

Sara snorted. 'Oh, we get along fine, as long as we don't talk. So far tonight, we've been doing *splendidly*. He's been with his buddies since he came on board.' Sara glanced at her watch. 'Well, I guess I've got him to myself now, for a few minutes, anyway.' She stood. 'You promise to tell me exactly what happens?'

'I'll videotape it.'

Sara smiled. 'I guess this is it.'

Jessica hugged her. 'I hope this is it for one of us at least.'

When Sara was gone, Jessica stood by the porthole for several minutes, staring out into the eerie night. Alice had loved the fog. Alice had loved everything. Jessica had been trying to tell Sara she had no hope for herself. Not for love.

'I'm going to the movies Saturday night. You won't believe

it, I asked the guy. His name's Michael Olson . . . That reminds me, where's that fantastic guy you were going to introduce me to?'

'Ask me after your date.'

And then Alice had lain down to sleep.

'I could go to sleep here and never wake up,' Jessica whispered, remembering her exact words.

The bathroom was small but neat. Jessica removed her robe and got in the shower. The water came out hot and hard at first, and she jumped back, almost slipping and falling. She had left her hair down, though she didn't want to wash it; she looked a lot better with it down. Well, it was going to get wet, there was no helping that. She wondered how long Bill would be. The shower curtain was translucent; at least it would have been without all the steam. She had read somewhere that steam was supposed to be very sensual. She hoped she started to feel sexy soon.

Several minutes went by. During that time she scrubbed herself from neck to toe using her own soap – just to be sure. The spray of the shower waved up and down in rhythm to the ocean swells. Finally there came a knock at the door. Naturally, she had left the bathroom door open – it was part of the plan. The distance between the two doors couldn't have been more than eight feet.

'Bill?' she called, pulling the shower curtain to the edge of the tile, on the small chance he did have someone with him.

'Yeah.'

'Come in.'

He opened the door to the suite, paused. She could see his outline through the curtain, but that was all. He was alone. 'Jessie?'

'It's all right. I'll be out in a minute. Come in.'

He entered, closing the door, and then sat on the bed. She peeped around the edge of the curtain. He had his hands folded in his lap and was staring at his feet. He was being a gentleman. 'Where's the party?' he asked.

'It's in Sara's room.' She added, 'I've been running around all night. I thought I'd grab a quick shower. I won't be long.'

'I could go on ahead of you.'

'No.' He was still looking down. 'Just let me wash off this soap.'

'OK.'

Now what? Sara and she hadn't given this enough thought. It would have been much easier had he come into the bathroom and tried to peep around the curtain or something. There was really no good excuse to invite him into the bathroom.

Fine, I'll give him a lousy excuse.

She turned off the water. 'Bill?'

'Yeah?'

'Could you hand me my towel?'

'Where is it?'

It was right outside the shower, on a hook on the back of the bathroom door. She could see it through her crack in the curtain, along with Bill, searching the bedroom. 'I don't know,' she said. 'Don't you see it?'

'No.'

'God, there's so much steam in here. Is it on the sink?'

He paused in the bathroom doorway. 'I don't see it, Jessie.'

She grabbed hold of the edge of the curtain and stuck her head around at him and smiled. He couldn't have been three feet away. He jumped slightly. She pointed to the towel with her wet and dripping arm. 'There it is,' she said sweetly.

He handed it to her, saving her a six-inch reach. 'You want me to come back?' he asked, his eyes down.

'That's all right.' She let go of the shower curtain and began to dry her face. 'I'm almost done.'

'OK. I'll wait for you.' He closed the bathroom door and returned to the bedroom. She couldn't believe how proper he was being. In all the teen movies she'd ever seen, guys were always dying to get peeps at cute girls in showers. And she was cute. She had almost been voted homecoming queen for God's sake.

She quickly dried herself, climbing out of the shower and slipping into her bathrobe. Sara had given it to her last Christmas. It was pink, thin, and it clung to her damp body in a number of important places. She glanced at herself in the foggy mirror. Wet, her hair appeared almost black, and the heat of the shower had flushed her face. In her totally unbiased opinion, she thought she looked pretty fantastic.

Just have to get him to kiss me. Just get him started.

She opened the bathroom door. Bill was standing by the window, admiring the fog. He jumped again when he saw her. She smiled to put him at his ease. 'I didn't know you'd get here so soon.'

'You said twenty minutes.'

'Oh, that's right, I did.' She gestured to the bed and reached for the towel around her neck. 'Have a seat, let me dry my hair.'

He sat on the bed. She stepped past his knees and sat beside him, on his left. They had the bathroom and its diffusing steam in front of them, the door to the hallway on their right. Bill still had on his yellow turtleneck and brown trousers. She reached up as if to fix his collar. Too bad he didn't have a collar. She brushed a hair from his neck, playing the role of the seductress to the hilt.

'I haven't got to talk to you much tonight,' she said.

'Yeah, where have you been?'

'Oh, I went for a little swim.' She giggled. 'I wish you could have joined me.'

He frowned. 'What are you talking about?'

'Nothing.' She turned to face him, tucking her right knee under her left leg while pressing her knee against the side of his leg. She had made a similar move months ago on his parents' couch without much success. But now they knew each other a lot better, and her bathrobe was split open and my, didn't her wet legs look fine. 'I'm glad you're here,' she said.

His gaze strayed to her legs. She was not sure how far up he could see, not exactly, nor did she care. Suddenly she began to enjoy herself. 'You're going to catch a cold,' he said.

'I'm not cold.' She smiled her naughtiest smile and moved her hand into his hair. 'Are you?'

'No.'

'That's good.' She tugged lightly on the hair at the base of his neck. 'If you were, I don't know what I would do.'

'Jessie?'

'Yes Bill.'

'What about Sara's party?'

'It'll wait.' She leaned closer, her wet hair hanging over the arm of his yellow sweater. 'I'm not making you uncomfortable, am I?' she asked.

'No.'

She continued to play with his hair, continued to smile as if she couldn't wait for him to kiss her, which was the truth of the matter. 'That's good, because I feel real comfortable with you. I mean, I like you, Bill. Did I ever tell you that?'

'Yeah. I like you, Jessie. You're a nice girl.'

She gushed over the remark as if he had just sworn his undying love. 'Really? Oh, that's neat. I mean, I wasn't sure if you felt that way.' She let her right hand slip from his hair to the top of his right shoulder and caught his eyes. 'You know what I liked most about the prom?'

'What?'

'When you kissed me afterwards.'

He took the hint. He kissed her. He might not have intended for it to be a deep and passionate kiss, but the moment his lips touched hers, she tightened her arm around his neck and pulled him close. She had not kissed many guys in her life. She was unaware of the finer points that constituted a great kiss. Nevertheless, she didn't feel Bill was giving her his all. She felt that way very strongly when he suddenly pulled back.

'It's late,' he said.

She laughed, tugging him towards her. 'It's early.'

They started again and things began to pick up, possibly because they rolled back on to the bed. This had nothing to do with her; it just happened. He put his right hand on her robe near her left breast. The kissing got harder, deeper. Yet she still felt as if she was doing most of the digging. She wished he would touch her breast. His hand kept moving towards it, then pulling away. It was driving her nuts.

'Jessie?' he mumbled.

'What?' She was having trouble with other parts of their bodies as well. Her legs were up on the bed. His feet were still on the floor. She tried swinging her left leg over his hip, but it kept slipping loose. Surprisingly, her robe continued to hold together; she must have tied the belt too tightly coming out of the shower. She took his right hand and put it on the knot, hoping he would work on it.

166

'Why are we doing this?' he asked, between heavy breathing and kissing.

'Because we want to.'

'I don't think it's right.'

'Don't think, Bill.'

He didn't loosen the knot. He put his hand on her hip instead. That would have been fine except his hand just stayed there, while his kisses became less and less passionate, until finally she began to feel as if she were chasing a strawberry around an empty bowl with a baseball bat. She had heard him when he said he didn't think what they were doing was right, but she hadn't *really* heard him. When she took his right hand and pressed it to her left breast, his reaction took her completely by surprise. He leaped off the bed and began to yell.

'What are you trying to do?'

She had never seen him mad before. 'Huh?'

'You're trying to seduce me!'

She sat up, very slowly. 'No. I was just, you know, being friendly.' There was something not quite right here. She still hadn't figured out where she had messed up. He looked positively livid.

'Look at you, Jessie. You're practically naked. And you're trying to undress me!'

'No. I was in the shower, and – '

'The shower! You knew I was coming. What kind of girl are you anyway?'

It hit her then – the humiliation. Her voice came out small and shaky. 'I'm a nice girl, like you said.'

He began to shout again, then suddenly balled his hands into tight fists and turned to face the wall, breathing heavily. She thought he wouldn't speak again, that he'd just leave. But finally he got hold of himself.

'I shouldn't have yelled at you like that, Jessie,' he

167

whispered, reaching out and putting his hand on the doorknob. 'I shouldn't have come.'

'Why did you come?' It could have been a stupid question. She had, after all, given him a legitimate reason to visit her cabin. But she had been a fool to think he had been fooled. He was nodding as he turned and looked at her, nodding to himself, asking himself the same question.

'I wanted to see, I guess,' he said.

'See what? Me?'

'No.'

'Oh.' His remark did wonders for what was left of her ego. And here all these years she had thought she was pretty cute. Oh, well, half the point in this whole seduction had been to run what was left of her self-esteem into the ground. It was funny how she had got exactly what she had wanted.

She began to tremble.

'This has nothing to do with you,' he said.

She nodded weakly. Of course her being unattractive to him had nothing to do with her. She may as well not have been in the room. She still couldn't believe this was happening to her. He took a step towards the bed, stretched out his arm to touch the side of her face, then thought better of it and pulled his hand back to his side.

'I'd better go,' he said.

She nodded again. 'All right.'

But he didn't leave immediately. Ignoring her for a moment, he stepped into the bathroom and picked up her brush beside the sink. He ran it under the faucet and began to comb his hair. She had run her fingers through his hair while they'd been kissing, but since he always wore it short, she hadn't really messed it up. From his perspective, however, she must have messed him up bad. Her eyes began to burn. He set the brush down and stepped to the door.

'I won't say anything to anybody about this,' he said gently.

She bit her lip. 'Thanks.'

'Bye.'

'Bye.'

He left. She picked up her towel and buried her face in it. She began to cry. A few minutes later someone knocked at her door.

CHAPTER TWENTY

Sara almost froze to death waiting for Russ to appear. The captain must have been scrimping on fuel. There was no hot water, and never before in her life had Sara taken a cold shower. She understood that only monks took those, and that they did so mainly for reasons of celibacy. Just what she needed – a cold shower to make her as horny as a statue and as desirable as a fish.

Why is he taking so long?

She had said twenty minutes. At least forty minutes must have gone by since she had last seen him. Maybe he'd gone with Bill to Jessica's suite. Yeah, the three of them were probably having a great time about now. Disgusted, Sara grabbed her towel and tried to stand at the far end of the shower out of reach of the spray. But every time *Haven*'s bow went under, the water splashed her legs. She had gooseflesh on her thighs ready to sprout feathers.

Someone pounded on the door.

'Who is it?' she called, pulling the old grey shower curtain tight. She'd left the bathroom door open, but she was beginning to wonder if that had been a good idea. He might have brought the whole cross-country team with him.

'It's me,' he called.

'Are you alone?'

He opened the door. 'What?'

'Are you alone?' She was afraid to peep around the edge of the curtain.

'Yeah.' She heard the door close. 'What are you doing?'

'I'm taking a shower. What do you think I'm doing?'

'Do you want me to join you?' He sounded as if he could have been standing in the bathroom doorway. She couldn't stop shivering.

'No. Close the door.'

'Whatever you want.' He closed the bathroom door.

He had to choose this moment to do exactly what I said.

She turned off the water and dried herself furiously, trying to get some warmth back into her flesh. All was not lost. She had a cute orange bathrobe waiting to put on. Jessica said she looked like a doll in it, even if autumn colours depressed Bubba. Sara knew as soon as Russ saw her in it, he would want to kiss her.

When she came out of the bathroom a few minutes later, he was lying flat on his back on the bed and staring at the ceiling. He had on blue jeans, a blue Pendleton shirt, and looked so masculine it made her legs weak. He hardly glanced over.

'Are you ready?' he asked.

'Sure, I'm going to go dressed like this.' She sat on the bed by his feet. The soles of his running shoes were dirty and he wasn't going out of his way to keep them off the sheets. She had to remind herself that she couldn't fight with him when she wanted him to make love to her. 'How are you doing?' she asked.

He yawned. 'Tired. I wish I could just stay here and sleep.'

'You can.'

'What about your friend's party?'

'We don't have to go.'

He sat up suddenly. 'No. I'll go. Hurry up and get dressed.'

She smiled. 'Don't you want to talk for a few minutes? I haven't really had a chance to talk to you all night.'

'We can talk at the party.' He glanced about restlessly. 'How come you and Jessie are the only ones to get your own rooms?'

'I'm ASB president.'

'So?'

She stopped smiling. 'It's me who rented this stupid boat. Why shouldn't I get my own room?'

He shrugged, doing an excellent job of not looking at her. 'I guess you're right. Come on, put on your clothes. Let's go.'

'No, I want to talk.'

'About what?'

She reached over and began to fiddle with the lace on his left shoe. 'Have you been able to train up there?'

'They have a track.' He was watching her hands. 'I run laps.'

'But you told me you never liked to run on the track?'

'They don't let you out, Sara.'

His saying her name – she didn't know why it touched her so. She squeezed his toes through his shoe and glanced up. He was looking at her now. 'It must be hard on you?' she said.

'I can take it.'

She was still cold from the shower. The thinness of her robe and the temperature of the cabin were not helping matters. She could have used a long hug. 'How come you never wrote to me?' she asked.

'I wrote.'

'Not really.'

172

'I didn't have anything to say. Every day there is the same.'

'But I wrote. You could have answered my letters.' She loosened his lace all the way and started to pull off his shoe.

'Don't,' he said, jerking his foot away.

'You're messing up the sheets.' She hadn't meant the remark to sound harsh. He got up.

'Let's go to the party.'

'No,' she said, watching as he leaned against the wall beside the bathroom door. His expression was inscrutable, and it depressed her; she'd always believed she could read his mind simply by looking at his face. He had changed while he was away. 'What's wrong?' she asked.

'Nothing.'

'Then why are you acting this way?'

'I'm not acting any way. You told me you wanted me to go to a private party with you. I'm here to go to the party. Let's go.'

'I can't go. I'm not dressed.'

'Get dressed.'

'You didn't really want to get in the shower with me.'

'What?'

'You just said that. You don't really like me.'

'What are you talking about?'

She began to speak, but found a lump in her throat. 'Nothing. Forget it. Forget the party, too. I don't want to go.'

'What do you mean, you don't want to go?'

'I don't want to go!'

'What?'

'And quit asking me what I mean. Isn't it obvious what I mean?'

'No. What do you mean?'

She put her face in her hands. 'Get out of here.'

Time went by. It could have been a whole minute. He finally sat beside her on the bed. 'I'm sorry,' he said.

'What are you sorry about?'

He hesitated. 'I'm sorry I don't know.'

She burst out laughing, although she knew he hadn't meant the remark to be humorous. She laughed until her sides were ready to burst, until she was ready to cry. Of course, she had felt like crying before she had started laughing. 'Oh, Russ,' she said, trying to catch her breath. 'You are a prince.'

He didn't respond to her raving, just sat looking at her. 'I know I'm not good enough for you,' he said without bitterness.

Sara stopped laughing. 'What do you mean?'

He glanced down at the dirty shoes she had criticised. 'You're ASB president. I'm just a beer-drinking bum out on a weekend pass from juvenile hall.'

She stared at him as if she were seeing him for the first time and discovering that he had two heads instead of the one she remembered. It sure was another side of him. 'How come you went to a bar after the homecoming dance and got drunk?' she asked. She had always wanted to know.

'Because you didn't want to kiss me.'

She knew instantly what he was referring to. Before the homecoming queen announcement, they had been dancing together and he tried to kiss her. She had stopped him because she felt uncomfortable with any public display of affection. At the time she figured he understood. He hadn't seemed upset. 'I was joking,' she said.

'After my race that morning, you said you didn't want me taking you to the dance.'

'I went to the dance with you!'

'We went in separate cars.'

'I had to get there early. I had to – You knew I was joking.'

He glanced at her. She wished again they hadn't cut his hair so short. 'Were you?'

'Yeah!'

'Oh. I didn't know.' He started to get up. 'It doesn't matter.'

She pulled him back down. 'It does matter, Russ. You didn't have to go out drinking that night.'

Now she could read his face. It was filled with regret. 'I wish I hadn't.'

'You do hate it up there, don't you?'

'It's a cage.'

'But you didn't cut down the tree?'

'No.' He showed a trace of annoyance. 'How could I when you took away my axe.'

'I didn't take your axe. Polly took it.'

'Polly took it? I thought that was you.'

'No.' She giggled. 'Does this mean you're in love with Polly now?'

He was insulted. 'Who says I'm in love with you?'

'Of course you're in love with me. Why else would you get all upset because I rejected you? And why would you go out drinking all night and try to kill yourself?'

'I didn't try to kill myself.'

'Anyone who drinks so much he can't remember where he drank is trying to kill himself. Don't be embarrassed. You can love me. You're an incredible person. I'm an incredible person. And I love you.' She stopped. 'I can't believe I said that. Never mind, I didn't say that.'

He kissed her. She didn't see it coming. She quickly decided those were the best kind of kisses. They fell back

175

on the bed and she felt his hands on her body. It was incredible. She couldn't even count the number of places he touched her. It was absolutely the most exciting thing ever! She didn't mind in the least that his twelve-hour beard was scratching the hell out of her face. She was just about to slip out of her robe and give him a night in heaven to make up for all his days in hell when he suddenly stopped and sat up.

'I shouldn't be doing this, Sara,' he said.

I shouldn't? She'd thought she'd been doing a few things of her own. 'What's wrong?' It was her ass, she knew it. He didn't like it, and he hadn't even seen it yet.

'I'm taking advantage of you. You're not even dressed.' He shook his head, ashamed. 'I can't treat you like you were just any old girl.'

She got up on her elbow, wishing she was a little older. 'You've slept with girls before?'

'Oh, yeah, loads of times. But they didn't mean anything to me.'

'Not like I do?'

'Well, yeah.'

'Do you love me?' she asked.

'Do you love me?'

She thought a moment. 'Maybe we should quit while we're both ahead.'

He laughed, hard and loud, as he used to laugh a long time ago. 'Come on, get dressed. Let's go to that party.'

She sat up. 'Oh, I forgot to tell you. It's been cancelled.'

He seemed disappointed. 'What are we going to do? Today and tomorrow are my only days out. I shouldn't waste them sleeping.'

She had this great idea. On the other hand, she didn't want to be one of *those* girls who meant nothing. She stood, heading for the bathroom and her clothes. 'Let's jog around the deck a few times.'

She'd have to do some creative thinking about what it had been like. She couldn't possibly tell Jessica she was still a virgin.

CHAPTER TWENTY-ONE

The late-night hours were hard on Michael. After questioning Bubba and searching unsuccessfully for Polly, he got trapped in a chess game with Dale Jensen – Tabb's first valedictorian to ever be impeached. Dale had not attended the graduation ceremony, but he had boarded the boat with a vengeance. He had sent out the challenge via Bubba: 'Meet me in the galley, twelve midnight. We'll see who's so smart.'

Michael didn't want to play. He had a lot on his mind and the pain in his head, rather than diminishing as the night wore on, kept getting worse. But Bubba sobering at a truly phenomenal pace – insisted that Michael play, and Bubba could be incredibly persuasive. He had always despised Dale. He even lent Michael an extra hat to hide his head wound. Michael had finally told Bubba about his run in with Clark. He hadn't planned to, but Bubba had started to ask about the gun. Seemed Kats was worried about it. Michael hadn't talked to Kats directly about the gun, of course, but as he searched the boat after the basketball game, he felt Kats was following him. Every time he turned a corner, Kats was there.

The galley was packed when Michael arrived with Bubba and Clair at his side. Dale had brought a chess set and cigarettes. Dale chain-smoked, and like everything else he did, he used the habit to irritate people.

Michael knew he would have smoke in his face until one of them was checkmated.

Although he had a despicable personality, Dale was not bad looking. Besides Bill Skater, and possibly Russ Desmond, he might have been the most handsome boy in the school. He was half Italian, with thick black hair, dark olive skin, and a wide insolent mouth Clair had once admitted looked mighty tasty. Dale was extremely slim, however, and he also had a chronic cough. He didn't care in which direction he coughed.

Bubba had warned Michael not to underestimate Dale, but Michael thought he would win easily. He had been playing chess regularly on his home computer since leaving school in January. He could beat the most sophisticated programs at the highest levels of complexity. He thought the contest would be over in less than twenty minutes.

He was still playing at one-thirty in the morning. Dale threw him off balance in the first few moves with a strategy Michael had never seen before. That was one of the weaknesses about honing chess skills against a computer; the programs had an almost endless supply of complicated attacks, yet they were often quite predictable. During the first hour of play, Michael had to use all his skill simply to defend his position. And then, when he finally did take command of the board, and his victory appeared certain, he allowed his mind to wander and made a disastrous mistake. He lost his only remaining rook, while getting nothing in return.

'Mike!' Bubba yelled, pounding the table beside the board and upsetting several of the pieces.

'I wanted to make it interesting,' Michael muttered, knowing that unless Dale made an equally careless blunder, the best he could hope for was a draw. Dale blew a cloud of smoke in his face.

'You won't be making a speech after this game,' he said.

Michael got his draw, but it took him until two, and left him feeling weak and drained. Dale surprised him afterwards by shaking his hand and complimenting him on an excellent game. Bubba did not approve of the result or the sportsmanlike gesture.

'Play him again and kick his ass,' Bubba whispered in Michael's ear as Dale got up to leave. Michael shook his head. He had to have another talk with Polly.

Unfortunately, once again, he could not find the girl. He decided to search *Haven*'s engine rooms one more time. He was seriously beginning to worry that Polly had jumped overboard. Before he started down, however, he stopped in the tiny bathroom he had used earlier. He needed a gulp of water.

That was the last he remembered for a while.

He regained consciousness on the floor of the bathroom in a pool of red, his heart thumping in his brain, his thoughts a grey fuzz. He must have knocked his cut open again. His watch said he had lost an hour. He was fortunate he had automatically locked the door upon entering. He sat up and stared in the grey-speckled mirror. The ghost image of Clark did not jump out to scare him as it had before, but his own appearance was frightening enough. A vampire could have got hold of him. His coat had blood all over it and he had to stuff it in the wastebasket, leaving him shivering in the damp night air.

The effect of the blackout went deep. After cleaning up, he stumbled outside and found he was trembling inside as well as out. He felt defeated, lonely. He had spent the whole year chasing an unseen enemy who might not exist, and running away from a girl who hardly knew he existed. He suddenly felt so weak he wanted to cry.

He had hit rock bottom.

It was precisely then he decided to tell Jessica he loved her.

He went searching for her. He brought his yearbook with him. She had said she wanted to sign it; it would give him an excuse to talk to her. But he couldn't find her either. He couldn't even locate Sara to ask where Jessica could be. He decided to go to Bubba for help. Bubba was supposed to know everything.

Except who killed Alice.

Michael found Bubba and Clair entwined in blissful slumber on a piece of foam on top of the bar. If they were to roll to the right or the left a couple of inches, they would surely get a rude awakening. Michael shook Bubba gently. Bubba half opened his eyes and smiled.

'Cabin forty-five,' he said.

'Jessie?' Michael asked.

Bubba closed his eyes. 'Forty-five.'

'Thanks.' Clair touched him with a warm hand as he was leaving.

'Tell her,' she mumbled, not raising her head or opening her eyes.

'I'll try,' Michael said.

Walking down the long hall that led to Jessica's cabin, Michael bumped into Bill. They had the space to themselves. Bill smiled broadly.

'I loved that speech you gave,' Bill said for the second time that evening.

'Thanks.'

Bill laughed. He appeared sort of jittery. 'So, where's our scholar off to now? Harvard? Yale? Stanford?'

'No place like that. I can't afford it.'

'No shooting, Mike? Did you apply for any scholarships?'

'No.'

181

'Why not?'

'I didn't feel like it.' And he sure didn't feel like talking to Bill at this very moment. He had to wonder where Bill had just come from. The neck of his yellow sweater was damp and he had water spots all over the arms.

'Does that mean you'll be around for a while?' Bill asked.

'I guess.'

Bill nodded to his yearbook. 'Hey, let me sign that. I'll give you my number. Maybe we can get together sometime for a movie or something. Just 'cause we're graduating doesn't mean we can't keep in touch. Right?'

'Sure.' Michael handed him the book. Bill whipped out a pen and scribbled something on the inside cover. Michael glanced down the hallway. Jessica's room must be at the end. Bill gave him back the book.

'I can run and get mine if you'd like to sign it,' Bill said. 'It'll just take me a minute.'

'That's OK, I'll sign it later.'

'You sure?'

'Yeah.' Bill followed Michael's glance down the hall. 'Looking for someone?'

'No.'

Bill smiled again. 'Catch up with you later, Mike.' He disappeared up the companionway.

Michael found cabin 45 three-quarters of the way down the hall. He stared at the number for a long time, remembering how he had felt when he had gone to Jessica's house to pick her up for their date. He had been scared then, but he'd had hope. He realised, suddenly, he didn't have a shred of hope now.

'I love you, Jessie.'

'That's sweet, Michael. I think you're a very special person, too.'

He knocked on the door, waited. No one answered. Maybe she was asleep. He was turning away when he heard a feeble, 'Who is it?'

'It's Mike.'

There followed a long pause. 'Come in.'

He opened the door slowly. She was sitting on the bed, wearing a pink bathrobe, a white towel resting on her lap, her hair wet. The air in the room was moist with steam. She must have taken a shower recently. Her eyes, however, were puffy, as if she had just awakened from sleep. She did not smile in welcome.

'I didn't wake you, did I?' he asked.

'No.' She glanced towards the bathroom and touched her head as if it hurt.' What are you doing here?'

'I'm sorry. I thought . . . I'll leave you alone.'

'No,' she said quickly. 'Come in, have a seat.' She picked up her towel and began to dry her hair, her attention obviously elsewhere. 'Please excuse the mess.'

The bed sheets were rumpled; otherwise the room appeared neat. A ceiling lamp in the corner swung back and forth with each rise and fall of the ship. It reminded Michael of a hangman's rope. 'I could come back later,' he said, closing the door.

'No, it's fine. I was just drying my hair. Have a seat.'

There was nowhere to sit except on the bed. He did not believe she had on anything beneath her robe. As it was, he could see more of her legs than he had ever seen before. He did not want to sit on the bed. He leaned against the wall near the bathroom doorway. 'You said you wanted to sign my yearbook?' He held it up. 'I have it here.'

'Oh.' She set down her towel and glanced around for her own yearbook. It was sitting on the stand three feet from her nose, but it took her several seconds to spot it. They exchanged books. 'Do you need a pen?' she asked, reaching for her purse.

'I have one.'

She found something to write with and flipped open his book, sitting cross-legged in the centre of the bed with her head down, her long hair hiding much of her face. She appeared to be having a hard time thinking of something to say. Michael took his pen out of his shirt pocket. For a moment, he considered telling her he loved her in her yearbook. Then he quickly discarded the idea. Everybody who signed her annual on Catalina would see it.

It was not going well. There was a gloom in the air that matched the gloom in his heart. He was probably the cause of it. His gaze strayed to the bathroom. A wet black brush sat on the counter beside the sink. There were a few hairs tangled up in its bristles. He leaned closer.

They were short blond hairs.

Bill's sweater had been wet.

Bill had been heading up the hall, away from Jessica's room.

Bill had just been here.

They had taken a shower together!

Michael closed his eyes and rolled into the wall, feeling sick to his stomach. The image of them naked together under the hot water stabbed into his mind like a needle. He had never known such pain. A hard knot formed in the centre of his chest and choked off his air. There was poison in his mouth. He couldn't swallow. *His* Jessie in Bill's arms – He simply could not bear the thought.

Not here! Get out! Get away!

He was going to cry, but he couldn't cry – not in front of her. He had sworn that to himself in Alice's studio after Alice's funeral. He swore it to himself again now with the last fibre of his shattered will. Yet he couldn't move. He couldn't get his head off the wall. And the tears were coming no matter how hard he fought to hold them back. He couldn't stop shaking.

She'll see you! She'll know!

'Michael?' She was standing beside him. She touched his shoulder. 'Michael, what's wrong?'

He tried to speak. He tried to disappear into the wall. It was not fair. They had been in the shower together in this bathroom having sex when he had been all alone in that other bathroom bleeding to death!

'Michael!' Jessica cried. 'You're bleeding!'

She pulled him off the wall and he fell sitting on the edge of the bed, his arm tightly locked across his eyes, his head down. 'I'm all right,' he managed to get out.

'What happened?' she asked, upset, sitting beside him. Her fingers touched the side of his head, cool and soft. He was able to draw in a breath, clamp down on the tears. He let his arm down, lowered his head further.

'Michael?' she said.

'It's nothing. I slipped and bumped my head.' He tried to get up, not looking at her. 'I'll go find a bandage.'

She stopped him and examined his scalp gently. He shouldn't have let her. 'You've split open your head! We've got to get you a doctor!'

'No.' He turned towards her, and although he didn't intend it to be so, a cold note entered his voice. 'Don't get me anything.'

She took back her hand, her fingers bloody. She swallowed. 'I can't let you go like this.'

'I'll be all right.' He did not believe it. He did not understand why her eyes were moist. He stood. 'Goodbye.'

She let him go, at least to the door. He had his hand

on the knob when she said, 'You forgot your year-book.'

He came back for it. Her hands trembled as she handed it to him. Then she burst into sobs, grabbing her towel and burying her face in it. 'You can't go,' she moaned.

He sat on the bed and put his hands on her back as she bent over. 'It's not that bad, Jessie.'

'But you're bleeding!'

'It'll stop.' He hadn't seen her this distressed since Maria had been hurt. She let go of the towel, looked at him with tears pouring over her cheeks.

'No, it won't stop.'

He was too hurt, too confused. He had no comfort left to give. 'I've got to go.' He picked up his yearbook. 'I've got to get out of here.'

He half expected her to grab his hand to stop him, to cry some more. Yet, suddenly, she stopped fussing and stared him in the eye. 'You can go,' she said. 'But you have to read it first.'

'What?'

'What I wrote.'

He opened the yearbook. He had not been passing it around. Few people had signed it so far: Sara, Clair, Bubba, Nick, Bill. Michael found Bill's note before Jessica's – something about getting together for a one-on-one game of basketball. Then he spotted Jessica's small neat handwriting tucked in the corner of a page at the back. It was not a long note.

I love you, Michael.

Jessie

Michael sat down again. People were always writing things like this at the end of the year in people's

186

yearbooks. It meant nothing. 'What does this mean?' he asked.

Her eyes never left his. They were a little red, but they were still pretty eyes. He had always thought so.

'I love you,' she said.

He looked down at the note, shook his head. 'I don't know what you're talking about.' He really didn't. Jessica couldn't love him. Only Alice had loved him.

'I've loved you for a long time.' A tear formed in the corner of her left eye. It was a quiet tear, not like the ones of a minute ago. 'I just wanted you to know.'

He closed the yearbook and stood. 'I have to go.'

'OK. Goodbye.'

'Goodbye.' He made it to the door, had his hand on the knob again. 'Why didn't you tell me this before?' he asked, his back to her.

'I was afraid.'

He understood that fear. He asked anyway. 'Why?'

'Alice didn't want me to meet you. She didn't think I was good enough for you.'

Michael turned to face her. She had lowered her head, hiding her face behind her long curtain of hair. 'That's not true.'

She nodded sadly. 'It is.'

He returned to the bed, to her side. She was crying softly. Setting down his yearbook, he put his arms around her. 'The first day I met you,' he said, 'Alice came to visit me in the computer room during fourth period. She had to leave the campus at lunch to see her doctor, but she told me about this wonderful girl she wanted to introduce me to at the football game. She didn't tell me her name, but that night, when I went to the game and spoke to you, I realised you were the girl.'

Jessica raised her head, sniffed. 'It was you?'

He smiled. 'It was me.'

187

A look of amazement filled her face. 'I'm glad.'

He brushed aside her hair and kissed her forehead. 'I have something else to tell you about that day.'

He had imagined the speech for almost too long. He couldn't live the moment without the memory of it already before him. On the other hand, nothing he remembered was exactly like this. Nothing was this sweet.

'When I met you at our locker that first day, I thought you were the most beautiful girl I had ever seen. I thought about you all that day, and the next day, and the day after that. Finally, Monday morning, I got up the courage to ask you out. You remember that time we spoke under the tree, when we talked about chemistry? I was going to ask you then.'

'How come you didn't?'

'You asked me first.'

Jessica sat back and put her hand to her mouth. 'No. This can't be. All this time – But you didn't ask me out later! Not once did you ask me out. I was the one who kept trying to set up a date.'

'Yeah, but only because you wanted to thank me.'

'Thank you for what?' She began to laugh. 'OK, I wanted to thank you. But I wanted to go out with you, too! Couldn't you tell?'

'No. Couldn't you tell I wanted to see you?'

'No. Every time we talked, you ran away.'

'I didn't want to bother you.'

She stopped smiling. 'Was there another reason?'

He hesitated. 'There was Bill.'

'Did you know that time I cancelled our date, I went out with him?'

He nodded reluctantly. 'Bubba told me.'

'I thought you might have known.' She sighed. 'I'm a bitch.'

'No.'

'Yes,' she insisted. 'I'm not who you think l am. Did you know Bill was just here?'

He honestly didn't want her to talk about it now, not right after saying she loved him. 'It's none of my business.'

She spoke seriously. 'But you should know about me. Bubba's going to tell you about it later anyway. I set up this whole scam to lure Bill here. I was in the shower. I was going to seduce him. I even stopped at a drugstore on the way to the harbour and bought contraceptives. Does this sound like the sweet innocent Jessie you think is cute?'

'Well.' He was beginning to feel a tiny bit sick again. She saw it, and hugged him quickly.

'I did it because I couldn't have you. I don't love Bill.'

'He's a nice guy.'

'He's not so nice.' Her face darkened and she looked towards the brush sitting by the sink. 'He told me I was just like all the other girls, loose. He couldn't get out of here fast enough.'

'Really?' That was excellent news, and he was glad to be hearing it first hand from Jessica rather than second hand from Bubba.

She chuckled. 'It happened just before you got here. He started screaming at me! It was so weird. I'm not that repulsive, am l?'

'Oh, no.' A faint idea touched the edge of Michael's mind, an idea so ridiculous and mean-spirited that he would have immediately dismissed it had it not been followed by the memory of a remark Bubba had made in the galley. ''Nothing. Absolutely nothing,' he whispered.

'What?'

189

'Something Bubba said about Bill.'

'Something Bubba said?' It was Jessica's turn to pause. ' "But if I were you, I'd keep Sara's receipt." '

'Did Bubba say that, too?'

'Yes.'

'When?'

She blushed. 'In the drugstore.'

They began to smile together. Then they started to laugh. They laughed so loud it hurt. It was the best laugh Michael could remember. But perhaps Jessica would not have said the same. She was beet red.

'Oh, God,' she cried. 'I've been trying to seduce a gay!'

'We don't know for sure he's gay,' Michael protested, trying unsuccessfully to stop giggling.

'Yes, we do! It all makes sense now, the whole year.' Jessica doubled up in embarrassment. 'I am so dumb!'

'Hey, there's nothing wrong with being gay.'

'I know that. It's just that I can't believe it,' Jessica said, still howling.

'We shouldn't be laughing.'

Jessica stopped suddenly, sat up. 'You're right. To each his own.'

'We shouldn't judge.'

Jessica nodded. 'I'm sorry.'

'He really is friendly.'

'He is, yeah.' Jessica kept her straight face approximately three seconds. Then she went into another fit. 'He's always liked you!'

Michael couldn't stop her. So he joined her. He could feel guilty about it later. If the truth be known, he was absolutely delighted with Bill's choice of lifestyle. Jessica's shower scheme might have ended a lot differently if Bill hadn't been gay.

But Michael preferred not to think about that.

Somewhere in the midst of their laughter, they began to kiss. Jessica started it; Michael had *never* kissed a girl before and would not have known how to begin. He was pleasantly surprised to discover it was easy to do. He had to assume he was doing it well; he was getting no complaints from Jessica.

They lay back on the bed, their arms wrapped around each other. He couldn't get over the fact that she cared for him! Or how warm and soft her body was. He seriously doubted any other girl would have felt like this. He ran his hand through her wet hair and she leaned into him, tilting her head back. Her mouth was a wonder, so soft and warm, tasting like – well, she tasted like toothpaste, which was fine with him. From now on, he knew, whenever he brushed his teeth, he would remember this moment. It was almost too much for him. He could see a *lot* of her legs. The knot in her robe was about to fall apart. He pulled back slightly.

'What's the matter?' she asked.

'Nothing.'

She smiled. 'I'm not too aggressive for you, am I?'

'No, it's not that.' He twisted his head around. 'I think maybe I'm bleeding on your sheets.'

She sat up with a start; leave it to him to put a halt to the happiest moment of his life. She touched the side of his head gently and grimaced. 'What really happened to you?'

He sat up. 'I can't talk about it.'

'Michael?' she protested.

He raised his hand. 'Not now, Jessie. But later, I promise, I'll explain everything.'

She continued to worry. 'Does it hurt?'

'No.'

'Liar. We should clean it at least.'

191

'I can't run water on the cut. It will only bleed worse.'

She touched a part of his head where the blood had already dried. 'We could wash here, if we were careful. I think it would help.' She slapped him on the back. 'Take off your clothes.'

He laughed. 'What?'

'I can't wash your hair in the sink. You're taking a shower.'

She was serious. 'I don't know,' he said.

She leaned over and kissed him briefly on the lips.

'Don't be shy. I'll join you.' She added hastily, 'We don't have to do anything. I know you're not feeling well.'

'I don't know,' he repeated, feeling a different sort of dizziness. She shoved him in the chest and giggled mischievously.

'Come on, Michael Olson, make my night.'

He had a sudden horrible thought of being eighty years old and looking back on this night with a feeling of profound regret. He took her hand. 'I'm not feeling that bad,' he said.

It turned out to be the best damn shower he'd ever had.

Later, when they were dry and dressed, he asked if she knew Polly's whereabouts.

'She's probably in her own room,' Jessica said, sitting on the edge of the bed, brushing her hair, a slight smile on her lips.

'She has a room, too? What number is it?'

'Twenty-eight, I believe. Why?'

'Stay here. I'll be back in a minute.'

When he knocked on cabin 28, no one answered. He tried the door without calling out Polly's name. It was unlocked.

192

The room was larger than Jessica's, far more plush. Polly had left all the lights on. An unopened grey overnight bag sat at the end of the undisturbed bed. No one had been sleeping in this room.

He checked in the bathroom. The bath was full. A double-edged razor blade lay in the corner soap tray beside several drops of bright red blood. Michael took a step forward, the joy of his time with Jessica fading rapidly. Sitting at the bottom of the warm bath – the hot water had been left trickling was a hair drier. Its plug rested less than two inches from a nearby socket.

'The man with the electricity.'

Had she accidentally dropped the drier into the water while blow-drying her hair during a bath, she would have received a terrible shock. Yet what did any of that mean next to a bloody razor? That nothing had been an accident?'

'I have to warm my blood.'

She had given Clark the form.

Michael reached down and touched the red drops beside the blade, rubbing them between the tips of his fingers. A strange sensation swept over him, similar to déjà vu but far more disturbing. It was a feeling of stumbling across the obvious and finding it utterly alien, a nightmare of staring into a mirror and seeing someone else. The realisation that had hit him on the deck at the end of his conversation with Polly returned. And this time it remained. He finally understood what Polly had been trying to tell him.

Russ had followed Sara's advice and was jogging laps around the deck in order to stay awake. Not being much of an athlete, Sara had decided to wait in the hall near Jessica's room. When Michael exited in a rush, Sara immediately ran to Jessica's door. She didn't knock; she just barged in.

'I knew you'd show up soon,' Jessica said, brushing her hair in the mirror on top of the cabin's built-in chest of drawers. Sara couldn't help but note Jessica's *glow*. She immediately felt insanely jealous.

'So how did it go?' Sara asked.

'Wonderful.' Jessica beamed. 'How about you?'

'It was great.'

'Did you and Russ *do it*?'

'Of course. How about you and Bill?'

'Three times,' Jessica said.

Sara leaned against the wall. 'How come I just saw Mike leaving?'

'He wanted to talk to Polly.'

'Yeah, but why was he here? I mean, what happened to Bill?'

'Nothing. Bill left, and then Michael stopped by.'

Sara thought a moment. 'He just stopped by to talk?'

Jessica grinned slyly. 'We didn't talk that much.'

Sara was shocked. 'You didn't screw both of them?'

'What's wrong with that?'

'That's disgusting!'

'No, it was fun. I had a great time. Especially with Michael. Bill just got me kind of warmed up.'

Sara almost choked with envy. Then she noticed the blood on the sheets. 'Was it painful?'

Jessica shrugged nonchalantly. 'It's sort of like having an itch. It bothers you at first, but then, when you scratch it, it feels great.' She set down her brush. 'You know what I mean.'

'Oh, yeah. Sure, yeah.'

Jessica laughed. 'I'm only kidding! I didn't have sex with Bill.'

'What happened to him?'

194

'Nothing. Absolutely nothing.'

Sara felt a small measure of relief. She hated to think she was missing out entirely. 'How about Mike?'

'Awesome.'

'If you're lying to me – How many times?'

'Simply awesome.'

'How many times?'

Jessica began to count on her fingers, then threw up her hands. 'I ran out of all the stuff we bought.'

Sara let her head drop against the wall. 'And I thought I was amazing.'

Michael reappeared a minute later. He looked a little pale. Sara didn't have a shred of sympathy for him. 'Hi, Sara,' he said.

'Hello,' she snapped. He paid her no heed.

'Could you two do me a favour?' he asked. 'Could you help me find Polly?'

Jessica sat up. 'Why? Is something wrong?'

'No, I don't think so,' he replied, his voice odd. 'But I want to find her. She's on board.'

'Of course she's on board,' Jessica said, concerned, watching him closely.

'Yeah,' he muttered, thoughtfully.

'What do you want with Polly?' Sara asked. He shook himself. His eyes cleared. 'I want to have a meeting of everyone who was at the party when Alice died.'

'Michael,' Jessica said, anguish in her voice. 'Don't.'

'Maria wants to have the same meeting,' Sara said, confused. 'I just ran into Nick a few minutes ago. She's sent him around to gather everybody together. She wants to have it down in the hull in half an hour.'

'Maria.' Michael chewed on that a moment. 'Interesting.'

'Why are you doing this?' Jessica asked, upset,

195

striding towards Michael. A look of sympathy touched his features, and he took her hand.

'It's all right. I understand everything a lot better now. It all makes sense to me, almost.' He hugged her. 'She didn't kill herself, Jessie.'

Jessica stared at him in disbelief. 'You don't know that.'

He touched the side of his head. 'You asked what happened – Clark did this to me.'

'Clark?' Sara muttered, more confused.

'Alice's boyfriend?' Jessica frowned. 'Is he on board?'

But Michael would not say.

CHAPTER TWENTY-TWO

In the dark and relatively deserted hull of *Haven*, Polly McCoy, last surviving member of her unlucky family, stood above Clark Halley and watched as he attached a potent charge of plastic explosive to the side of the ship's huge black fuel tank. He glanced up at her as he turned the setting on the timer, his thin, sweaty red hair plastered over the sides of his white bony face like streaks of caked blood, his dry cracked lips pulled back from his huge teeth in a skull's grin of ecstasy.

'I'll set it for an hour,' he said. 'It will be almost dawn then.'

'If the tank goes, hardly anyone will survive,' Polly said.

'It can't be helped.'

Polly was cold, even though she had on her biggest and warmest jacket. It was waterproof, but she didn't know how well it would hold up in a fire. 'When I was coming down here after you,' she said, 'I saw Maria. She told me everyone who was at the party will be meeting here soon.'

The explosive looked like a lump of dirty orange Play-Doh. Twin red and black wires trailed from it to the tiny square clock. Polly had seen similar explosives and detonators at her parents' construction company. Philip Bart had been in charge of the stuff.

'So?' Clark said.

She knelt beside him and put her right hand over his hands. A drop of blood from the incision in her wrist fell on to his clammy skin. 'They are the only ones who matter. Let the rest go.'

He chuckled. He was in a great mood. He loved twisting the blue dial on the timer. 'The boat's going down, babe. Ain't nothing going to change that.'

'It could go down slowly.'

He looked at her, holding her eyes. She had never realised before how similar their eyes were – both green, both red. 'None of them would shed a tear for you,' he said. 'Not a one.'

'Give them a chance. Please?'

He noticed her blood on the back of his palm, and his mouth twisted into a ravenous grin. 'I told you a drop of it seeped through the floor.' He held up his stained hand proudly. 'See, it escaped the room. It's free now.'

'I don't know what you're talking about.'

He licked the drop away with his long tongue and bade her lean close, whispering a single black word in her ear. 'Madness.'

'It's you who's mad,' she replied angrily.

He chuckled and let it pass. 'All right, babe. For you, I'll let the sleeping innocent try to swim back to shore. As long as you swear to keep our party people down here for the fireworks.'

'How can I keep them here if they want to leave?'

He showed her a few minutes later, after he had detached the bomb and dragged her into a small colourless room down the hall from the fuel tank. Here there was a tall metal cabinet pressed against the hull; he opened it, squeezing the plastic explosives into the bottom corner.

'It's always darkest before the dawn,' he sang as he decided on a final setting for the timer. The bomb couldn't have been more than three feet from the ocean water.

His answer to her question about how to keep the others from leaving was already in the cabinet, in the green sack he'd brought to the cemetery – a double-barrelled shotgun, covered with dirt. It looked familiar. He loaded it with fresh fat shells, and then set the weapon on the topmost shelf, almost beyond her reach.

'It belonged to your father,' he said. 'Before he burned.'

'I know.'

He looked at her. 'Sure you do. I've been telling you that all along. But it never mattered what you knew. It only mattered how much you cared. Me, I'm free as a corpse. I don't care about nothing.' He added softly, perhaps even with a note of regret, 'It's too late to start remembering, Polly.'

'Too late,' she agreed.

He climbed into the closet, turned, and spread his arms. 'Love me, babe, before they get here. It'll feel good, like old times.'

'If you stay in there, you'll die,' she said. Yet she followed him, into his arms, into the darkness. He was a liar. There were no old times. The door closed at their backs. She could feel his breath in her ear, like the whispering breeze in dreams she had long ago forgotten. But she could not feel his arms, only the cold steel of the closet, surrounding her on all sides, like a metal coffin.

'We'll die together,' he promised.

Kats strode *Haven*'s deck alone, wearing the thick fog as if it were a cloak personally given to him by the night. The lounge was crammed with unconscious bodies. The few kids still awake had gathered in the galley to await

199

the dawn. Kats felt as if he had the ship to himself, and the thought of it made him giggle. It was true what they said about the taste of revenge being sweet. He had a natural buzz singing cool music between his ears.

Kats knew about Maria and Michael's desire to have a meeting below deck for all those who had been at Alice's party. Both of them had told him to be sure to come. They hadn't asked him if he wanted to come; they had simply given him the order. It was just like those jerks. Well, he had no intention of attending – at least, not until his plan was fully hatched. Then he might swing by, if only to see them squirm. He could get into that.

Kats leaned over the rail and spat into the fog. The foam tip of a swell caught his eye as it broke against the side of the ship. The waves were riding high; solid five-footers. It would be rough out there on the water.

Kats whirled and headed for the stern. He needed his bag, his equipment. It was almost time to set the trap. He'd hidden his materials well. He knew they'd be waiting for him, safe and ready.

He poked a lifeboat along his way and howled at the invisible sky. He loved it.

CHAPTER TWENTY-THREE

The reason Jessica wore glasses instead of contact lenses was because of the unusual sensitivity of her eyes, and this, in turn, was largely the result of allergies. When she was a little girl, she had suffered terribly with a runny nose and itchy eyes, particularly in the spring when Southern California's many olive trees bloomed. Occasionally she had even been bothered with asthma. As she had grown older, she had left the majority of her symptoms behind, but her eyes had continued to remain easily irritated by dust and pollen. Also, probably as a psychological carry-over from her few childhood asthmatic attacks, she had a strong dislike of closed and stuffy places. On several occasions during her high school days, she had left an exciting movie right in the middle simply to get a breath of fresh air.

Haven's lower deck was as bad as a submarine as far as Jessica was concerned. It was not only cramped, it had an overall battleship look. There were huge thick pipes running along the grey walls and ceiling, and the door to the room Michael had chosen to meet in had a *wheel* on it. Michael had closed the door a second ago and turned the wheel. He had locked them in. Jessica could feel the tightness in her lungs and had to consciously remind herself to relax.

Why am I afraid? I am surrounded by my friends.

With the exception of Kats, everyone who had been

at the party when Alice had died was present. Maria in her wheelchair sat near the door. Nick stood behind her – it was Nick who had carried Maria and her chair downstairs. To their left were Sara and Russ, sitting on what appeared to be a huge toolbox. Clair and Bubba stood opposite the door, leaning against the steel hull and looking sleepy. Bill was in the corner with The Rock, and he wasn't giving Jessica a lot of eye contact, which was fine with her. Jessica didn't know how Michael had persuaded Bill to come.

Polly was by herself; she was the only one sitting on the floor, a few feet to the right of a tall metal cabinet. Her bulky navy-blue ski jacket dwarfed her under-nourished figure, and she'd tied her dark hair back in a ponytail, making her look all of twelve years old. As Jessica watched her, she noticed Polly's gaze drifting between Michael, a red light above the door, and the cabinet to her left. Just these three places, nowhere else.

'Aren't we going to wait for Kats?' Maria asked Michael. Outside the door, a few paces down the hall towards the rear of the ship, was *Haven*'s colossal fuel tank. Beyond that were the engines. Coming down the ladder, they had passed the engineer on duty, a big bearded gentleman taking an open-mouthed nap against a control panel. They pretty much seemed to have the space to themselves.

'He won't come,' Bubba said.

'I could go look for him again,' Michael said to Maria, apparently not bothered by Kats's absence.

'I'd like everyone to be here,' she said.

'He won't come,' Bubba repeated.

'How do you know?' Michael asked, the white gauze strip Jessica had obtained from the captain wrapped in a single strip around the top of his head. But Bubba simply waved his hand, as he often did when asked a

202

question that wasn't in his self-interest to answer. Although he was being sensitive to Maria's desires, Michael obviously wanted to get on with things. 'It's up to you,' he said to Maria.

'Maybe he'll show up,' she said, glancing up at Nick.

'I told him twice about the meeting,' Nick said.

Michael turned and paced in the centre of the room, collecting his thoughts. The room fell silent. Watching him from her position in the corner behind the door, Jessica felt both love and fear. She was still sailing the sky from their time together in cabin 45. Of all the strange and wonderful things in the universe that could be true – he liked her! In the shower she had been amazed at how excited she had been, and at the same time, how comfortable; it was as if they had known each other intimately for ages. Yet there was still much about him that she did not understand.

Why didn't he tell me he loved me?

It didn't matter, he'd told her enough to let her know she was important to him, even if perhaps he meant more to her than she meant to him. You couldn't have everything. Yet that was exactly Michael's problem. He wanted the impossible. He wanted to change the past.

'I had a reason for calling this meeting,' Michael said. 'But before I begin, I'd like to know your reason, Maria?'

'You go first,' she said.

'I would appreciate it if you could give me some idea?'

'So would I,' Nick said. But Maria never could be hurried.

'Later,' she said.

'All right,' Michael replied, pausing and scanning the room. 'My purpose in gathering you here is to prove that Alice did not commit suicide. I know most of you have heard me say that before, but this morning I hope

– with your help – to put together a number of clues I have gathered to show that suicide had nothing to do with it. I'll start by explaining a couple of alternative theories I gave to the police a few days after the party. I won't spend a lot of time on them, though, because I now realise they are fundamentally flawed.'

He returned to pacing, and Jessica noticed he was leaning slightly to the right. She continued to worry about his head wound, and exactly how he had received it.

'I told the officer in charge of the investigation that Alice's murderer could have hidden in the bathroom after killing her, and stayed there until after we left the bedroom. Looking at it from a slightly different angle, I also suggested that the murderer could have stepped out of the bathroom and secretly slipped into our group moments after we found the body. But both of these scenarios have major problems. The murderer would either have had to enter the bedroom – with Alice – immediately after Nick had been in there, or else the murderer would have had to have been in the bedroom with Alice when Nick got there. With the first possibility, the time would have been incredibly tight. Nick was back outside the bedroom only a few seconds later. And with the second – I just can't imagine Nick not knowing someone was in the room, even if it was dark.'

'I didn't hear anyone, that's for sure,' Nick said.

Michael nodded. 'Because that isn't what happened. Let's get into that now. Let's back up. Let's go downstairs before the gun went off. There were three of us in the living room: Maria, Nick, and myself. Then Jessica and Sara entered. Sara, what was the first thing you did?'

Sara thought a moment. 'I don't remember.'

'You complained about how loud the music was,' Jessica said. 'Then you turned it down.'

'That's right,' Sara said.

'The music was loud,' Michael said. 'I find that interesting. For all practical purposes, the party was over. But let's not dwell on this point right now. Just remember it. Anyway, Sara lowered the volume on the stereo, Jessica and Sara sat down, and the five of us talked a bit. Then Polly came in.'

'I remember,' Polly said softly, her eyes big on Michael. He crossed the room and stood above her.

'You turned the stereo off,' he said. 'You said your head hurt. Then you went outside to check on the chlorine in the pool. Isn't that right?'

'Yes.'

'On your way out, you shut the sliding-glass door to the patio. I saw you walk over to the pool.'

'It needed chlorine,' Polly said.

'So you tested the water?' Michael asked.

'Yes.'

Michael resumed his striding back and forth. 'Let's pick up Nick's story. He asked where the bathroom was. Sara said there was one in the games room, but that she thought someone was using it. She, in fact, said somebody was in there throwing up. Why did you say that, Sara?'

'When I passed it a couple of minutes before, I noticed that the door was closed and the light was on.'

'But you didn't actually hear anyone throwing up inside, did you?' Michael asked.

'I was speaking figuratively.'

'Did you hear *anyone* in the bathroom?' Michael asked.

'Not really,' Sara admitted.

'Was I in there?' Russ asked Sara.

'Shh,' she said, and patted his arm. 'Stay out of trouble.'

'Jessica told Nick to try one of the bathrooms upstairs,'

Michael said. 'So Nick headed for the stairs. Tell us, Nick, about that little walk you took, step by step.'

Nick cleared his throat. 'I went to the stairs. I saw Bill in the kitchen. He was bent over the sink. He looked sick or upset. He didn't look good.'

Bubba glanced at Clair, who took the occasion to stare at the floor. 'What was wrong, Bill?' Sara asked.

'I was – I'd had too much to drink,' Bill said.

'You hadn't drunk that much,' The Rock said. 'What was bothering you, buddy?'

'Nothing,' Bill mumbled.

'Come on, Mr Treasurer,' Sara insisted. 'Tell us what the problem was?'

'This isn't important,' Michael interrupted.

'How do you know it isn't important?' Sara asked.

'It's not,' Clair said.

'But I want to know,' Sara said.

'Sara,' Jessica said, not exactly sure how this related to Bill's homosexuality, but knowing it must. 'Shut up.'

'Go on, Nick,' Michael said.

'I went up the stairs, both flights. In the first part of the hall there were four doors: three on the left, one on the right. I didn't know which one led to the bathroom, but Jessie had said it was halfway down the hall, so I skipped the first door on the left.'

'Let me interrupt just a sec,' Michael said. 'The police later checked that door. It was locked from the inside. I'm sorry, Nick, go on.'

'I tried the second door on the left. It was locked. I thought I heard water running inside.'

'I was in there,' The Rock said. 'I was taking a shower.'

'You come to a party and you take a shower?' Sara asked, still smarting from the rebuff over Bill.

'I was washing out my eyes,' The Rock said defensively, glancing at Polly, who gave no sign that she remembered the chlorine she had thrown in his eyes.

'I tried the door on the right,' Nick continued. 'It led on to a porch that overlooked the backyard. Kats was out there.'

'Did he see you?' Michael asked.

'I don't think so.'

'But you could see him clearly?' Michael asked.

'Yeah. There was some light from the pool. It was Kats. I didn't say anything to him. I tried the last door on the left. It was locked, too. But I thought I heard someone inside.'

'Was I in there?' Russ asked.

'Were you?' Nick asked.

'He doesn't have to answer that,' Sara said. 'Not when our quarterback won't tell us why he was crying in the kitchen sink.'

'I crashed somewhere upstairs,' Russ said.

'You were in that room,' Michael said confidently. 'Please continue, Nick.'

'The hallway turns. There were another two rooms, both on the left. I tried the first door. It was locked. There were people inside. I heard someone groaning.'

'That was Clair and me,' Bubba said without hesitation. 'She was acting out a role in a play for me.'

'You told the police the two of you were outside looking at the stars,' Sara said.

'That was a misunderstanding,' Bubba said with a straight face.

'You're not an actress,' Sara told Clair.

'So what?' Clair said.

'This isn't important either,' Michael said. 'All that matters is that Clair and Bubba were together in that bedroom and that they were so occupied that they

207

couldn't hear what was going on in the next room.'

'Why couldn't they hear?' Sara wanted to know. This time everybody simply ignored her. Nick went on.

'I went to the last room. The door was wide open. It was dark inside. I tried the light switch, but the light wouldn't go on.'

'What was wrong with the light, Polly?' Michael asked.

'It was broken,' Polly said, taking her wrist away from her mouth. She'd been holding it to her lips for the last minute. She looked exhausted.

'Had it been broken long?' Michael asked.

'I broke it when I tried to fix it.'

'When? How?' Michael asked.

'That night.' Polly shivered. 'My hands were wet. I turned it, and it went on. Then it broke.' Polly lowered her head. 'I fell off the ladder.'

Michael stopped dead. 'You fell off the ladder?'

Polly nodded, her head still down.

'Did you get a shock, Polly?' he asked, his voice falling to a whisper.

'Yes.'

'Did it hurt?'

She looked up, her face sad. 'Yes.'

Michael stood staring at her for a moment and something in his expression softened. Then he seemed to shake himself inside, throwing off whatever troubled him about Polly's remark. He turned back to Nick. 'Go on, and please give us as much detail as you can.'

'I stepped into the room,' Nick said. 'It was cold, dark. The east-facing windows were wide open. The blinds were up. But the other windows – the ones that faced the backyard – they were closed. The blinds were down at least. I could hardly tell there was a window there. Polly must have turned off the pool light. I went into the bathroom and closed the door. I didn't even try to turn on the light. My eyes were beginning to adjust a bit. I could see what I was doing. I wasn't in there but a minute.' He shrugged. 'Then I came back out into the hall.'

'Stop,' Michael said. 'You skipped something. The day of Alice's funeral, you told me that while you were in the bedroom, you felt something. Tell us about that.'

Nick hesitated, and it was obvious to Jessica that he would have preferred not to have been pressed on this point. Jessica did not like the course of Michael's analysis. It was too *real*. It brought it all back, the whole night. The claustrophobic dimensions of the room were not the only thing pressing down on her chest. She was beginning to feel – it frightened her as much as it gave her hope – that perhaps Michael *had* uncovered a truth beneath the obvious. A suicide was horrible to contemplate, but a murder – that wasn't something she could simply forget.

Especially if the murderer was in the room with them.

'I felt scared,' Nick said.

'Of what?' Michael asked.

Nick moistened his lips. 'I don't know.'

'You didn't see anything? You didn't hear anything?'

'No.'

'What exactly were you thinking when you were scared?'

'What?'

'People don't just feel scared when they're scared. They have scary thoughts. What were you thinking?'

Nick had to stretch his memory. 'I was thinking of Tommy. He was a friend of mine. He died in a gang fight.' Nick glanced at The Rock. 'Stanley killed him.'

The Rock scowled. 'That bastard.'

'Who's Stanley?' Sara asked, for all the good it did.

They ignored her again. Something in Nick's remark had made Michael pause once more.

'Were you with Tommy when he died?' he asked.

Nick fidgeted. It must have been a painful memory. 'He died in my arms.'

'How did Stanley kill Tommy?'

Nick took a breath. 'He got him in the heart with a switchblade.'

'I'm sorry,' Michael said. 'I had to ask.'

'It's OK,' Nick said. 'Should I go on?'

'Please.'

'Should I tell . . .' Nick glanced down at Maria.

'It'll be OK,' Michael said. 'Honestly, Nick, you can trust me on this.'

'I trust you,' Nick said, uneasy. 'Like I said, I left the room and went into the hall. I got all the way back to the top of the stairs. Then the gun went off. I – I froze, for a second, and then ran down the stairs.'

'*Down* the stairs?' Sara asked.

'Yes, he *instinctively* ran *down* the stairs,' Michael said. 'This is very important. He wasn't the only one who ran down the stairs. Kats did the same.'

'How come we didn't run into Kats then?' Sara asked. She was intrigued with the way things were unfolding, Jessica could tell. Bubba, also, seemed very interested in what Michael was up to.

'Before starting down,' Michael said, 'Kats checked out the backyard from his vantage point on the second-storey porch. The only one he saw was Polly, running towards the back door. Go on, Nick.'

'I bumped into Maria on the landing. I knocked her down. I had to help her up. Then we went back up the stairs. All of you know the rest.'

'Not quite,' Michael said. 'When the four of us – Jessie, Sara, Polly, and me – came up the stairs, we heard you and Maria talking around the turn in the hall. That's why we went straight to the last bedroom. But you also went straight to that room. Why?'

'I'm not sure I understand your question,' Nick said.

'You had five doors between you and the last bedroom, four rooms. How come you didn't stop to check any of those rooms?'

Nick was perplexed. 'I don't know.'

'How come you ran down the stairs?' Sara asked.

'I don't know,' Nick said.

'Do you know, Mike?' Bubba asked.

'You'd better,' Clair said, nervously rubbing her hands together. 'The suspense is killing me.'

'I do know,' Michael said, stopping beside Polly. 'The shot we heard that night did not come from the bedroom. It did not kill Alice. It came from outside, from a spot in the backyard on the east side of the house directly beneath the bedroom window.'

No one spoke for a long time. Yet it was interesting, Jessica noted, that everyone in the room appeared to believe Michael. He sounded so sure of himself. Even Bubba, who spoke first, had no doubt in his voice when he made his one-word request.

'Explain,' Bubba said.

'Nick and Kats were upstairs,' Michael said. 'They were the only ones upstairs who were – fully functional. They were the only two people in the house familiar with guns. And when the gun went off, they *instinctively* thought the shot came from *beneath* them. Think about it for a minute. Then think about how the group of us downstairs would have heard a sound originating from the side of the house. The sliding-glass back door was shut. The games room and the aunt's bedroom windows were all shut. But the east-facing windows in the upstairs bedroom were open. The bulk of the sound from a shot fired beneath that bedroom would have reached our ears via the second-storey hallway. It was no wonder Sara and Jessie and me – and even Maria – thought the shot came from upstairs.'

'Interesting,' Bubba said, thoughtful.

'There's more,' Michael said, getting excited, pulling a folded square of white paper from his back pocket. 'Alice was supposedly killed by a twenty-two shell. Now I'm not a gun expert, but a twenty-two is a pretty small bullet. The shot we heard was loud.'

'Fire any gun in a quiet house and it will sound loud,' Nick said.

'Yeah, that's what the police told us,' Michael said, unconvinced, stepping towards Nick and carefully holding his paper. 'Look at this.'

Nick studied Michael's secret evidence without fully unwrapping it. 'Where did you get these?' he asked Michael.

'What is it?' Sara demanded.

'Shotgun pellets,' Nick said.

'Fascinating,' Bubba said.

'I removed them from a torn wooden shingle,' Michael said. 'A shingle located at the edge of the overhang of the roof directly outside the bedroom where Alice died.'

'How was the shingle torn?' Bubba immediately asked.

'It was splintered upwards,' Michael said.

'But she had the gun in her mouth,' Jessica said, her voice shaky. Suddenly she wished he would stop. Alice was dead. Nothing was going to bring her back. The feeling belonged to a coward, and that was exactly how she felt – as if she wanted to run away and bury her head in the sand. Yet that was only half of it. As Bubba had said, it was *fascinating*. 'We all saw it,' she insisted.

The reminder of how they had found Alice appeared

to dampen Michael's enthusiasm. He leaned against the tall metal cabinet off to Polly's left, and Jessica could not remember when he had ever looked so frail. She wished to God they had a doctor aboard who could examine his wound. He was white as a sheet.

'That's true,' he said. 'But the question is, how did the gun get in her mouth? Let's look at Nick's account just before we heard the shot. He went into the bedroom. It was dark. It was quiet. He couldn't see or hear anything. Yet he was scared. Now why was he scared? He's no chicken. It wasn't the dark that was bothering him. It was something else. There was something in that room that made him think of a stabbing years ago. What was it?'

'He smelled something,' Bubba said suddenly.

'Exactly,' Michael said. 'Nothing was coming to him from his eyes or his ears. But his nose – the dark doesn't affect your nose. He thought of Tommy dying in his arms from a knife wound to the heart because he smelled blood.'

'And that's why he ran to the last bedroom instead of checking the others,' Bubba said, nodding to himself, enjoying the intellectual puzzle.

'Does everybody understand?' Michael asked.

'No,' the others said.

'It is clear,' Michael said. *'Alice was lying dead in the room before Nick even got to it.'*

More silence followed, longer and deeper than the previous spell. And again it seemed that everyone believed Michael. Jessica sure did, and yet she did not know what it meant, other than that everything they had believed about that night had been built on a faulty foundation.

Michael glanced down at Polly, and she stared back at him, or so Jessica thought at first. But Polly's eyes were focused slightly to the side, behind Michael, on the cabinet. Her red lips trembled. She must have had lipstick on — Jessica had never seen them quite so red. Polly was suddenly the centre of attention.

'You fired the shotgun,' Michael said.

'Yes,' Polly replied softly.

'Then you threw the shotgun into your garden and ran into the house.'

'Yes.'

'Why?'

'Clark told me to.'

Jessica jumped from her position in the corner. 'Did he shoot Alice?'

Polly nodded.

'Oh, God,' Clair said.

'No,' Michael said.

'But, Mike, maybe she saw him do it,' Nick said.

'No,' Michael repeated, still watching Polly. Now she was looking at him, and she may have been looking to him for help.

'I didn't,' she whispered.

'How did Clark get the gun in Alice's mouth?' Michael asked. Polly only shook her head. He came and knelt beside her. He wasn't there to help her. His tone hardened. 'Where did he go after he pulled the trigger?'

'I don't know.'

'How did he get her fingers on the trigger of the gun?'

'I don't remember,' she said, begging to be believed.

'Where did he go after he did all these things?' Michael demanded, grabbing her arm. 'How come *none* of us saw him?'

'Michael!' Jessica cried. 'She didn't shoot Alice!'

Polly had closed her eyes. She was not crying, but Jessica could hear her breathing, shallow and rapid. It was the damn room. No one could breathe in here. It was almost as if they were back in the bedroom with the body. Michael let go of Polly's arm and sat back. His next words went off like a silent bomb.

'Alice was dead before anyone shot her,' he said.

Polly pressed her wrist to her mouth. Jessica could have sworn she was sucking on it; a child in desperate need of a bottle. They were all going nuts. Jessica looked again to the locked door with longing. If only there was a window they could open that wouldn't let the ocean in. Michael had finally lost them all with his last remark.

'Did she have a heart attack or something?' Nick asked.

'No,' Michael said.

'A stroke?' Sara asked.

'I read the coroner's report,' Michael said, his eyes never leaving Polly's. 'I talked to the coroner. That night someone broke Alice's nose. They broke it badly. She had brain damage the bullet didn't cause.'

'You'd have to hit someone just right to kill them that way,' Nick said doubtfully.

'How about it, Polly?' Michael asked. 'Did Clark do it?' When she didn't respond, he reached over and grabbed her hand away from her mouth, yanking up on the sleeve of her jacket. Jessica felt dizzy.

Polly's wrist was all red. She had been sucking on her own blood.

'Did Clark do this?' Michael yelled.

She nodded wearily. 'He does whatever he wants.'

Michael threw her arm down. 'Liar.'

'He's not here, is he?' Clair asked anxiously.

'He is,' Polly said.

'Really?' Michael asked. 'Let me see him.'

'I can't,' Polly whispered.

'Let me see him,' Michael insisted.

215

'Let me see if I can find him,' Polly said, giving up, trying to get up.

The madness was still a few heartbeats in the future, but even before it arrived, Jessica felt the brush of the razor's edge. It was not the same blade that had cut Polly's wrist. It was a sharp point in time. As Polly stood and walked towards the metal cabinet Michael had been leaning against, Jessica felt the weight of the entire year behind her, focusing down upon this one moment. That was why the air in the room felt so heavy, she realised, so hard to breathe. Polly started to turn the handle on the cabinet.

'What is that?' Clair suddenly cried.

'What?' Michael asked jumping to his feet.

'People are shouting,' Nick said, frowning. 'Something's happening.'

Michael strode towards the door. He was halfway there when the red light above the door suddenly began to blink off and on and a screaming alarm pierced the air.

'The ship's sinking!' Sara cried.

With the exception of Maria, Polly, and Bubba, they all converged on the door. Nick took hold of the wheel and turned it counterclockwise. It didn't open. He spun it the other way.

'It's stuck,' he said, pounding the metal with his fist.

'Oh, God,' Sara said.

'Let me try it,' Russ said, shoving Nick aside.

'No, I'll do it,' Michael said, pressing Russ out of his way. He pulled up on a metal lever beneath the wheel and spun the wheel counterclockwise again. The siren continued to wail. The door cracked open. In a tangled knot, the group pressed forward.

'Stop,' someone ordered at their backs. Jessica turned to see who it was. She didn't recognise the voice. She did not know why; it was only Polly, good old Polly, closing the door on the cabinet with her right hand, holding a double-barrelled shotgun in her left. She had her finger on the trigger. They were her target.

'Polly!' Jessica cried. 'Put that down.'

Bubba, standing quietly off to Polly's right, made a sudden lunge for the shotgun. He didn't make it. Even though she was bleeding from her wrist under her jacket, and floating above a space mountain between her ears, Polly was still mighty quick. Bubba caught the tip of the barrels on the bulge of his gut. He froze in mid-stride and slowly raised his hands, giving Polly his warmest smile.

'Never mind,' he said.

Polly's face was dark. She herded everyone into the corner of the room opposite the door with a few silent gestures of her gun. Then she reclosed the door with her shoulder and locked it. Trapped in her wheelchair a few feet away, Maria watched calmly, unmoving. Polly slumped against the door, clasping the shotgun with both hands as if it might suddenly vanish into thin air.

'We have to stay,' she said finally, her voice barely audible over the panicked shouts from the decks above. Jessica could hear people running, screaming. She would scream next. She smelled smoke. Michael took a step forward.

'Why?' he asked.

'Clark,' Polly said. 'He'll kill them all if you don't stay.'

'But we have to get out of here!' Clair pleaded. 'The ship's on fire!'

'No,' Bubba said, reaching a hand out to comfort Clair. Then he hesitated, glancing at Polly. He let his arm drop to his side. He had not finished what he was going to say.

217

'What is it?' Michael asked Bubba.

'Nothing,' he replied.

Michael turned his attention back to Polly, took another step forward. 'Where's Clark?' he asked.

'Near,' Polly said.

Another step. He was practically daring her to shoot. 'Tell him I want to talk to him.'

'He won't talk,' Polly whispered, perspiration pouring over her face. 'Stay.'

Michael circled to the left, putting the cabinet at his back and drawing the barrel of the gun away from the others. Jessica could not bear to watch.

He'll sacrifice himself to get us out of here.

Jessica stepped out from the group. The Rock tried to grab her hand, but she shook him off. Michael didn't notice; he was too preoccupied.

'I don't really want to talk to him anyway,' he said. 'It's you I want to talk to. Do you want to talk, Polly?'

'About what?' she asked. Her wrist appeared to be hurting her. She stopped supporting the barrel of the gun with her right hand and hugged the cut to her side. The red light continued to flash above her head like an unholy halo. The smell of smoke kept getting stronger. Jessica decided to circle to the right, towards Maria's side of the room.

'Alice,' Michael said, taking another step towards her.

'No,' Polly pleaded. 'Stop there. He pushed . . . He told me – I'll have to shoot you!'

'I don't think so,' Michael said, ignoring her order to halt.

'But you don't understand,' she cried, pulling back on the trigger with her left index finger. 'You must stay here.'

'All right, Polly,' Michael said, stopping less than a yard from the tip of the shotgun. ''Whatever you want.'

What followed next happened quickly and was confused. Jessica had closed to within approximately six feet of Polly's left side. When Michael paused and began to reassure Polly everything was all right, Jessica took that as a sign that he was about to try for the gun. Since he had to cover three feet in the time Polly had to squeeze her finger a fraction of an inch, Jessica did not believe he would survive such an attempt. She decided to make a dive for the gun.

Jessica had barely begun to move when Polly swung the gun towards her face. The twin holes at the end of the double barrels were wide and black – very frightening. Jessica froze. Then Michael made a try for the gun. His heroic attempt was also stopped short. Polly was simply too quick for the two of them. She snapped the gun again on Michael, then on Jessica, back and forth, holding them both at bay.

Then something incredible happened.

Jessica did not see Maria stand from her wheelchair. Maria was just there, up on her two feet, at Polly's side, forcing the gun down. Unfortunately, whatever magic had suddenly given the small girl the ability to walk had not given her an extra dose of strength. Polly threw her off easily. Maria hit the side of her wheelchair, letting out a cry and falling on her side.

But by then Michael had reached Polly.

He probably could have got the gun from Polly more quickly if he hadn't been so overly concerned with where it was pointed while he wrestled with her. It was good he took his time. Whether Polly did so intentionally or accidentally, the trigger was pulled.

The shot hit the side of the tall cabinet, ripping through the metal. Jessica thought she screamed. Maybe the whole room did. Except for Michael. He was in control. He had the gun in one hand, Polly's bloody wrist in the

219

other. Jessica noticed for the first time that the shotgun was caked with dried mud.

'Now you stop,' he said.

'I can't,' Polly moaned, nevertheless collapsing into him as if he had just come to her rescue. Michael tossed the gun to Bubba and wrapped his arm around Polly.

'Let's get out of here,' he called.

'You can walk!' Nick exclaimed, helping Maria up.

'Mike, there's something I've got to tell you,' Bubba said. 'Later,' Michael called, spinning the wheel on the door.

'I *can* walk,' Maria said calmly as Nick hoisted her into his arms on the off chance that her reclaimed legs might disappear.

'Did that goddamn Clark light the goddamn ship on fire or what?' Sara yelled over the din as once again they pressed towards the door.

'No!' Bubba shouted.

Everybody stopped. Bubba never shouted. 'What is it?' Michael demanded. Before Bubba could respond, the heavy metal door swung open. It was Kats, grinning the full length of his greasy moustache. He stepped into the room as if he were captain of the ship.

'Are the kids all right?' he asked, pulling the door closed at his back.

Had he been expecting a royal reception, Kats was in for a big disappointment. Michael leaped to a quick conclusion. 'You bastard,' he swore, throwing Polly to Jessica and drawing back his fist. 'What have you started?'

'Hey, Mike, it was only a prank,' Bubba said, jumping in front of Kats, the dirty shotgun still in his hands. 'Kats just let off a few smoke bombs to scare everybody into the lifeboats. There's no fire. The ship isn't sinking. There's nothing to get shook about.'

220

'We have to stay,' Polly moaned softly in Jessica's arms.

'Why?' she asked, repeating Michael's question. Polly's head sagged back on Jessica's shoulder. She looked up at Jessica with eyes both sad and angry.

'You talked me into it.'

'Into what?' There was a hard lump inside Polly's jacket. Jessica wondered what it could be. It didn't feel like a gun. Polly's gaze slipped past Jessica to the cabinet where she had got the shotgun.

'Go look, Jessie,' she said. 'You'll see, it's dark in there, like the tunnel we got lost in when we were small.'

The shotgun was in safe hands. The fire apparently didn't exist. Yet the fears of the whole night suddenly coalesced above Jessica and fell over her in a smothering wave. Polly's gaze had been moving to the cabinet since they had come down to this wretched room. Had Polly been pointing to something worse than a hidden weapon?

Jessica pulled a handkerchief from her pocket and handed Polly over to Russ, telling him to bind her wrist. Sara quickly moved to help. Everybody seemed to be talking at once. The alarm continued to blare. Jessica hardly noticed. The tall grey cabinet, its side ripped and twisted from the blast of the shotgun, held her attention. She stepped towards it.

The world exploded in her face.

CHAPTER TWENTY-FOUR

Orange fire. Black water. And a naked fist of thunder. Time could have come to the Bible's cataclysmic end. Except there came pain – terrible pain.

Since she was closest to the cabinet, the shock wave hit Jessica the hardest. Her eyes had no chance to absorb the blinding flash when she was literally swept off her feet and thrown backwards. Her moment in the air existed in her mind all out of proportion to reality. It lasted for ever, and yet it remained incomprehensible to her. She couldn't fly. *Haven* didn't carry nuclear warheads. What was going on?

Then she hit the far wall, and the agony almost consumed her. It pulsed throughout her body, shrieked inside her right arm. A long thick pipe had whipped loose from the ceiling and pinned her to the wall.

Flames danced in short-lived fury and tried to claim the ceiling. But the blaze could not go down. The ocean was pouring in. Jessica tried to draw in a breath and gagged on fumes. Dark numbing water swam around her ankles and up her calves. Cries wailed in her ears. Everyone was trying to open the door again, and this time they were in a hell of a hurry.

Jessica could hardly see. She had lost her glasses. There was a lot of smoke and the blast had knocked out the overhead lights. Yet the red light above the door remained functional, throbbing like a maddened heartbeat in the closing darkness. The fire was going out already. The water was rising. A shadow stumbled against her, grabbing on to the wall for support.

'We have to get out of here,' Michael said, taking her left hand and giving it a tug. Jessica screamed.

'I'm stuck,' she gasped. Out the corner of her eye, she saw the group manage to force the door open against the pressure of the rising water. For a few seconds, the water around her knees dropped. Then something crashed outside the hull and it quickly rose again, faster than before. The cabinet was gone; a gaping hole into the underworld had taken its place. She realised then how close she was to dying.

Michael pulled himself past her and tugged on the pipe pinning her right arm to the wall. It didn't budge at all, and yet the effort somehow shot the pain in her arm into the region of the unbearable. She teetered on the edge of blacking out. It was only the swelling current, and the horror of drowning beneath it, that kept her conscious. Michael called to the others.

'Jessie's stuck. I need help.'

Several had already escaped out the door, if it could be called escape; the flood was sweeping away everything that stood in its path, and who knew where it was taking them. Jessica could not find Bill or Clair or Bubba. But Sara and Russ were in the corner to the right of the door, fighting to hold up what might have been an unconscious Polly, and Nick was still hanging on to Maria, trying not to go under. It was only The Rock who seemed to hear Michael. He splashed towards them. Michael pointed to the pipe.

'We've got to bend this back,' he said.

The Rock grabbed hold of the pipe with his thick hands and pulled with everything he had. The pipe creaked. Jessica screamed again. The blood must be squeezing back over her shattered bone. She knew it was broken; it felt like a meaty pancake beneath the hard metal. The Rock leaned his head close to her face.

'Can you pull it out?' he shouted.

'No!'

'Can you try?'

'It hurts!'

'Mike,' Nick called, one arm wrapped around Maria, the other hugging another steel pipe that had fallen from the ceiling. 'Can you get her loose?'

Maria must have taken in a lungful of salt water; she was coughing horribly. Michael looked to The Rock, and to Sara and Russ struggling to save Polly. 'I don't know!' he called back.

'Theodore?' Nick shouted.

Who in God's name is Theodore?

'I'm working on it!' The Rock replied.

'Tell them to go,' Jessica said.

'Not yet,' Michael said, fighting to get around The Rock in order to grab the pipe from above. 'Not till you're free.'

'Go!' Jessica screamed at Nick and the others. 'Get out!'

'Jessie!' Sara called, flailing in the river flowing through the door. Russ had finally got a handle on Polly; he had her swung over his back. He looked as if he could get her to safety, but he glanced over at Jessica before he left.

'Just go!' Jessica yelled. 'I'm almost free.' Her brave lies amazed her. She had always thought brave people were not afraid. The water was now up to her waist.

Russ left with Polly and Sara. Nick got out with Maria a few seconds later. It was down to the three of them. *Haven's* alarm cried on. It was a death cry. The floor

224

lurched to the side. Jessica could not bring herself to tell The Rock and Michael also to flee. She almost wished Polly's shotgun blast had caught her in the head. The thought of coming to the end choking beneath the sea was too much for her. She had to fight not to faint.

'We have to pull at the same time!' Michael said. He was to her right, his hands on the pipe above her head, while The Rock was directly in front of her, gripping the pipe inches below her trapped arm. The Rock had decided upon a strategy. He had his feet planted to either side of her waist; he would be able to use the strength in his legs to pull harder.

'Let's do it!' The Rock shouted back. 'One! Two! Three!'

They pulled. The pipe creaked again, and she screamed again. It made no sense – freezing on the outside like this while she burned on the inside. The water level passed her breasts, heading for her mouth.

'You must pull, too!' Michael yelled at her, probably not knowing he was asking her to pull her bones apart.

'I can't,' she wept. 'It hurts.'

He let go of the pipe and grabbed her chin. Through the pain, the smoke, and the haunting red light, she hardly recognised him. 'Please, Jessie,' he said.

He was begging her. She couldn't let him down. 'I'll try.'

Michael repositioned himself. They counted to three again. The Rock leaned back and howled as if he was on a football field. The pipe squealed. Jessica closed her eyes and prayed for it to end. She pulled.

My God.

The pain was not natural. It soared upwards like a light beam fleeing the spectrum. Perhaps it momentarily yanked her soul out of the top of her head. She might have blacked out. She didn't feel her arm snap free. The next thing she knew, she was bobbing loose, with Michael holding on to her. She opened her eyes.

'We'll be all right,' he said.

'Honestly?' she asked.

They had outwitted the pipe none too soon. Even as they turned to leave – holding on to the wall to keep from being sucked down – the water level passed the top of the door. That was a problem. Not only did she not know how to swim, she did not know how to hold her breath underwater. She was really a pathetic girl to have to rescue. She stopped.

'What is it?' Michael asked behind her. While freeing her, The Rock had accidentally taken in a mouthful the wrong way; he was caught in the throes of a coughing fit.

'I'm afraid,' she said. Her one healthy arm was hardly able to hold on against the power of the current pouring through the submerged door. The ceiling was less than two feet from the tops of their heads and getting closer. The red light would go under next and then it would be pitch black. The Rock continued to choke. Michael spoke with amazing patience.

'There is nothing to be afraid of. This is a big ship. It will take a while to sink. Once out of here, we'll be halfway home. Go on, just hold your breath, let go, and duck down. It might even be fun.'

'All right,' she said. But she didn't move. Michael turned round to The Rock and patted him on the back as if he were a baby needing burping.

'You OK?' Michael asked.

The Rock nodded, although he was obviously far from OK. He had taken in a lot of water. She was killing them all. The Rock motioned for them to get going. Michael reached for her hand that was holding her in place.

'Michael,' she said anxiously.

'I'll go with you,' he said.

'No. You go first.'

'Close your mouth, Jessie.'

'But –'

'Close your mouth.' He pulled her protesting fingers loose. She did close her mouth, but forgot to duck down. It didn't make much difference. The current took hold of her and pulled her under. She was in a washing machine set to black and tumble. Water shot up her nose. *Nothing* could have been worse, not even burning at the stake. Panic consumed her reason. She was smothering! She had to take a breath! Not even the knowledge that she would drown if she did could stop her. She opened her mouth, tasting the salty cold, her bitter death. It was over. She couldn't believe it. She started to suck in.

Then she burst to the surface riding a foaming wave towards the huge fuel tank.

'Eeh!' she screamed.

Michael had caught the same wave. He grabbed her uninjured arm, and the wall, preventing her from a nasty collision.

'The ladder's around this room,' he said, pulling her to her feet. 'We're going to be fine.'

There were more red lights on in the hall. Fortunately they were not blinking, nor were they about to go under. The water level was about three feet. It was, however, a torrential three feet; it was hard to stand. Glancing back the way they had come, Jessica noticed an equal amount of water rushing from the room beyond the one that had held them prisoners. The blast must have torn through the wall and the hull. *Haven*'s crew was at a minimum. Those on duty must have raced to the top deck the instant the smoke bombs had gone off to help evacuate everyone; obviously, none of the crew had had a chance to return to the hold and seal off the flooding section. Michael was wrong. This ship was going under soon. The floor lurched again as they began to round the corner.

'I hate ocean cruises!' she complained.

'They're usually not this bad,' Michael said philosophically.

Someone had forgotten to turn off the engines. The turbines were freezing up and were not happy about it. The grinding noise vibrated the insides of Jessica's skull. It was as if a whale had swallowed them whole and then been harpooned.

'Up you go!' Michael yelled over the noise when they got to the ladder. Every other deck on the ship had stairs except this one. The pain in her arm had not gone away with the pipe. The ladder looked as insurmountable as Mount Everest.

'I'll follow you!' she gasped, trying to hold up her right arm.

'You can do it with one hand,' he insisted. 'I'll be right behind you if you fall.'

The rungs were smooth and wet. Her foot slipped before she had got halfway up and she banged her nose. It was a good thing Michael had his hand on her butt.

The next deck was dry. But their pace didn't improve. *Haven* had gone beyond lurching to shaking. Twice they stepped on to the companionway only to be thrown off. Both times Jessica landed on her broken arm. She could actually feel the bones grinding against each other. All around them, the lights went out, including the emergency lights. Tears poured over her face. She couldn't bear to move another inch. In the black, Michael pulled her off the floor.

'Think of the story we'll have to tell our grandchildren,' he said, trying to give her courage. She clung to him. She couldn't talk. He dragged her back on to the stairs.

As Bubba might have said, the gods were finally kind. They escaped the darkness, and the lower decks. Stepping on to the top deck, tasting the fresh air, and watching her close friends preparing to launch a lifeboat, Jessica almost forgot her pain.

They almost forgot something else. They were all aboard and lowering the small boat off the davit and over the side when Michael suddenly leaped to his feet.

'The Rock!' he exclaimed. 'He's still aboard!'

They were approximately twenty feet beneath the topdeck, bobbing against the hull. The fog had cleared somewhat, and there was a hint of dawn in the misty night, but the bow of the ship was still invisible. Working the ropes together, Russ and Nick looked up and shook their heads.

'We can't pull this thing up with everybody on it,' Russ said.

'And we're going to have to get clear soon or we'll get sucked under,' Nick said.

Michael caught hold of one of the ropes, the side of his head plastered with blood. 'I'll climb back up. I can't leave him.'

'When did you last see him?' Bubba asked, sitting beside Clair.

'In that room,' Michael said.

'You can't go back down there,' Bubba said.

'I can do it,' Michael said confidently. Jessica grabbed his leg with her good arm.

'No!' she yelled, feeling instantly selfish. The Rock had, after all, saved her life.

'I'll get him,' Nick said. But Maria grabbed him.

'It's going to go under any second,' she said.

'I'll get him,' Russ said, gripping the rope and preparing to hoist himself up. It was Sara's turn to stop her man.

229

'The hell you will,' she said.

'I'll save him,' Bubba said gallantly. Everyone stared at him. He waited for a moment without budging an inch, then turned to Clair. 'Aren't you going to stop me?'

'You're not that dumb,' she replied between chattering teeth.

'Don't look at me,' Kats told everybody.

'I'll go,' Bill said, getting to his feet.

'If he got caught in that room, he's dead,' Bubba protested.

'He's my friend,' Bill said quietly.

'I'll go with you,' Michael said, undoing Jessica's hold on his leg. But Bill stopped him.

'I can do this one,' Bill said.

'You might drown,' Michael said, looking him straight in the eye.

'Maybe,' he said. 'Maybe not. Stay here, Mike, you can't do everything.'

Michael held his eyes a moment longer, then nodded. Before Bill climbed up the rope, he leaned over and hugged Jessica.

'I'm sorry,' he said in her ear. She kissed his cheek.

'I'm sorry, too,' she said. 'Come back to us quick.'

Bill had strong arms. He was up the rope and over the rail in a few seconds. Nick and Russ continued to lower the lifeboat. They hit the water a moment later. The swells of an hour ago had vanished. Yet the ocean beside the ship was in turmoil, bubbling like a steaming pool above a geyser about to burst. Nick and Russ disengaged the ropes and shoved off.

'We have to wait for them!' Jessica protested. Michael sat down across from her and shook his head.

'We can't wait this close,' he said.

The lifeboat came equipped with two oars. Nick and Russ took them out fifty yards off the stern. No other lifeboats were visible through the fog. They could hardly see the ship. Without her glasses, Jessica was particularly handicapped. Yet five minutes later even she saw enough to know when the *Haven*'s tail suddenly dropped.

'No!' she cried.

It happened unbelievably fast. The nose rose up like a great white whale readying to launch towards the heavens. Only this whale had a grievous wound. As they watched in horror, it began to slide backwards, bellowing loud blasts of spray as if it, too, felt the pain of drowning.

Then it was gone, and they were alone on the water.

CHAPTER TWENTY-FIVE

They drifted aimlessly through the strange night. They could have been trapped in the centre of an underground lagoon. The water was *flat*, and the fog seemed a thing risen from below, possessed of evil purpose. It would unfold far enough to tempt their eye, and then suddenly close over, as if it were playing a game of hide and seek that only it could win. Yet the hint of dawn continued to gather strength in the mist. It was now no longer completely dark. Far away, Jessica could hear the faint sounds of people shouting to one another. She hoped most of the class had had a chance to get clear. It was Bubba who spoke first.

'Those were pretty powerful smoke bombs you had there,' he said to Kats.

'My stuff didn't blow open that hole. Mine only made smoke,' Kats said defensively, casting a worried eye on Michael.

'I suppose,' Bubba said, frowning, perplexed at the cause of the explosion.

'Could either of them have escaped?' Michael asked Bubba.

'Don't ask me to quote odds.'

Jessica was sick with grief, cold, and pain. The Rock and Bill both gone – she couldn't grasp it. She couldn't stop shivering. The lifeboat didn't come equipped with blankets. Her arm hung limply on top of her trembling knees. It was no longer straight. Looking at it made her nauseated.

'What the hell *did* you do?' Michael asked Kats.

'It was just a prank, like Bubba said,' Kats replied uncertainly. 'I just wanted to scare everybody off the ship.'

'Why?' Michael demanded.

'I thought it would be funny,' Kats said with a trace of bitterness.

Michael scowled, before turning to Jessica. 'How's your arm, Jessie?' he asked.

'It's all right,' she lied.

'It looks like it could be broken,' he said.

'I'm all right. Don't worry.'

'How many life jackets do we have?' he asked the group.

They had four. They were stored in small compartments spaced around the inside of the lifeboat. Clair, Maria, and Sara each put one on. Michael tried to get Jessica into a jacket but she just shook her head; she wasn't sticking her arm through any strap for anything. Michael then tried Polly; she ignored him altogether. She didn't appear completely recovered from whatever blow she had received when the bomb had gone off. Nick took the last life jacket. Apparently he couldn't swim either. Nick still had his big question.

'Since when can you walk?' he asked Maria.

'Since my back healed,' she said.

'But you were paralysed,' Jessica said.

'I was, yes, but it was temporary. The fall didn't cut my spinal cord. It merely bruised it. There was a lot of swelling and pressure near where the vertebrae broke. The feeling did not begin to return to my legs until I got to the rehabilitation clinic.' She put her hand on Nick's knee. 'I'm sorry I couldn't tell you.'

233

'Why couldn't you?' Nick asked, hurt.

She glanced at Michael. 'I wanted what Mike did. That's why I called the meeting.'

'How could you be sure the person who killed Alice was the same person who tampered with the float?' Michael asked.

'What were the chances Tabb High had two psychotics?' she asked.

'That's logical,' Michael said.

'How did you know – how *do* you know someone killed Alice?' Sara asked.

'I knew her for only a short time,' Maria said. 'But I knew her well enough to know she wouldn't have taken her life.'

'What was your plan?' Michael asked.

'I wouldn't actually call it a plan,' Maria said. 'I thought I'd have you all together in a room, and then I would stand and walk across the room. I would be watching all your faces, and in one of them, I knew, I would see the disappointment, maybe even the guilt. But only if I took you completely by surprise.' She spoke to Nick. 'You see why I kept silent. I was afraid the truth of my injury would leak out, and then I could never have my surprise, and catch the person who hurt me.'

'I would have kept your secret,' Nick said.

'I'm sorry,' Maria repeated. 'I felt I would only have the one chance. And I must apologise to you also, Jessie, for what I said the morning after the dance. I have no excuse – except I couldn't feel anything below my waist. The doctors hadn't explained to me yet that the paralysis might pass. I was scared. I just needed someone to blame, I guess.'

'I understand,' Jessica said. 'But why didn't you write me later?'

It was hard for Maria – who had always been as

proud as she was kind – to answer the question. 'I was too ashamed,' she said miserably.

'But now you've lost that one chance you wanted,' Nick said.

Maria looked at Polly, who sat with her head bowed at the end of the raft, holding on to her wrist, silent and unmoving. 'Maybe not,' Maria said.

'But what about Clark?' Sara asked, confused. She wasn't alone in her confusion. *Haven* had sunk. It may have taken some of them with it. But they had unfinished business to complete. They looked to Michael, thinking he would take them back to the party to finish the investigation. But he went back further, to many years earlier.

'Polly,' he said. 'We need to talk some more.'

She pulled her jacket tighter and did not look up. 'I'm cold.'

'I want to talk about your parents,' Michael said.

Now he had her attention. Polly slouched deeper. 'You have the same name,' she said.

'That's right,' Sara said. 'Michael McCoy.'

'Does that matter?' Michael asked.

'No,' Polly said.

Jessica understood. Polly had idolised her father. She – and not Alice – had been the light of her father's life. Polly was trying to tell Michael to help her, not hurt her. Jessica doubted that Michael cared. It was clear who he thought was responsible for Alice's death.

'You were in the car with your parents when they crashed,' he said. 'Tell us what happened?'

Polly fingered her cut wrist nervously. 'They died.'

'Why did the car go off the road?' he insisted.

'I don't know.'

'Did you start an argument in the car and distract your dad?'

235

How could he know that?

Michael was probably using simple deduction. He knew Polly and her parents had been on a deserted road. If a tyre hadn't blown, then the father must somehow have become distracted. Michael had hit the bull's-eye. Polly's face crumpled.

'I just wanted another soda from the cooler. That's all I wanted.'

'It wasn't your fault,' Jessica said quickly.

'They burned,' Polly said, distraught. 'And I got away. I didn't even get scratched.'

'Then why did the doctors keep you in the hospital?' Michael asked.

Polly's head snapped up angrily. 'To hurt me! They taped me up with wires. They gave me shots. They tried to make me go to sleep and forget. But I didn't go to sleep. I remember everything that happened!'

Michael apparently had her where he wanted. He pounced hard. 'Was Clark in the room with you and Alice?'

'Yes.'

'There was a ladder in the room. There were Christmas lights hanging out of the closet. Alice told me you wanted her to find some paper cups. Was she up on the ladder getting the cups from the closet?'

'Yes.'

'Were the wires in her way?'

'Yes.'

'What happened?' Michael asked.

'Clark pushed her! She fell! She landed on her nose!' Polly stopped, horrified with what she had just said, or maybe at the memory of what had happened. Tears filled her eyes. 'It made this terrible cracking sound.'

'So that's what happened,' Sara gasped. 'That bastard.'

'Wait a second,' Clair said. 'Who shot Alice?'

'Clark did!' Polly said.

'What else did Clark do?' Michael asked in a mocking tone.

'He took Sara's money!'

'Huh?' Sara said.

'He took it. He hated you and Jessie. He blamed you for making me have the party. He tried to kill Jessie. He tampered with the float!'

'Did he chop down the tree?' Russ asked, interested.

'Yes! Then he went home and smothered Aunty!'

'That's gross,' Sara said. 'How did he get my money?'

'He can do anything! He's a sorcerer! He has the spirits of dead Indians do whatever he wants!'

'I've got to meet this guy,' Bubba said.

'You've already met him,' Michael said. He leaned towards Polly, obviously unimpressed with her outburst of information. 'Let's go back to the bedroom, Polly. Before Clark shoved Alice off the ladder, was he arguing with her?'

'Yes.'

'About what?'

'She wanted him to come to the party, but he came – No, she *didn't* want him to come, but he came anyway.' She nodded to herself. 'That's it.'

'Did you want him to come?'

Polly regarded him suspiciously. 'No.'

'Polly?'

'Well, he was mine at first. She took him away from me, you know.' She added softly, 'I just wanted to see him again.'

'Did Clark take the form I wanted your aunt to sign?'

Polly hesitated. 'I told you he did.'

'Did Clark set the bomb on the ship?'

'Yes.'

Michael reached into his back pocket and removed a soggy piece of paper. He handed it to Polly. She could not look at it. A strange light had entered Michael's eyes. Jessica didn't like it. He was a hunter closing in on his prey.

'That's the form, Polly,' he said. 'I found it in your backyard yesterday.'

Polly winced, putting her hand to her head as if it hurt. 'He must have dropped it.'

Michael got on his knees, rocking the lifeboat, moving close to Polly. 'No, Polly. You didn't give it to him.'

'Yes, I did.' She swallowed painfully. 'I did.'

'He didn't push Alice off the ladder.'

'He must have!'

'Where is he, Polly? Where's Clark?'

'He's there!' she cried, pointing desperately into the fog. 'He's there on the ship!'

Michael grabbed her by the shoulders and shook her. 'The ship's gone. Clark's gone. He's been gone all along. He never came to the party. He never came to see you after the party. He didn't push Alice off the ladder. It was you, Polly, it was you who pushed her!'

He's been gone all along?

Jessica's brain did a double take. What Michael was saying was preposterous; it made no sense. It was insane . . . yet he was talking about insanity. Something inside Jessica suddenly clicked. Polly had been going on about all the evil things Clark had done, and yet not one person had seen him at the party. No one had seen him at the homecoming dance. And yet Clark *had* to exist. He had to be real. Michael had said Clark was the one who had hit him on the head.

He is saying there are two Clarks: the real one, and the one Polly talks to – an imaginary Clark.

238

He was saying Polly was insane.

'No,' Polly moaned, collapsing in his arms. He would have nothing to do with her. He threw her back into the side of the lifeboat, almost throwing her overboard. A year of pain and bitterness twisted his face and voice.

'She was up on the ladder,' Michael said. 'You were arguing about Clark. She was trying to get the paper cups down for you. There were the Christmas lights, a bunch of wires. Her hands must have been tangled up in them. She wouldn't call Clark and ask him to come. You were mad. You shoved her. She wasn't able to get her hands out in front of her to brace her fall. She hit the floor with her nose, the hard wooden floor. She died, Polly, and you snapped. You couldn't take it. You had to make it look like she had killed herself. Or maybe you thought you would make it look like Clark had killed her since he was the one that had made you lose your temper. You went to the garage and got your father's shotgun and hid it around the side of the house. But you needed another gun. You knew where to get it. You knew Kats. You used to get petrol at his station. You knew he always carried a gun. You went out to his car and stole the gun from his glove compartment. You turned up the music in the living room. You went back to the bedroom. You put on gloves and you stuck the gun in Alice's mouth. You wrapped Alice's fingers around the trigger. But you made a mistake there. You put the gun in her right hand. You should have put it in her left. It didn't stop you, though, that mistake. You got a couple of pillows or something and held them around the gun to smother the noise. Then you pulled the trigger, Polly. You blew a hole in your sister's head. But you weren't half done. You hid the pillows or whatever in the first upstairs bedroom. They probably

239

had gunpowder stains on them. You locked the first bedroom door. Then you came downstairs and turned off the stereo. You wanted to be sure we heard the shotgun. Then you went around to the side of the house after checking the pool and fired it off. I noticed on the boat the shotgun had dried mud on it. You must have thrown it into the garden where no one could find it, and left it there. You're pretty clever. When you ran inside, you had the whole house fooled. Is this what happened? *Do you remember, Polly?*

Polly had listened to Michael's speech with her face buried in the side of the lifeboat. But now she sat up and brushed her dark hair from her green eyes. The gesture seemed symbolic; it was as if her inner vision had just cleared. She looked at Michael.

'I remember,' she said calmly. 'You're right.'

The admission took the wind out of Michael's sails. He was right – it was over. There was no mystery left to drive him on, Jessica saw, and also, perhaps, no reason to be bitter over what had befallen his Alice. He sat back on his ankles and touched his head much the way Polly had a minute earlier. It was still bleeding. He was in worse shape than any of them.

Jessica also knew that he was wrong.

'Why?' he asked.

'I have no excuse,' Polly said, unzipping the front of her bulky navy-blue jacket. She had something hidden inside in a clear plastic bag. 'I'm a bad girl.'

You can't have a soda, you're a bad girl.

He had been so quick to condemn her a moment ago, but now Michael appeared no longer interested in confessions or revenge. He glanced at Jessica, and she believed he was remembering back to the day of the funeral when he had yelled at her in Alice's studio. He had been looking for someone to blame then. He had

240

been through a lot since then. He was wiser. 'It was the light bulb,' he said to Polly. 'The electrical shock. It was – a mistake.'

He was referring to the doctors who had treated Polly years ago. Polly heard him, but wasn't listening. Too late Jessica realised what was in the plastic bag: red and black wires, a timer, a lump of orange dough, a detonator. Another bomb. Polly pulled it out and flipped a switch. 'It was a mistake,' she said.

'Oh, no,' Bubba said, sitting up.

'I don't deserve to live,' Polly said, her attention on Michael. 'I *can't* live with what I remember.' She turned the dial on the timer. 'You have five minutes. Leave while you can.'

'Polly,' Jessica said. 'Don't do this. You have your whole life in front of you.'

Polly was not spaced. She was resolved. 'I died in that room when Alice hit the floor. I've been killing time since.' She coughed. 'I am going to do this. Nothing will stop me. Leave.'

'How about you leave,' Bubba suggested hopefully. Clair elbowed him in the side.

'Shut up and let Mike handle this.'

'Polly,' Michael said. 'We don't have anywhere to go.' He held out his hand. 'Give me that thing.'

Polly nodded to the fog, to the faraway voices. 'There're other kids out there. You can find them.' She glanced down at the timer. 'You have four and a half minutes.'

There was something in her voice that made Michael take back his hand. He looked at Bubba, who in turn leaned forward and took a closer look at the mechanism Polly held. Michael's unspoken question was clear: *If I pull it out of her hand, will it go off?* Bubba considered a moment and then shook his head.

'Don't try it,' he said.

'I don't want to spoil the party,' Russ said. 'But we should get the girls off the lifeboat now. That thing could blow any second.'

'I'm not leaving without you!' Sara cried.

Russ frowned. 'Who said I was staying?'

'Oh.' Sara turned to Jessica. 'You don't have a jacket?'

Jessica gestured vaguely towards her butt. 'There's one under my seat.'

'Russ is right, Mike,' Nick said. 'It could blow any second.'

It was seldom Michael appeared lost. He quickly scanned the ocean. Then he slapped the side of his leg with his fist. 'Dawn's coming and the fog's lifting, but we could be in the water an hour.'

'I'd rather tread water that long than be spread all over it,' Kats said.

'Bubba?' Michael asked.

'I can float till the Coast Guard gets here.' Bubba stood and grabbed Clair. 'Let's go for a swim.'

'Mike?' Clair asked, tightening her life jacket. They were all waiting for him to tell them what to do. He threw his hands up.

'Go then, get away. Swim towards the voices. There have got to be other lifeboats out there.'

The gang jumped overboard almost as one, sending the lifeboat rocking. Nick didn't even stay. Jessica understood. He had to take care of Maria. They disappeared within seconds in the fog. Michael sat back down across from Jessica. 'Get out that jacket.'

'There's no jacket,' Jessica said.

He did a double take. 'You're kidding?'

'No.'

He glanced anxiously at Polly. She had the bomb

hugged to her chest, her eyes half closed. 'It doesn't matter,' he said. 'You'll be OK. Just swim after the others. You can catch up.'

'You're not staying,' she said.

'I'll be along in a few minutes.'

He was a lousy liar. The minute she was gone, he s going to try to talk Polly into giving up the bomb. And if that failed, he would attempt to take it from her by force. He would risk his life in order to save Polly's. 'You go after the others, and I'll be along in a few minutes,' she said.

His anxiety increased. 'This is no time for games. Get out of here, Jessie!' Holding on to her right arm, she came and sat beside him. He was so beautiful; it made her heart ache to think she'd only been given one night to love him. 'My arm's broken,' she said.

'*What?* Why didn't you say something?' He whirled in the direction the others had disappeared. 'All right, it doesn't matter. I'll go with you. We can still catch them. You can swim with a broken arm.'

'No.'

'Yes, you can! I'll help you.' He stood and tried to take her hand. 'Come on.'

'I can't swim.'

He dropped back down. The life went out of his eyes. 'No?'

'No. I have to stay. *You* have to go.'

He turned away from her and stared at Polly. A minute went by and he didn't say anything. Then he burst out crying. 'I *can't* leave you,' he whispered.

She pressed her left hand to the side of his cheek. He was shaking with fear, and she was suddenly calm. The fear was still there, but it was as if deep inside she understood that it was supposed to end this way. Her destiny had come to her. It was a relief in a way.

'She's my friend,' she said. 'We've been together since we were children. I can't leave her.' She wiped at his tears. 'It's all right. I love you, and I got to tell you that. I remember the night we went out. You told me you sometimes swim around the pier in the morning for exercise. You're hurt, but you're still a swimmer. You'll catch the others. Now go ahead, get out of here.'

He bowed his head and covered his eyes. 'You're going to die.'

'Nothing's decided yet.' She hugged him as best she could. 'Please, Michael, before it's too late.'

'I can't.'

'Yes, you can. You can do it for me. For us. Please, go.'

He shook his head. He wouldn't look at her. And she suddenly realised he wouldn't leave. Not Michael. Not for anything.

Except possibly to give her some kind of chance.

Polly was watching them. She caught Michael's eye, subtly shifting her hold on the bomb's wires. Polly didn't have to speak the threat aloud. It was there in the air. If he didn't leave, she would blow the three of them up right then.

'Damn,' Michael whispered. Beaten at last, he did turn to Jessica, looking at her for the longest time. And she remembered the first time she had seen his face, how she had admired the warmth and intelligence in his eyes. From that point on, the whole year, she had wondered what he thought of her.

'I love you,' he said.

She smiled. 'That is good.' He kissed her goodbye once. Then he was in the water and swimming away. The fog swallowed him up as it had the others. She turned her attention to Polly.

'Do you want to talk?' she asked.

244

Polly had seen everything. 'You could have taken Sara's life jacket. Sara can swim like a fish.'

'I could have.'

'Why didn't you?'

'I wanted to talk to you alone.'

Polly looked away. 'Oh, Jessie.'

'What happened to your wrist?'

'I cut it with a razor blade. I'm crazy.'

'You seem sane enough now.'

'I suppose I have Mike to thank for that.'

'He doesn't know everything. How come you didn't defend yourself?'

'I used Clark for that. But Mike is right. Clark never came back to see me after Alice died. No one came.'

Polly shrugged. 'Mike knows enough.'

'You didn't smother your aunt. You'll never convince me of that.'

'When I came home, after I chopped down the varsity tree, I thought I saw Clark leaving my house. And then I went inside . . .' Polly drew in a weary breath. 'She was hard to take care of. There were so many times I wished she was dead.'

'That doesn't mean you smothered her. She was old. She just died.'

Polly paused. 'I suppose that's true.'

'And you didn't take Sara's money.'

'Yes, I did do that. I remember she had just got it out of the bank. She had to run back inside for a receipt or something. She had it less than five minutes when I took it.'

'Did you have a reason?'

'I was afraid she'd lose it. She had all cash.' It was coming back to Polly in bursts of clarity. 'Yeah, I took it out of her bag and put it in mine. And then, when I got home, I put it in our safe.' Polly chuckled without mirth. 'And then I forgot about it. I forget my name sometimes. I'm crazy.'

'Stop saying that.'

'It's true.'

'You didn't kill Alice.'

Polly looked away again, hugging the bomb closer. Jessica wondered how much time was left. She supposed she wouldn't feel anything when it went off. But that remark Kats had made about being spread all over the water . . . She couldn't go out this way – torn to tiny red pieces. She couldn't help thinking of her mother receiving the news. Not everything that was left of them would sink. The calm and silence of the surrounding sea remained, but her internal calm began to waver.

'Get out of here,' Polly said.

'I have nowhere to go.'

'Well, it's your own fault.'

'I don't care how mad you were at Alice. I don't care if everything else Michael said about that night is true. You didn't push her off that ladder. You loved her.'

In response Polly yanked open a compartment on the side of the lifeboat. There was a life jacket inside the compartment. She threw it to Jessica. 'Get out of here.'

'No.'

Polly checked the timer, tension spreading across her face. 'There's less than a minute left.'

'I don't care.' Jessica set the life jacket aside.

'What are you doing? Go!'

'Did you push Alice off the ladder?'

'I'm not bluffing!'

'Did you push Alice off the ladder?'

Polly blinked. 'No. We were arguing about Clark. Her hands got all tied up in the Christmas lights like Mike said. And then, she slipped. She fell forward. She landed on her nose.' Polly closed her eyes and grimaced. 'I was always arguing with her about something.' Then her eyes popped open. 'Oh, Christ.'

'That's it. It was an accident. It was an accident your father drove off the road. You didn't do anything wrong.'

The immensity of the revelation had Polly stunned. Yet she would not easily abandon her madness. It had a hold on her stronger than the most potent drug on the most hopeless addict. 'I sunk the ship,' she said.

'The Rock probably got out some way. And Bill's an athlete. I bet he was able to swim clear. What's one old boat? You've got millions. Buy the captain a new one.' Jessica paused. 'You didn't do anything wrong.'

Polly began to cry. '*You're* wrong. I did tamper with the float. I thought you would be elected homecoming queen. I blamed you for making me have the party.'

'I forgive you.'

'I tried to hurt you! I was jealous of you!'

'Why?'

'Because everybody loves you! I heard what Mike just told you! No one's ever told me that!'

Jessica picked up the life jacket and threw it overboard. Immediately it began to drift away from the lifeboat. 'Does this tell you something? You're my friend, Polly.'

Polly stared at her in utter amazement. 'You'll die.'

'Maybe we'll both die. But we don't have to.'

'You would do this to Mike?'

'No.' Jessica got to her knees and slowly crawled towards Polly, wincing with the pain in her arm, the fear in her heart. 'If I die, *that* will be your fault. You're not crazy now. You know what you're doing.' Jessica stopped and stuck out her left hand. 'Give it to me, Polly.'

Polly held her eye. 'Alice told me you would end up with Mike.'

'Let's not disappoint her. Give it to me.'

'I don't even know how to turn this thing off!'

'That is not a problem,' Jessica said, losing patience. 'Give it to me!'

Polly's anxiety evaporated, being replaced by an indignant expression and tone that was almost comical given the circumstances. 'Really, Jessie, you've got a broken arm. I can get rid of it myself.' And with that Polly stood and – holding on to the detonator and the plastic explosives as one unit – threw the bomb as far as she could into the fog. Polly's choice of direction seemed commendable; she had thrown it opposite the direction towards which the gang had disappeared. Of course, it was always easy to end up going in circles in the fog.

The bomb exploded. A couple of seconds later they felt the spray. A couple of seconds after that they heard an irate shout. It was Bubba.

'Hey, girls! Lighten up!'

'Come back!' Polly yelled happily. 'Come back! Everything's OK! I'm OK!' She plopped down beside Jessica and the two girls laughed and cried together as they used to in the good old days before time had made them into terrible teenagers. But there was one thing Jessica still didn't understand. 'Why did you chop down the varsity tree?' she asked.

'I used to hate seeing all those jocks and cheerleaders gather under the tree every afternoon at lunch. They're such a bunch of snobs.' Polly smiled. 'That's one thing I don't regret.'

There was a reason the ocean had been so flat. *Haven* had sunk less than a quarter of a mile off Catalina. The swells that had rocked the ship earlier had been effectively blocked by the proximity of the island.

This was fortunate. Not a single passenger or crew member drowned as a result of the bomb. When the sun rose half an hour later and the fog cleared, all of Tabb's senior class – including The Rock and Bill – could be found either drying out on the beach or floating about on a lifeboat offshore. Some called it a miracle. *Haven*'s captain, though, was quick to credit one passenger with keeping his head in the middle of the crisis and hurrying everyone into the lifeboats. He was Mr Carl Barber, better known as Kats.

Very few people realised that Kats had started evacuating the ship *before* the bomb went off. From then on, he was considered something of a hero.

EPILOGUE

It was a different morning from the previous one. There was no fog. There were no bombs. There was nobody on the beach. Michael was glad the school year was finally over.

It was Sunday. He could hardly remember Saturday. He had spent the whole day – and night – in Catalina's small but efficient hospital. The diagnosis had not been too bad. Twenty-four stitches in the scalp and 'a moderate concussion'. Michael would have hated to have seen a serious one. He still had a slight headache. They hadn't wanted to release him so soon. Then he had told them how poor he was.

The sun was an hour into the clear sky, dazzling on the gentle blue Catalina water; he was still on the island. Michael sincerely believed the morning shore was the best place in the world to sit while waiting for someone. He had recently adopted that belief. He stretched his bare feet through the cool grainy sand. Jessica was supposed to meet him soon.

He had a girlfriend. He had a sister. He had vindication.

A good day to be alive. I need a lot more of these.

Lieutenant Keller had called him and asked if he could interest him in pursuing a career as a detective. Keller had sounded properly chastised, but to his credit, he had also seemed happy to be proven wrong.

Michael had a visitor before Jessica arrived. The fellow

seemingly came out of nowhere. He wore black leather as if he had been born with it on. His red hair shone in the morning light. He carried a brown paper sack in his left hand.

'Hi, Clark,' Michael said, not getting up to greet him.

'Hello.' Clark glanced at the white bandage wrapped around Michael's head. He apparently decided to remain standing. Michael felt no fear, not even when Clark removed a gun from his coat pocket. 'This is yours,' Clark said.

Michael accepted it. Clark had removed the bullets. 'Thanks. Just what I need.'

Clark gestured to Michael's bandage. 'Did I do that?'

'Yeah.'

Clark chuckled. 'You should have known better than to come to my door in a hundred-degree heat with a sports coat on.'

'You knew I had the gun?' Michael wondered what Clark had in the bag.

'Sure. But I didn't know what you were going to do with it.'

In his own way, Clark was apologising. Michael decided he had no reason to hold a grudge since he had been the one who had brought the gun. 'I wasn't going to shoot you,' he said.

'Should have told me before I clobbered you.'

Michael studied Clark's face. He wanted to make sure he had the real one. 'I chased you the whole year.'

'I knew you followed me from the petrol station that one day.'

'You were on a fast bike. Why didn't you ditch me?'

'I wanted to know why you were following me,' Clark said.

'Were you really stoned that night I met you at the game?'

'Probably. Why?'

'Honestly? You're a weird guy, Clark. I followed you because I thought you might have killed Alice.'

'Why would I kill Alice?'

The proverbial question. It was good to finally understand there was no answer to it, that it had been an accident. 'It doesn't matter. How come you're here?'

Clark's green cat eyes brightened. 'I heard about what happened on the radio. I called the hospital to see how Polly was doing. They referred me to her doctor. He wants me to come and meet with him and Polly. He told me she was starting therapy. He thought I could help her.' Clark shifted his paper sack into his right hand. 'What's the dude talking about?'

Polly must have been placed into the hands of an innovative psychiatrist. Michael approved. Confronting a flesh-and-blood illusion couldn't be any worse than being struck by lightning.

Clark hadn't actually answered his question. 'I don't want to spoil the surprise,' Michael said. 'But you definitely should go. You'd find it fascinating.'

Clark showed interest. 'How's she looking these days?'

'Thin and sexy.' Michael had to shake his head. 'What did Alice ever see in you?'

Clark was not offended. When he spoke next, though, there was a strange authority in his voice. 'She used to talk about you. She thought you were all right. I guess you thought the same about her. But your Alice was not mine. She was an artist. She could have been great. She had my passion.' He wiped his nose with the back of his arm. 'She couldn't stand me most of the time, but she saw something in me most people don't.'

'What was she to you?'

Clark handed him the bag. Inside was an achingly beautiful painting of Alice walking alone on an ocean shore beside a wide desert, wearing a long white dress, a string of jewels around her neck. It was on the small side, twelve inches by twelve inches, and had yet to be framed, but the colours pulsed with life; they literally took Michael's breath away. He understood. Alice had meant a great deal to him.

'You cleared her name,' Clark said.

'So you came all the way over here to give me this?'

Clark nodded. 'You're right, I'm a weird guy.'

He walked away before Michael could even thank him. Michael stood and threw the gun into the ocean. A few minutes later he heard Jessica call his name.

The doctors had put a pin in Jessica's arm. It was a nasty break, they said, but they were optimistic she would have a hundred per cent recovery. With her cast in its sling and the wide black-rimmed glasses her mom had brought her from home on her nose, she was a fine sight. She even had her hair pinned up; she hadn't been able to wash it since – well, since she had taken a shower with Michael. But she didn't care how she looked because she knew Michael wouldn't care.

He was sitting on the beach near the water and looking at a paper or book or something. She was amazed at the pleasure it gave her simply to watch him and know that she was going to see him tomorrow, and the day after that. Although they had been in the same hospital, with rooms down the hall from each other, they had hardly spoken since the lifeboat. She raised her left hand and waved.

'Michael!'

Putting away his object of interest in a brown sack, he stood and walked towards her. She was relieved to see he had got over his slight limp. She met him halfway. It was cute – the awkwardness in his greeting. He gave her a light pat on the shoulder. She gave him a sloppy kiss on the lips.

'Hi,' she said. 'Love your hat.'

He touched his bandage. 'Bubba wanted to sign it.'

'How do you feel?'

'Great. How about you?'

'Fantastic.'

'You look good.'

'Liar. But it's OK – I'm a liar too. My arm is actually killing me. And I just swallowed two of those yellow pills the doctor gave me.'

'I hope they weren't Valium.'

'Me, too! My mom dropped me off, but how did you get out here?'

'Hitchhiked. It's easy to get a ride when you look like a war vet.'

They began to walk down the beach, holding hands, Michael carrying his brown bag. *Haven* was underwater but not forgotten. They passed three plates, a chair, one soggy pillow, and a dozen beer cans before they had gone a hundred yards. A gentleman from the Coast Guard had said debris from the sunken ship would wash ashore for a long time.

'I suppose your trip to Hawaii is off?' Michael asked.

'Postponed,' she corrected. 'Sara and I are going later in the summer. In a way, I'm glad we have to wait.'

'Why?'

'It will give you a chance to arrange your schedule so you can come with me.' She added quickly, 'Sara's bringing Russ.'

'Oh, yeah, he's a free man now. How are those two getting along?'

'They're at each other's throats. They're in love. He's helping her with her PPB – Post Presidential Blues. She doesn't know what to do with herself now.' She smiled. 'You haven't said yes yet.'

'What would your parents say?'

'Nothing. I won't tell them you're coming. What would your mom say?'

'That you only live once. To tell you the truth, Jessie, I don't know if I could afford it.'

'Do you *really* want to come with me?'

'Absolutely.'

'Then it'll be my treat. And don't say no. My parents gave me a bunch of cash for graduation that I've got to get rid of immediately, before I get materialistic.'

'I don't know. That's a lot of money.'

'Michael!'

'I'll come.'

She laughed. 'Had to twist your arm, didn't I? That's great. I'll have my cast off. You can teach me how to swim. But you're sure getting the time off won't be a problem?'

'I'm quitting my jobs at JPL and the 7-Eleven. I'm going to bum around all summer and write a book.'

'Can you write?' she asked.

'I hope so.'

'What's it going to be about?'

'This year.'

'Hah! No one will believe it.'

'I'll turn it into a novel,' he said. 'Where did you say you were going to go to school next fall?'

'I'm not. I've been thinking about what you said about my awesome voice. I'm starting a rock-and-roll band. What are you laughing at?'

'I'm sorry. It's such a coincidence. I told Clair Friday morning I was going to start a band. She told me to get you for a singer.'

'*Clair* said that?'

255

'Yeah. Can I be in your band?'

'Can you play an instrument?' she asked.

'No.'

'It doesn't matter. I'll teach you piano if you promise to put me in your book and make me real sweet.'

'I wouldn't know how else to make you.'

'Hang around with me for a while. You'd be amazed.'

They had company – half a dozen sea gulls hunting for lunch in the leftovers from *Haven*'s galley. And far off, perhaps half a mile up the beach, somebody was scouring the sand with a garbage bag in hand.

'Is that The Rock?' Jessica asked, squinting through her glasses.

'Yeah. I spoke to him earlier. He had a story to tell. Right after we swam out of that room, the door closed on him. He had to go out the hole in the hull. I don't know how he did it.'

'He deserves his nickname. What about Bill?'

'He says he was still on the top deck when the ship suddenly went belly-up. He was thrown clear.'

Jessica pointed down the beach. 'What's The Rock doing?'

'He doesn't want a cameraman from a news station coming over to Catalina and seeing what drunks we have for a senior class. He's picking up all the beer cans. Did you know that yesterday when the tide was out people were able to spot the *Haven*'s antennas sticking from the water?'

'Really?'

Michael looked wistfully out to sea. 'I'd like to rent scuba equipment and check her out.'

'For something in particular?'

'Well, I'd like to find my yearbook for one thing.'

She poked him. 'Why?'

He blushed. 'No particular reason.'

256

'Liar!' she called him again, bouncing away to the water's edge. 'I'll write it in the sand with my toes.' She kicked off her shoe. 'Michael Olson is the greatest *lover* Jessica Hart has ever – '

He stopped her. He was easy to embarrass. They continued their stroll, the sun warm on their faces. They found a yearbook a few minutes later. Talk about coincidences – it was Sara's, and it was sitting next to Bubba's sombrero. Jessica picked it out of the foam and shook it off. The paper Sara had glued over the inside cover had come loose. The handwriting beneath was smeared but still legible.

'Listen to this,' Jessica said. ' "My dearest Sara. My heart patters at the thought of us making love tonight above the deep ocean swells, our bodies locked in passion, the salty sweat on the burning flesh of our entangled limbs mingling like oil and wine, ready to burst into flaming ecstasy. My head swoons . . ." ' She read all the way through, giggling like a schoolgirl by the time she came to the last line. ' "Love you always, in so many different positions. Bubba!" '

'Now there's someone who knows how to write.'

'Do you think he slept with her?'

'She's your friend.'

'I doubt it. She says she did it with Russ when it's obvious she didn't even untie his shoes. Then again, Bubba is *your* friend. What do you think?'

Michael started to scratch his head, but ran into his bandage. 'Ordinarily I would say yeah. But Bubba and Clair are getting married tonight in Las Vegas.'

'*What?*'

'Bubba has a ticket waiting for me at Los Angeles airport. I'm flying out there this afternoon. I'm going to be his best man. You should come. Maria and Nick are getting married also.'

'This is a joke.'

'No. If Nick marries Maria, she is automatically allowed to remain in the country. They're all eighteen. I think it's great. Nick said Maria wants you to be her bridesmaid.'

'You're serious? Who's going to be Clair's bridesmaid?'

'It might be you. As you can imagine, this is all sort of short notice.'

'But Clair and I hate each other.'

'Pretty girls always hate other pretty girls. It's biological. That's what Bubba says. Maria's counting on you.'

'Then I'll come. Clair must be pregnant again.'

'Bubba says no.'

'I don't believe it.'

A smile lit up Michael's face. 'I can tell you someone who's not pregnant any more.'

'Your mom! What did she have?'

'A seven-pound six-ounce girl.'

Jessica dropped Sara's yearbook and hugged him. '*Brother* Michael! Are they both OK?'

'Yeah, they're fine. Mom had the baby about the same time we were in the lifeboat.'

'What did she name it? No – let me guess. Alice?'

'Mom wanted to, but I said no.'

'Why?'

It might have been a delicate question. Michael let go of her hand and looked down at the paper sack he carried. 'Life has to go on.' He shrugged. 'I'm still learning to let her go.'

'I understand. I shouldn't have – What's in the bag?'

He showed her, and it brought tears to her eyes, and not just because it was so beautiful. 'I had this dream,' she said, staring at the painting in her hands. 'It was

258

the morning we were together at the hospital waiting to hear about Maria. There were four of us in a black tunnel. You, me, and these two little girls. One of the girls was Alice. When we got to the end of the tunnel, we were in a place like this. Who did this painting?'

'Clark.'

Jessica made a face. 'The *real* one. Not Polly's imaginary one.'

'Yeah,' Michael muttered, a faraway look in his eyes. 'What is it?'

He didn't seem to hear her question at first. 'I had this dream,' he said finally. 'I had it many times this year. It started a couple of days after I met you. In it I'm standing on a bridge over a roaring river. There's a desert in front of me and a forest behind me. And there's this girl — I never see her face. But she tells me to go forward, that she will follow.' He glanced at the sky. 'I always used to wonder if it was Alice.'

'Who do you think it is now?'

'My sister.'

'How did you feel in your dream?' she asked.

'Happy. But also sad. I felt I was leaving paradise.'

'I felt very happy in mine. I didn't want to wake up. I felt like I was being reborn.'

Michael was impressed. 'Maybe that's how it really was.' Then he shook his head. 'We'll never know.'

She took his hand. '*I* know. I was supposed to meet you. Alice knew it. That's why she wanted you to meet me. She was wise.' Jessica smiled. 'She knew how far out I am.'

Michael smiled, too, briefly. The sadness of leaving paradise, however, was still there. 'If there is a design to our lives, and Alice was sensitive to it, then maybe I messed things up. The night of the party, she was upset she didn't get to introduce me to you. I could have let

259

her, you know. She felt as if somehow a wrinkle had been put in the canvas.' He took the painting back and put it in the bag. 'I don't know why it bothered her then, or why it bothered me later.'

'She didn't die because you avoided me. You don't think that, do you?'

He shrugged again. 'I shouldn't have brought it up.'

'Michael, you have a guilt complex. You've done more good for more people than anyone I know. I grew up with Alice, but I deserted her the night she died like everyone else. I went by the obvious facts. You went by your gut feeling, and you used your head. You saved her memory.'

'I was late doing it.'

'Not at all. The truth is coming out. It hurts Polly's image, but that's OK. Polly's got something out of all this. Her memory was saved. You gave it back to her.'

Michael was doubtful. 'I was hard on her.'

'You had to be hard.' Jessica paused. 'She told me to thank you.'

'You spoke to her?'

'Late last night, on the phone. She's in another hospital. This one's supposed to be the best.' Her voice faltered. 'We had a long talk.'

'Was it painful?'

Jessica nodded. 'But I'm glad we had the chance. Her doctor arranged the call. I understand her a lot better now. We're going to talk again soon.' A sea gull ran across their path with a Ritz cracker in its mouth, fleeing from another almost identical bird. Jessica smiled at the sight, although it touched her with strange sadness. Birds of a feather, and best friends – they were sometimes each other's worst enemies. 'I asked her why.'

'Why?'

'Why Clark. Of all people to dream into her life, why

him? Her response really hit me. She said she just needed someone to love her, but that any time she ever did love someone – in real life – it always brought her pain. She couldn't help who she invented. Her lover had to be her tormentor. Clark was just someone who fitted the bill.'

'She said that?'

'Yes.'

'It sounds to me like she's on the road to recovery. She has you to thank as well. You saved her life. It was you who got the final truth out of her.'

Jessica took his hand and pulled him close. 'OK, we're both heroes. Now let's talk about happy things or I'll leave you and go out with Bill again.'

'That isn't much of a threat.'

She shoved him away. 'Hey, he's as big a hero as they're making Kats into.'

Michael groaned. 'Don't remind me.'

'Oh, you never answered my question. What – '

'Ann,' he interrupted. 'We chose it together.'

'Why Ann?'

'Why not? It's a nice name. It's easy to spell.'

'Ann was Alice's middle name.'

He was amazed. 'I didn't know that.'

'Are you sure?'

'Positive.'

She smiled. 'What's in a name? Maybe everything, huh?'

'Let's wait and see who she grows into before we try to answer that one. But speaking of names . . .' He set the painting down and pulled a heavily wrinkled envelope out of his back pocket. 'Last autumn I built a telescope. I used to take it out to the desert a lot. Anyway, to make a long story short, I discovered a comet.'

'You what?'

'A comet. They're these big balls of ice and dust that –'

'I know what a comet is. That's incredible. Are you going to win the Nobel Prize?'

'If Bubba uses his influence.' He handed her the envelope. It looked as if it had been underwater. Jessica realised it was the sealed envelope his mother had given him before the graduation ceremony. It *had* been underwater. 'This is the confirmation of the sighting,' he said.

'How come you haven't opened it?'

'I spoke to the observatory on Thursday. I already know what it says. Besides, I wanted you to open it. That's why I brought it to the all-night party.'

She let go of his hand and got to work; it was a lot harder getting to a sealed letter with only five fingers. 'When will it be visible?'

'It won't, not without a telescope. In fact, it's already passed its closest approach to the earth. It's heading back out into space. But if you want, I can take you out to the desert and show it to you in my telescope.' He watched her fumbling. 'Need help?'

'I can manage, thank you. Is it like Halley's comet? Will it come back?'

'Sure.'

'When?'

'In a couple of thousand years.'

'Then you had better take me to the desert soon.' She finally got the paper out. There was an official seal on top, and words of congratulation and numerous astronomical notations below that made about as much sense to her as did the name given to the comet. She frowned. 'I don't understand?'

'They always let the person who discovers a comet choose its name.' He stopped. 'What's the matter? I thought you would be flattered.'

'I am. It's just the way you put our names together – '

Michael snapped the letter from her hand. He quickly scanned it and his forehead wrinkled. 'I told them to name it Jessica-Michael not Jessica-Olson.'

She nodded. 'Uh-huh. Are you sure you're not trying to tell me something?'

'No, honestly. It's a mistake.'

'Right. Who's getting hitched tonight in Las Vegas? And why is it *I* have to be there?'

He turned red. 'I didn't mean that.'

'I believe you.'

'Jessie!'

'The nerve of the guy. He washes my back in the shower once and he thinks I've got to marry him.'

Michael started to protest again. Then he stopped and grinned. 'I washed a lot more than your back, sister.'

'I haven't forgotten.' She kissed him shyly. 'Maybe I should marry you.'

THE END

Also available

CHRISTOPHER PIKE

CHAIN LETTER

When Alison first read the chain letter signed 'Your Caretaker', she thought it was some terrible sick joke. Someone, somewhere knew about that awful night when she and six other friends committed an unthinkable crime in the desolate Californian desert. And now that person was determined to make them pay for it . . .

One by one, the chain letter was coming to each of them, demanding dangerous, impossible deeds, threatening violence if the demands were not met. No one out of the seven wanted to believe that this nightmare was really happening to them. Until the accidents started happening —and the dying . . .

CHRISTOPHER PIKE

SPELLBOUND

They found Karen Holly in the mountain stream, her skull crushed. There was only one witness to the tragedy — Karen's boyfriend, Jason Whitfield. He said a grizzly had killed her. But a lot of people didn't believe him. They thought Jason had murdered her in a fit of rage.

And now weeks have passed, and Jason has another girlfriend, Cindy Jones. And there are the new kids in town. Joni Harper, the quiet English beauty that Cindy's brother, Alex, cannot get out of his mind. And Bala, the foreign exchange student from Africa, the grandson of a powerful shaman.

Together they will return to the place where Karen was killed.

Some will die.

The others will come face to face with a horror beyond imagining.

CHRISTOPHER PIKE

LAST ACT

Melanie was the new girl in town, a little lonely, a little bored. Then she auditioned for the school play and won the starring role. Suddenly she had a whole gang of exciting friends. But these friends shared something that Melanie did not know, something from the past. Something so terrible that none of them would ever talk about it. Until the police came for the body, and for Melanie . . .

CHRISTOPHER PIKE

WEEKEND

The dream became a nightmare.

The weekend in Mexico sounded like a dream vacation. Four guys, five girls—and a gorgeous oceanside mansion all to themselves. It should have been perfect.

Except nothing was going the way they'd planned. There was the girl upstairs who was fighting for her life. The phone lines that went dead. And the explosion in the garage that could have killed them all.

But not even that prepared them for what happened next. Because while they were getting some sun, someone else was getting revenge—and the terror wouldn't stop until the weekend was over.